Duel of Desire

The village festivities were at their height. Long-repressed emotions sought release in ancient rites of revelry. And for a moment Marietta did not sense what it meant when Coll, the man she loved, strode up to Richard Wynter, the darkly handsome English officer who had proved so firm a friend to her.

Then she saw Coll extend a sword hilt-first to Richard, and watched the Englishman grasp it in acceptance of the challenge.

As the two men faced each other, sword against sword, Marietta knew that this was no mere sporting contest for them but something more earnest—a duel of pride and jealousy and blood hate . . .

. . . and as Marietta tensely followed the intricate dance of swordpoints, the piercing clash of steel against steel, she realized with mounting horror that she was not sure whom she wanted to win. . . .

THE FIRES OF GLENLOCHY
A novel of passionate love and spellbinding suspense

"YOU'LL BE HOOKED FROM THE FIRST PAGE TO THE FINISH!"
—AMARILLO GLOBE

Big Bestsellers from SIGNET

The Fires Of Glenlochy

Constance Heaven

Ⓢ
A SIGNET BOOK
NEW AMERICAN LIBRARY
TIMES MIRROR

Copyright © 1976 by Constance Heaven

Library of Congress Catalog Card Number: 75-44091

This is an authorized reprint of a hardcover edition published
by Coward, McCann & Geoghegan, Inc.,

SIGNET, SIGNET CLASSICS, MENTOR, PLUME AND MERIDIAN BOOKS
are published by The New American Library, Inc.,
1301 Avenue of the Americas, New York, New York 10019

First Signet Printing, May, 1977

1 2 3 4 5 6 7 8 9

PRINTED IN THE UNITED STATES OF AMERICA

For CARL and KAY
who also love the Highlands

Author's Note

Glenlochy is an imaginary castle set in an imaginary valley on the West Coast of Scotland and, so far as I know, there has never been a Clan Gilmour though it is an ancient Highland name. The legends and superstitions have been culled from memoirs, travel diaries and collections of ancient folklore or have been gathered during my own wanderings in the Highlands. They do not belong to any specific person, place or district.

Whither is fled the visionary gleam?
Where is it now, the glory and the dream?

WILLIAM WORDSWORTH

Chapter One

ᛁᚹᚲᛟᛁᚲᚱᛁ

Glenlochy Castle is now a burnt-out ruin. There is little left but the stone walls of the great hall and one solitary turret, smoke-blackened and stark against the sky. My husband has built a new house for us further up the glen, tucked under the massive shoulder of the mountain, and not exposed to the fierce Atlantic winds and the incessant pounding of the surf. Sometimes I still dream of fire, the devouring flames, the fierce heat, the suffocating smoke, the agony of that terrible night, and yet when I walk down there on summer evenings with the children and the dogs racing ahead and the sun going down in unearthly glory over the grey misty shapes of the islands, I cannot help remembering the day I saw it first and foolishly, helplessly, fell in love with a dream and a man.

I used to think that it was my stepfather's unwelcome attentions that drove me from Paris to Scotland, but I know that is not really true. The day my mother came upon me struggling in his arms and boxed both my ears and his had its amusing side. Maybe it was because I hated her so bitterly that I snatched at any excuse to escape, but that is not entirely true either because I had long known all about her. She had been deceiving my father since I was twelve years old and Henri was only the last in a string of lovers though he was the one she married barely six weeks after my father died. He was rich and had pretensions to gentility and she was anxious to nail him down. Mainly I think it was the sheer helpless disgust that grew inside me at the way she had tricked my father, belittling him, making fun of him, trying to pull him down to her level so that I burned with a passionate desire to justify him, to make his dream of the Scotland he had loved

1

through the long years of exile come true for him and for me.

It was a bitterly cold day in the late March of 1770 when the ship sailed at last into Leith. Even wrapped in my fur mantle the icy wind bit into me with scurries of sleet. Up in the Highlands, the Captain told me, the snow would still be lying thick in the glens. There was no welcoming gleam of sun in the bleak grey skies and yet in some indefinable way that I could not explain I felt as though I were coming home.

I was still shaken from the miseries of the stormy voyage. Jeannie, my maid, had been prostrate with sea-sickness for most of the journey and in caring for her I had been forced to conquer myself. Now while she finished the packing and strapped down my trunk in our tiny cramped cabin, I stood on the deck, watching the bustle of loading and unloading among the brigs and hoys crowded into the harbour. Across the wide waters of the Firth of Forth I could see a faint blue line of mountains. There were few passengers at this season of the year. I was alone except for the man who stood a few yards away from me. I had glimpsed him once or twice during the voyage when I had come up on deck glad to drink in the cold fresh air after the sour-smelling cabin. He was always alone, speaking to no one. Even on this bitter day he wore no hat. His dark hair blew about his forehead and his long caped cloak flapped in the wind.

The cook threw out a pail of scraps from one of the portholes below me and the seabirds swooped down on them in dizzying arcs. I forgot my idle curiosity about the stranger in facing up to my own doubts. I wondered, not for the first time, if I were indeed the trusting fool my mother had called me on that last day before I left the neat little house in the Rue Chantelle which was all the home I had ever known.

'Go if you must,' my mother had said, looking at me sideways out of her slanting green eyes. 'I won't pretend I am sorry. Why should I be? What woman like me wants a grown-up daughter of twenty-two forever tagging at her heels? You and I have never seen eye to eye, have we, Marietta?'

'Has that been my fault?'

'Yes, I think it has, in part at any rate.' She stood by the window, a good-looking woman still and I think she was speaking honestly to me for perhaps the first time. 'You have always been so besotted with your father, you've never even tried to see my point of view.'

I had moved away restlessly not willing to quarrel with her when so soon I would be gone. 'Why bring all this up now?'

'Yes, you're right. It's too late, isn't it? Twenty years too late. Ever since you were old enough to understand, your father stuffed your head with grand tales of the Gilmours, of the castle and lands given to his ancestors by Robert the Bruce, just as he once talked to me. And I, fool that I was, listened to him just as you have done, only it didn't take me long to see through him. Master of Glenlochy, he called himself, and one of these days he would be Chieftain in his father's place. He would take me to Scotland. I would know what it was to be a great lady, I, daughter of a lodging-house keeper and a sergeant in the artillery who took himself off before I was born!' My mother laughed, a bitter scornful sound. 'Words, empty words, he was always a master of those! He was an exile, living on a miserable pittance, and so he remained to the end. He would have starved in the gutter but for me.'

'That's not true,' I interrupted passionately. 'He worked, he earned money when he could . . .'

'When it wasn't beneath his damned Highland pride,' she retorted sourly. 'Where did they get him, those handsome looks, those fine manners, the book-learning? A beggarly tutor to our neighbour's brats and they laughed at him behind his back. He should have died with his brothers at that outlandish battle he and his half-starved friends never stopped talking about.'

I rounded on her fiercely. 'How can you say that? Was it his fault the English defeated the Prince at Culloden? My father fought for the Scotland he believed in, he was true to his ideals . . .'

'True to his beloved Charles Stuart,' said my mother with a wealth of contempt. 'My God, how weary I grew of that damned name! You should have seen the Prince as I did last time he passed through Paris . . . a drunken sot fumbling at his mistress and all those fools pressing forward to kiss his hand calling him Majesty, your father among them. He cared no more about the men who had died for him than the German king who sat on England's throne and hunted them down.'

I hated her then most bitterly because she tarnished the dream that my father had cherished so long, the brave hopeless dream that had ended only in bloodshed and tragedy. I hated her as I hated the English. I would have flung away from her but she caught me by the shoulder and turned me back.

'And now you have some romantic notion in your head that Glenlochy is your home too instead of what I have given you. You're like him, Marietta, a head full of dreams and not an ounce of common sense. Did your father ever have a single reply to any of his letters? What do you suppose was happened all these years? Your grandfather may have married again and sired another brood of sons; he may be dead, the house razed to the ground . . . who knows? And when you find you're not wanted, I suppose you'll come creeping back to me like a beaten puppy bitch with your tail between your legs, begging like he did.'

'No, I won't, you needn't be afraid of that, never, never! I'll find work for myself, I'll teach, I'll scrub floors rather than ask you for anything.'

'Brave words,' said my mother with her little smile. 'Well, we shall have to see, won't we? You're a strange girl, Marietta. Any other young woman in your place would have been married by now. There have been plenty of men, God knows. You've got looks, you know, my looks, but you won't make the best of them.'

She was right, I knew that. Ever since I was sixteen, there had been men who wanted me and I loathed the look in their eyes, the touch of their hands. If my mother had had her way I'd have been married to one of them long since but my father had stood firm.

'Marietta shall not be forced to take a man she doesn't love,' he had said.

'Love!' my mother had exclaimed impatiently. 'Will love keep her in good clothes and feed her children?'

I had trembled and been glad of my father's arm around my shoulders and the certainty of his strong support. She knew nothing of the day I had come home early from the convent where I was a day pupil. My father was out and I had gone unthinkingly into my mother's bedroom to ask where he was. They had been lying naked on the bed, my mother and a brown-haired stranger, too absorbed in themselves even to notice the door opening. I had stared at them, horrified yet fascinated. Then I had fled to my own room, shutting myself in, shaking, sick with shock and disgust.

There was one other thing she did not know either because more than anything I feared her laughter. Three weeks after my father died I wrote myself to my grandfather addressing the letter to Sir Alasdair Gilmour of Glenlochy. Four months later there had come a reply, if you could call it that . . . a single sheet of paper and the words printed: 'Do not come to Glenlochy. You will be sorry.' It had frightened me only I was too proud to admit it and by that time I had grown very afraid of Henri. So I hid it and told no one.

I thought of it now and shivered as the wind blew the sleet into my face. But I had not let it prevent my coming to Scotland and to do my mother justice she had seen me well provided before I left Paris. 'My daughter is not going to these high and mighty relatives looking like a pauper,' she said flatly. So there were gowns of silk in my trunk as well as those of velvet and warm wool. My mantle was lined with squirrel and there was some of my stepfather's gold locked safely in a steel box.

Jeannie had come up on deck to join me swaying unsteadily from the movement of the ship and clinging to the rail. She looked with disgust at the brown huddle of mean houses, at the slimy mud and heaps of filthy snow.

'If that's Scotland, Miss Marietta,' she said, 'then I wish we were safely back in the Rue Chantelle.'

'That's because you're still feeling the effects of the sea,' I said cheerfully. 'Father used to say Edinburgh was a grand city. You'll feel differently when you've had a good dinner.'

'I shall never eat again,' she exclaimed shuddering.

I laughed. 'We shall soon find out.'

The boats had already been launched to carry the passengers to the shore. One by one they were climbing down the swaying rope ladder, a sailor standing at the top and another steadying it at the bottom.

'Merciful God,' said Jeannie faintly. 'Have we to climb down that thing?'

'Yes, we have. It's easier than it looks. Come along.'

Jeannie went first and reached the waiting boat safely.

Then I took the first unsteady step. Halfway down there came a great gust of wind billowing out my cloak like a sail. I missed a rung and hung for a moment suspended, terrified lest I should fall into the water and trying hard to stifle a scream. Then two strong arms gripped me around the waist. I was lifted bodily off the ladder and for an instant I was aware of a lean cheek very close to mine. Then I was in the boat, Jeannie was clinging to my hand and breathlessly I tried to thank the tall dark passenger who had come to my rescue. He nodded but said nothing, seating himself in the prow of the boat as we were rowed ashore.

There were very few hackney carriages on the quay and there was a scramble among the travellers to secure those available. I was hampered by Jeannie and anxiety about my baggage. By the time it was gathered together, I realized that the cabs had all driven away with the exception of one by which my rescuer was standing looking impatiently around him.

He had a stern forbidding appearance but the icy mud was already penetrating my thin kid boots. It might be hours before the others came back. We couldn't stand there and simply freeze to death. I was trying to pluck up courage and ask if we might share it with him when there was a sudden commotion. A fashionably dressed young woman came running down the quay towards him, veil and furred cloak streaming out behind her as she ran heedless of the filthy slush splashing her velvet skirts.

'Richard,' she exclaimed, 'dearest, dearest Richard! I meant to be here hours ago but the carriage stuck in the ruts and James couldn't get it to move. How wonderful to see you again. Are you really quite recovered? Was it a terrible journey?' She threw her arms round his neck kissing him warmly. They were locked in each other's arms and just for a moment I was filled with envy. How comforting

It would have been if someone had come to meet me like that, someone out of my father's past who could greet me for his sake . . . then I pulled myself together. Quick as a flash I signalled to the cab driver and in no time at all he had us both safely installed inside, our personal baggage piled at our feet.

'Edinburgh if you please,' I said breathlessly as he prepared to close the door on us.

'And where in Auld Reekie would ye be wanting to go, mistress?' he asked humorously. He was a little man muffled to the eyebrows and speaking in so thick a dialect I found it almost impossible to understand what he said.

I knew only one address. My father had written it down not long before he died.

'We were boys together, Marietta, but he was the canny one, not like me,' he had said smiling wryly. 'He always knew how to look out for himself. He's a lawyer now and has risen high so they say. If ever you go to Scotland, then go to him for my sake.'

'Mr Duncan Cameron,' I said hesitantly. 'He has a place of business in the High Street. Do you know of him?'

'Aye, I do that. There's no many as havena' heard o' Duncan Cameron. Away then wi' ye, mistress.'

Excitement tightened my nerves as the carriage bumped over the cobbles emerging out of the slums of the quayside into clean green fields. It was bitterly cold. Jeannie was shivering and my feet felt like lumps of ice despite the evil-smelling straw on the floor. We skirted a stretch of water and came down a hill into a street of tall houses, the little turrets, the balconies and outside staircases reminding me in a strange unexpected way of the France I had left behind me.

Jeannie's teeth were chattering and I was worried about her. She needed warmth and food more than I did. Ahead on our right I caught a glimpse of a large inn. I saw the arched gateway into the yard and the swaying sign of a White Hart. I hammered on the side and the driver grumbling pulled up his horse on the icy cobbles.

'We'll stay here,' I said.

'It's no place for young leddies,' he began but I cut him short.

'Never mind. It will do well enough. Please to carry our baggage inside.'

The inn was crowded. A stagecoach had just arrived and several passengers were seeking accommodation. There was a heated argument in which our driver played a vigorous part. Then a room was found for us after toiling up two flights of stairs.

Jeannie said anxiously, 'You'll not go alone to this Mr Cameron. It wouldn't be decent, Miss Marietta.'

'Don't be silly. He's an elderly man, older than my father, a respectable lawyer. You stay here, Jeannie. Order yourself coffee, or tea if you prefer it, and unpack some of our clothes. I'll not be long.'

I tidied my dress and took a hasty look in the mirror before I went down to the waiting cab. The young men who had tried to kiss me had paid me compliments and called me beautiful. Perhaps it was so, I don't know. There was a look of my mother about me and that I bitterly resented though her hair was black as ink and mine was a deep fiery red, the red hair that had been the badge of the Gilmours since the first of them had bloodied his sword for the Bruce at the battle of Bannockburn. I had my mother's slanting green eyes too, the lashes dark and curling. 'Cat's eyes,' my father used to call them, laughing because a cat reared itself on the Gilmour coat of arms, a wild cat with a crown on its head and the one word 'Courage.'

I had a small bag with me that I never let out of my hands. In it I carried my birthright, the one thing that I hoped would prove my rightful claim to the name of Gilmour even if Mr Cameron doubted my red hair and the written proofs of identity.

It did not take long to reach the High Street. My driver stopped outside one of the tall narrow houses and waved his whip to the first floor.

'Mr Duncan Cameron hangs his plate outside there,' he said.

'Would you wait?' I put a coin in his hand with little idea as to its value.

'For a piece of siller the like o' that, I'd wait till the crack o'Doom,' he said with a grin on his monkey face so that I knew I had paid him far too much. Well, I would learn.

I climbed up to the first floor and rapped at the heavy nail-studded door. After a moment it creaked open and a thin man in a dusty snuff-coloured coat peered out at me.

'Mr Duncan Cameron?' I asked.

'Have ye an appointment?'

'No, but I think he will see me,' I said as firmly as I could. 'Tell him it is Mistress Gilmour of Glenlochy.'

He stared at me for a full half minute before he swung the door wider. 'Aye, I'll tell him. Come ye in, mistress.'

It was a small room panelled in dark oak but well furnished with a Turkey red carpet and a great number of large heavy books. The man disappeared and came back in a few seconds.

'Mr Cameron has a client with him. He begs you to wait. Please take a seat.' He pulled forward a chair, wiping the dusty leather with a sweep of his sleeve and then went back to his high desk under the window.

It seemed a long time before Mr Cameron's client took his leave. Once there was the sound of raised voices and the clerk gave the inner door a startled glance. Then all was quiet again except for the scratch of his quill on the parchment. Nervous tension built up inside me until I could sit still no longer. I got up and began to look idly through the books piled on the table, ancient volumes of law of which I understood not one word. Then the inner door flew open and a gentleman came out with a rush that sent him halfway across the room. The hat in his hand caught the books beside me and sent them crashing to the floor. Both of us bent to retrieve them, our heads bumped and to my surprise I was suddenly face to face with my tall dark rescuer from the rope ladder.

'I beg your pardon,' he muttered as he took the books from me. Our hands touched. I was looking up into remarkably luminous grey eyes under straight black brows. 'Miss Gilmour, is it not?' he said abruptly.

'Yes, it is,' I replied wonderingly.

'You stole that cab from under my very nose,' he said accusingly.

'I'm sorry but I thought . . .'

'That yours was the greater need. Well, maybe it was. Forgive me. I'm in haste.' He replaced the books on the table, gave me a slight bow, crammed his hat down on his head and went swiftly from the room.

'I am afraid that Colonel Richard Wynter has a way of coming in and out of my chambers like the East wind,' remarked Mr Cameron dryly and I turned to see the lawyer standing in the doorway of his inner office, a rosy-cheeked genial man in a neat black coat and wearing a neat grey wig. He held out his hand.

'Come in, my dear Miss Gilmour. I am sorry to have kept you waiting.'

He ushered me past him, shut the door and motioned me to a chair. Then he sat down behind his desk, pushing up the spectacles that tended to slip down his nose and looking at me shrewdly.

'My clerk tells me that you claim kinship with the Gilmours of Glenlochy.'

'I am the daughter of Ian Gilmour.'

'Indeed. I was not aware that Ian was ever married.'

'My mother is French.'

'I see.' His manner was very cool. 'Have you proof of identity?'

'I have papers and letters, Mr Cameron, all of which you may see, but I also have this.'

I felt in my bag and brought out what my father had given me when he knew he could not live much longer, something about which my mother had known nothing. He had been only too well aware that once seen she would never have been able to keep her greedy hands from it.

I unfolded the handkerchief with its rusty brown stains. Within its folds lay a blood-red stone large as a pigeon's egg; two serpents twined themselves around it in an ancient setting of pure gold.

Mr Cameron stared down at it. 'My God,' he breathed at last. 'It is the Sìthen Stone.'

'Yes. It is the Faery Brooch of Glenlochy, Mr Cameron,' I said half smiling. 'You see I know all about the legend, about Donald Ruadh who married a daughter of the King of Elfland. I was even named for her. I too am called Marietta. She brought this with her as her dowry.'

'With the promise that while it remained in the castle, the Gilmours would never lack either honour or courage,' went on Mr Cameron smiling in his turn. 'Alas, for the truth of these old tales. In my father's time, I remember, Sir Alasdair had it examined by an English expert in London. It is probably Eastern in origin, Saracen most likely, brought home by some crusading Gilmour.' Then his friendly tone changed. 'Where did you get this? I was never informed of its loss.'

'Sir Alasdair, my grandfather, had three sons, Mr Cameron, Andrew, Donald and my father Ian. He gave it to Andrew when he left Glenlochy to fight for the Prince. When he was killed at Culloden, it was my father who took it from him wrapped in this very handkerchief stained with his blood. It was he who gave it to me. His dearest hope was that one day I would bring it back to where it belongs.'

Mr Cameron was looking at me steadily and his eyes behind the steel spectacles were very cold. 'Miss Gilmour, I hesitate to cast doubts on your pathetic story but we had certain information that Ian Gilmour was taken prisoner after the battle, carried to the gaol at Fort William and there died of his wounds.'

'But he didn't. He escaped. It took weeks and he nearly perished from hunger and cold but somehow he reached Paris. He died there six months ago,' and suddenly, unexpectedly, the weariness and the unforgotten grief swept over me. I felt the tears prick behind my eyelids and turned away my face to hide them.

'My dear young lady,' said Mr Cameron more gently, 'I have to question you. You understand that.' I nodded and groped for my handkerchief. 'If this is true, then why did he never write to his father? He could not return, he would still have been under sentence of death, but letters did get through despite the English.'

'He did write, more than once,' I interrupted quickly. 'Only he never had any reply and he thought . . .'

'He thought what?'

'You see his brother Donald had been taken prisoner with him. He was wounded and very sick. My father could not save him as well as himself and the memory tortured him. He was bitterly ashamed because he left his brother to die. All his life he believed that his father blamed him for his lack of courage.'

'He could have written to me. I was his friend.'

'My father was a proud man. He would never beg for any man's help.'

Mr Cameron looked at me for a moment, then he got up and walked over to the fire warming his hands absentmindedly at the cheerful blaze before he turned to me again.

'What is it you want from me, Miss Gilmour?'

'I want to go to Glenlochy. I want to see my grandfather. Does that seem so strange?'

'It is not strange at all. In fact now . . .' he broke off and looked at me curiously. 'Do you know what has been happening in the Highlands since the rebellion was crushed?'

'I know how savagely the English have behaved,' I burst out indignantly. 'There were many in France who had to flee from the brutes who robbed them of wives and children, who burned and ravaged and slaughtered . . .'

'Yes, yes, that's only the half of it,' said Mr Cameron sombrely. 'But there is something that concerns you closely if indeed you are whom you claim to be. Many chieftains lost their homes and their lands because they took up arms against England and King George.'

'It was a good cause, a noble cause . . .'

'All lost causes are noble,' said Mr Cameron cynically, 'but I am not concerned with political ideals at the moment. The plain fact remains that Sir Alasdair sent his sons to fight but remained himself at home. Glenlochy was left untouched.'

I stared at him still not grasping his meaning. 'Is that any reason why I should not go there?'

'On the contrary. It is every reason why you should. The estates are not as extensive as they were, part of the land has already been sold. The clan was always a small one and many died in the rebellion, but there must be more than a hundred families still living beside the loch and in the glen, all of them claiming kinship. My dear Miss

Gilmour, when Sir Alasdair dies and he is an old man and in poor health, all this will belong to you.'

'To me? Do you mean . . .?'

'You will be the Mac'Ghille Mhoire, the seventeenth Chieftain of Glenlochy.'

The Gaelic title stirred my blood. I gazed at him stupefied, quite unable to take in what he said, thinking that either he must be mad or I was.

'But it can't be,' I said at last. 'Surely there were other children, other sons. My father had two brothers and a sister.'

He shook his head. 'Andrew and Donald died unmarried and as for your Aunt Kathryn . . . indeed there is no legitimate male heir. It has been a great grief to Sir Alasdair. It is still a splendid inheritance.'

I saw it written on his face as if he had spoken his thoughts aloud . . . a splendid inheritance indeed, five hundred years of it, for a girl who was half a foreigner with some doubtful whore of a French mother . . . I had never dreamed of such a thing. That scrap of paper in my bag which I had thought I might show him suddenly assumed a new significance. 'Do not come to Glenlochy. You will be sorry.' With a little shiver I realized that someone else knew, someone who hoped to frighten me away. 'Courage'—that was what the Sìthen Stone bestowed on its owner and it was mine now, I had every right to wear it if I chose. I raised my head defiantly.

'Mr Cameron, how soon can I leave for Glenlochy?'

'Oh come now, Miss Marietta, there is a great deal to be settled first. I have to make sure that everything is in order, you know. Besides it is winter still in the Highlands and it is a long and arduous journey. You might well be advised to wait for the mail boat that will be sailing up the West Coast very soon now.'

'No, no more boats,' I said with a shudder. 'I have had enough of the sea already.'

He smiled, his manner changed as if he had accepted me without further question. 'Leave it with me, my dear. I will think of something. Where are you staying?'

'At the White Hart. My maid is there already.'

He exclaimed in horror. 'You cannot remain there. It

is no more than a rough and ready coaching inn, not fit for a young lady like yourself. You must come to us. Our house, I fear, is small and my two young sons not yet returned to the university, still I am sure my wife can find room . . .'

'You are very kind, Mr Cameron,' I interrupted sturdily, 'but I would prefer to be independent and not trespass on Mrs Cameron's goodness of heart. We shall do well enough, Jeannie and I. After all we have already travelled from Paris and have met with no harm.'

'A young lady of spirit, I can see that. It is a pity that the town house of Glenlochy is closed up at present. There is no one there and in fact your grandfather has contemplated selling it if he can find a buyer.'

'Where is it?' I asked curiously.

'Further down the hill in the Canongate on the corner of Ramsay's Wynd.' He sighed. 'At one time it was a gay place. I remember it well.'

'Did you go there with my father?'

'Aye, we were young then, madcap students thinking only of amusing ourselves . . . ah well, those days are gone,' he went on briskly. 'The day after tomorrow my wife and I give a party, some music, a little dancing perhaps. You will come, I hope. I will send my carriage. By then perhaps I shall have news for you.'

I gave him the papers I had brought with me and he escorted me down the stairs. The cab was still waiting, the driver hunched on the box with an old brown blanket pulled up to his chin. He opened one eye nodding familiarly to Mr Cameron as he helped me into the carriage. Then he turned his horse carefully in the frozen snow. At the White Hart he climbed down to open the door for me.

'There was a gentleman askin' after ye, mistress,' he whispered confidentially, 'wantin' to know where you were staying.'

'A gentleman?'

'Aye, a dark body. He came down Mr Cameron's staircase as if the de'il himself were after him. I told him naething.'

'Thank you. It was kind of you.'

I dropped a small coin in the outstretched hand and went into the inn thoughtfully, a little disturbed because I could think of absolutely no reason why Colonel Richard Wynter should be asking questions about me.

Chapter Two

When I reached our room on the second floor I found Jeannie had unpacked all our baggage and was stretched out on the bed fast asleep. In one way I was glad. I was still dazed. I still could not quite believe in what Duncan Cameron had told me. I had set out from Paris with no fixed purpose, no plan of campaign, no certainty as to whether I would be made welcome at Glenlochy. I had longed only to escape from my mother and see for myself the place where my father had grown up; the long beautiful beaches of white sand where the seals basked on the rocks, the forests of oak and ash and pine haunted by deer and fox and badger, the simple kindly people whose crofts lay scattered up and down the glen, the green knolls where the faery folk go to and fro with silent printless step, the ice-cold waters of the loch where the *each uisge,* the water-horse in harness of gold, rears and plunges threatening disaster to anyone unlucky enough to catch a glimpse of him.

These were some of the tales my father had learned from his Gaelic nurse and they had become the fairy stories of my childhood. Now they were to be my inheritance; one day they would become part of my children's dreams. It was too wonderful to be spoken of carelessly lest it should vanish like the magic gold at the foot of the rainbow. I dreaded Jeannie's sturdy common sense. She was a practical level-headed little body, the daughter of one of the Scots who had followed his chief into exile and had died leaving wife and child penniless. My father had pleaded for them until my mother in exasperation had taken Jeannie into our household. She had been maid of all work at the Rue Chantelle for four years ever since she was twelve, and she had not been above speaking her mind on occasions. I think my mother had not been sorry to be rid of her just as she had gladly freed herself of me.

When Jeannie sat up sleepy-eyed but eager to hear all that had happened, I told her little except that Mr Cameron had been kind and would advise us as to the best way of reaching Glenlochy.

We spent the next day quietly. I was more exhausted from our journey than I realized and was glad to rest while Jeannie clucked disapprovingly over the creases in my gowns and borrowed a smoothing iron from the chambermaid. If I were to meet members of Edinburgh society at Mr Cameron's party, she said sternly, then it was important that I should do her credit.

By late afternoon I was beginning to find the room stifling. I have always had a lively curiosity and I made up my mind to take a short walk. Jeannie reached for her bonnet but I shook my head.

'There is no need to come with me. I am only going out for a breath of air. I shall not be long.'

Outside I found the weather had improved. It was still cold but there had been a few thin streaks of sun during the day and I felt an enormous exhilaration as I gazed up at the castle on the crest of the hill sailing like a full-rigged ship against a sky of pink-tipped clouds. The stall-keepers in the market were packing up their butter and cheeses. Ragged barefoot children stared at me and then darted away screaming to one another. Hens squawked and I was jostled by sheep and cattle and black-faced goats. Then I was free of them and walking swiftly down the hill past St Giles's Cathedral with its lantern tower and eight flying buttresses until I reached the Canongate. Ahead I could see the stately grace of the palace of Holyrood in its circle of low green hills. Snow and slush piled up against the gilded gates. This was where my father had danced at a grand ball when Highland chieftains gathered around their handsome Prince and every heart was radiant with hope. Now English soldiers in red coats paraded at the castle and rubbish blew about the neglected palace of the Scottish kings.

The sun had gone down. It was already dusk when I retraced my steps and looked curiously around me. This was where the Gilmours lived when they came to Edinburgh. Many of the houses were empty or turned into slum tenements with ragged washing hung across courtyards and sullen faces staring from broken windows. One of them still retained its dignity. It stood alone on the corner of Ramsay's Wynd. Above the lintel was a coat of arms carved in the stone, a rearing cat with a crown on its head. I stared up at it and wondered what lay behind the shuttered windows. Tempting visions chased through my mind. Maybe one day it would be I who would open it up again. It would know children's laughter, all the bustle and gaiety of living. Then I came back to reality shivering in the cold wind that whistled up the alley. I was reluctantly turning away when the door opened and a man came out on to the step. I could see little of him, his hat was pulled down and a long cloak hid his figure but the woman in the doorway held a candle in her hand and I saw the pale face, the long unbound black hair hanging to her waist over a gown of dark red wool. She had a wild beauty like the heroine of some ancient ballad. The man turned back pulling her close to him. There was a lingering passion in his kiss, then the door was shut and he came swiftly down the steps, pushing past me to make his way down the Wynd.

It seemed strange when Mr Cameron had been so sure that the house was shut up. I was tempted to knock and then thought how embarrassing it would be to explain myself even if only to servants. The hand that touched my arm nearly made me jump out of my skin. I shrank back against the iron post at the bottom of the steps.

'Isn't it rather late to be sight-seeing, Miss Gilmour?' said Richard Wynter quietly.

He seemed to have the habit of cropping up at unexpected moments and I said with exasperation, 'Have you been following me, Mr Wynter?'

'Certainly not. Like yourself I have been taking a stroll and admiring the curiosities of Edinburgh. It's a fine old house, isn't it, but badly in need of repair. Do you see how the roof sags? There must be pools of water in those attics.'

His cool practical tone irritated me. I said acidly, 'I don't really see that it is any concern of yours.'

'It could be,' he said unexpectedly, 'if I made up my mind to buy it.'

'Buy it?'

'Why not? Quite a large stretch of Glenlochy land belongs to me already.'

I stared at him in disbelief. 'Mr Cameron never told me.'

'No reputable lawyer discloses the business of his clients.'

'But I have a right to know.'

'I would have thought that right belonged to Sir Alasdair.'

'He is my grandfather.'

'Indeed. I did wonder.'

'Is that why you were asking questions of my cab driver?'

'Mere idle curiosity, Miss Gilmour, I assure you. Don't you think you had better allow me to see you to your hotel?'

I had no wish to encourage him but it seemed churlish to refuse so we walked on in silence side by side until I said, 'Why should you, an Englishman, be buying lands in the Highlands?'

'Why indeed?'

'I suppose it is easy to obtain a fine bargain when poverty forces an owner to sell,' I said with some anger thinking of my grandfather.

'It is a point worthy of consideration certainly,' he replied calmly, 'but you mistake me, Miss Gilmour, I am not buying, at least not yet. In actual fact the land is an inheritance and a damned awkward one too if you will pardon my bluntness.'

I stole a glance at him as we passed under one of the lanterns hung at infrequent intervals along the street. He was looking straight ahead and there was a grim set to his mouth. I said impulsively, 'If you dislike it so much it should not be difficult to rid yourself of it.'

'It's not so simple, believe me. An inheritance carries obligations with it, don't you agree?'

It seemed a curious way of putting it. I was beginning to wonder how much he knew about me when suddenly without any warning he seized my arm and dragged me into the middle of the highway just in time to escape a pail of filthy slops poured down from one of the upper windows.

'That was lucky,' he exclaimed, 'I saw it just in time. The Scottish housewives have an unpleasant habit of emptying their buckets regardless of anyone passing underneath. We had better keep ourselves at a safe distance.'

'Oh, how disgusting!' I gasped, searching for a handkerchief and holding it to my nose. 'How did you know?'

'I've been in Edinburgh once before. I was not so fortunate that time.' For the first time he smiled and it had a way of lighting up the grey eyes and giving a humorous quirk to the stern mouth.

I might have warmed to him then except that he was English, one of the hateful race who had ruined my father's life and were brutally destroying the Scotland he had loved. I hurried on and he kept pace with me until we stopped outside the White Hart.

'You should be safe enough now,' he said looking down at me still with the same quirky smile. 'I greatly fear that much as you dislike me we shall be meeting again in Mr Cameron's drawing-room tomorrow.'

'I never said I disliked you.'

'Not in so many words but I felt it, you know, bleak as a wind off the snow. Goodnight, Miss Gilmour.' He bowed and walked quickly away from me up towards the castle.

I dressed myself with exceptional care for Mr Cameron's evening assembly. Jeannie had pressed the flounces of a green silk brocaded gown with a rose-pink petticoat embroidered with tiny flowers. My mother might be only the daughter of a lodging-house keeper but she had excellent taste. It emphasized the green of my eyes and set off my red hair to perfection. At the last moment I took the Sithen Stone. I pinned it amongst the laces at my breast.

'And where in the name of God did ye find that?' gaped Jeannie. 'You'll surely not be wearing it. It's awful large.'

She was right. It was the kind of clasp that a man

might wear on his shoulder to hold his plaid but I felt gay and reckless. I was Mistress Gilmour of Glenlochy and I was proud of it. Why shouldn't I flaunt my claim to all the world?

Promptly at five o'clock the carriage arrived. Jeannie put my fur mantle around my shoulders and I waved to her as the coachman closed the door on me. Mr Cameron lived in a fine substantial house in one of the new-built squares to the north of the city. The moment I entered the white panelled drawing-room I knew my gown was a mistake. It was cut very low in the French style despite the cream lace that foamed around my bare shoulders. There must have been about thirty people present and as I came into the room, all eyes turned towards me.

Mr Cameron came to greet me, kissing my hand with an old world courtesy and introducing me to his wife. I read strong disapproval in the look she gave me and in the cold glances of the ladies in their high-necked provincial gowns. Well, let them think what they pleased.

I chatted gaily as I was led from one to the other. I answered questions, I spoke of Paris and my grandfather, very aware of their curiosity. Later we sat down to listen to music. A young man played the harpsichord excruciatingly badly, an elderly lady who should have known better screeched her way through an Italian song. We applauded politely. Mr Cameron was at my elbow again.

'I am sure you sing too, Miss Gilmour. Won't you delight us with a French ballad?'

'Oh no, I really couldn't.'

'Oh come, please do.' He twinkled at me. 'What has happened to your Glenlochy courage?'

It was a challenge and I could not resist it. I let him lead me to the instrument. I had been well trained. My mother had seen to that. 'A man likes his wife to have a few social accomplishments,' she had always said, as if I was a package to be sold to the highest bidder. I sang a French air, light, sweet and slightly daring. The young men applauded vigorously. I had risen and would have gone quietly back to my chair when I saw that Richard Wynter had arrived. He stood in the doorway, his plum-coloured coat elegantly cut, his dark hair curled. I did not like him but I had to admit his distinction and he was the only one amongst the guests who was not applauding and calling for an encore. I cared nothing for any of them but his slight sardonic smile piqued me. I sat down again on the music stool. I let my fingers stray over the notes and began to sing. It had a haunting melody. I had sung it often among my father's friends and they had wept for what they had lost.

> 'Sweet the lav'rock's note and lang,
>   Lilting wildly up the glen,
> And aye the o'erword o' the sang
>   Is "Will he no come back again?
> Will he no' come back again?
> Will he no' come back again?
> Better lo'ed he'll never be
> And will he no' come back again?"'

I felt the change in the atmosphere at once, the shifting of the feet, the uneasy glances, the half-hearted applause. I did not care. I took pleasure in hitting at their smug complacency. I had shown how I felt. My father had fought for a noble cause and I was not ashamed of it.

As I passed Richard Wynter on my way back to my chair, he stayed me with a hand on my bare arm.

'You have been very bold, Miss Gilmour.'

'It's a fine Scottish ballad,' I said defensively.

'True and you sang it very movingly, but it has reminded them of something they would rather forget.'

'Does it matter?'

'I think it does. Isn't it rather foolish to stir up old hatreds? It is not our quarrel. I was six years old when my father fought for King George at Culloden and you had not even been born.'

'My father suffered all his life because of what the English did to him.'

'Perhaps, but I still don't believe that he would have wished you to insult his good friend who happens to be your host.'

There was rebuke in his cool tone and it made me angry because I knew it was justified. I drew away from him and was instantly aware that someone was staring

at me. Across the gilded chairs I met the gaze of a tall
woman in a plain dark red dress, her black hair drawn
up and away from her pale face and I was almost sure
that it was she whom I had seen the night before on the
steps of the Glenlochy house. For an instant her eyes held
mine and my hand instinctively went to the Sìthen Stone.
Then she moved quickly away mingling with the other
guests so that I thought I must be mistaken. The next
moment Mr Cameron had come hurrying up, taking my
arm in his friendly fashion.

'You sang like an angel, Miss Marietta,' he said warmly.

'I did not mean . . .' I stammered. 'I hope I have not
offended you.'

'No,' he answered quietly. 'I know how you feel. I am
not without sympathy but you cannot go on regretting
the past. The future is what matters now. Come with me.
There is someone I want you to meet, a charming young
lady like yourself. She will be a companion for you when
you travel to Glenlochy.'

'Companion? But how do you mean? I don't understand . . .'

'You will in a moment.' He beamed at me from behind
his spectacles obviously very pleased with himself. We
crossed the room to where a group of guests were laughing together and helping themselves from the liberally
spread buffet table.

'My dear Lady Janet,' said Mr Cameron, 'may I present
Mistress Marietta Gilmour?'

One of the ladies turned round. Frivolous pink ribbons
tied up bright brown hair and trimmed an elaborate gown
of cream silk. It was quite unmistakably the young woman
who had thrown her arms around Richard Wynter on
the quay at Leith. A pair of blue eyes looked me frankly
up and down. Then she smiled and held out her hand.

'How delightful to meet you and how exciting that you
should be wanting to go to Glenlochy at the same time
as we do. I was quite dreading the journey but now it will
be different. I am sure we shall have great fun together.'

I was so taken by surprise that for an instant I could
find no words and Mr Cameron supplied them for me.

'I thought of it only this morning when Colonel Wynter

told me that he intended to leave at the beginning of next week. To travel across Scotland alone would be quite unthinkable especially at this season of the year, but now you will have company and an escort. Nothing could be more suitable.'

'But I cannot, really I cannot be such a burden to anyone,' I exclaimed. 'There is Jeannie as well as myself. It is impossible.'

'Of course it isn't,' said the young woman in pink ribbons. 'Don't take any notice, Mr Cameron, I'll talk to her. Come and sit down, Miss Gilmour. Let's get to know one another. Tell me about yourself.'

I was quite appalled at the prospect of spending days and days in the company of Richard Wynter but I let myself be led to a sofa. The young girl, for she could not have been more than a year or two older than myself, pulled me down to sit beside her.

'Now let's have a cosy chat,' she said, comfortably settling herself. 'I've been admiring your gown from the moment we came in. It's French, isn't it? So elegant and stylish. I'm always telling John he ought to let me buy my clothes in Paris but he's such a stick-in-the-mud. He says he loves me just as I am. Very sweet of course, but I do like to be fashionable. John is my husband, you know, Sir John Thorpe. He's abroad at the moment with the army. Such a bore being away so much but there it is. A man likes something to do. He and Richard served in the same company. That's how I met him when Richard brought him home on leave to Laverstoke. That's in Sussex. Father is Lord Wynter.'

I tried to disentangle what she was saying. 'Then Mr Wynter is not . . .'

'Did you think that Richard was my husband? Oh dear, no.' She laughed merrily. 'He's my elder brother. Oh, he's a darling and I love him very much but I couldn't possibly be married to him. Richard can be very stern, you know, not a bit like John.'

'I thought, you see, when I saw you both on the quay at Leith . . .'

'Oh yes of course. You were there too. You stole our cab and Richard was so annoyed. You must have travelled together on the same ship from France. Was the crossing very dreadful? Thank goodness we are not taking the boat up the West Coast. I put my foot down about that. Richard is never sick of course but I know for a certainty that I should be absolutely prostrate and then he would be so cross with me.'

'How unkind.'

'Oh no, you mustn't think that. Richard is very considerate really. It's just that he expects such a lot from everyone and I'm always afraid I'll never measure up to his high standards.'

If possible that made me dislike him even more but there was something very engaging about Janet. I had never had many girl friends. I suddenly thought that it might be pleasant to travel in company with this charming young woman even if it meant that I had to put up with her difficult brother.

She was still rattling on happily. 'We shall be able to travel in the carriage together and Richard will ride. Nothing would induce him to be shut up with me. He says my chatter would drive him out of his mind in an hour.'

That was a relief anyway. It meant I should not see much of him during the day at least. I said curiously, 'If I am not being very impertinent, may I ask why you are going with your brother to Glenlochy?'

'Oh, it's rather a long story. I expect you'll hear most of it before we arrive there. It's all rather an adventure really. You see, it's like this . . .'

'You talk too much, my dear,' said a cool voice and I looked up to see that Richard Wynter had come up behind us and his hand was on his sister's shoulder. 'I am afraid, Miss Gilmour, that Janet is an incurable romantic.'

'No, I'm not,' she said irrepressibly. 'It is I who am the practical one. I'd like to know how you'd manage alone in that gloomy old place in Glenlochy without me to make it comfortable for you.'

'Oh I'm grateful, my dear, very grateful, you know that.' His fingers touched her cheek and she looked up at him smiling.

'Nothing to be grateful for. I'm bored to death without John and you know it. I've been making friends with

Marietta—you don't mind me calling you Marietta, do you, and do please call me Janet—and I do think it is the most romantic thing in the world that you are going to meet your grandfather for the first time when up to now he didn't even know you existed. You must agree about that, Richard.'

'Indeed I do. I only hope that it turns out to be as romantic as it sounds,' he said dryly. 'I'm afraid you must prepare yourself for a tiring journey, Miss Gilmour. We can only use the carriage for part of the way, then I understand we must take to ponies.'

'You needn't concern yourself, Mr Wynter. I can ride. I shall not fall off.'

'Of course you won't. What a ridiculous idea! Don't be such an old bear, Richard. You mustn't mind my brother, Marietta. He regards all females as silly frivolous creatures constantly subject to fits of the vapours. Just because you've had one bad experience, Richard, it doesn't mean that all women are like . . .'

'Jan please!' For an instant it was as if a mask slipped and I was startled by the look of pain that crossed his face and was gone almost before I realized it. His sister was immediately contrite.

'I'm sorry, dearest. I didn't mean to remind you. Don't take any notice of me, Marietta, I'm always rattling on without thinking. Oh look! They are going to begin the dancing already.'

While we had been talking the floor had been cleared of chairs and a fiddler had come to stand beside the harpsichord.

Richard Wynter said abruptly, 'Will it break your heart if we leave before the dancing, Janet?'

I fully expected her to protest but she didn't. She got up immediately, slipping her arm through his.

'No, of course it won't, you silly old thing. I know just how you feel. I don't mind at all. I'll say goodnight, Marietta. It's been so nice talking to you and we'll be meeting again very soon.'

Richard bowed and murmured something polite and they moved away together. Obviously she would have loved to dance and I thought it very selfish of him to drag her away even though she was looking up into his face and laughing. She might call him an old bear but she seemed very fond of him despite his autocratic manner.

I did not stay much longer myself. Mr Cameron pressed me to join in the dancing but I shook my head. I looked around once for the woman in the dark red dress meaning to ask him who she was but I could not see her anywhere and the question suddenly seemed unimportant.

He came down with me to the waiting carriage. 'I hope I have done right in arranging for you to travel with Colonel Wynter and his sister,' he said a little anxiously. 'There was no time to consult you and I thought it too good an opportunity to be missed.'

'I am very grateful.'

'Janet Thorpe is a pleasant young lady and her brother is very reliable. I knew their father at one time. He has succeeded to the title now, you know, but then he was just the honourable Robert Wynter.'

That must be the father who had fought for King George. I said, 'Why didn't you tell me that they own part of Glenlochy land.'

'The question did not arise. It was a few years ago. Your grandfather needed money desperately and sold the hunting lodge and the woods surrounding it. There was some trouble over it.'

'What trouble?'

He looked at me for a moment and then went on quickly. 'I don't think you need worry about it. It is all done with now. Glenlochy is a lovely spot but lonely. You may find it pleasant to have neighbours only a few miles away. I have written already to Sir Alasdair. The letter will go up by the mail boat and should reach him before your arrival. I will call on you tomorrow and we will settle the details.'

'Thank you.'

I was tempted then to tell him about the cryptic message warning me to keep away from Glenlochy but something stopped me. It was foolhardy perhaps but I was afraid that it might prevent my leaving so I said nothing as he handed me into the carriage and we clopped away over the frosty cobbles.

Later that night long after I had answered Jeannie's

questions and she had fallen silent, I lay restless and
wakeful, the events of the evening turning over and over
in my mind. That black-haired woman . . . who was she?
. . . and had I only imagined the searching look she had
given me? I was annoyed with myself because in some odd
way the face of Richard Wynter persisted in coming between me and sleep. If someone had once made him suffer, no doubt he thoroughly deserved it. I buried my head
in the pillow deliberately thinking of my father and wondering if on the desperate and bloody battlefield of Culloden Ian Gilmour had ever confronted Robert Wynter
sword in hand.

Chapter Three

Nothing that I had ever experienced prepared me for my first sight of the Highlands, the grandeur, the overwhelming majesty, the queer sense of belonging which I could only feel but never explain.

We left Edinburgh a week after Mr Cameron's evening party, quite a cavalcade of us. Janet and I travelled together in the large roomy coach that had been specially reinforced for the rough roads, followed by Jeannie and Rose, Janet's hard-faced elderly maid, in a second carriage with the baggage. Richard Wynter rode ahead, pistols in his saddle holsters since there was no telling what dangers we might meet on the road, and James, the groom who had accompanied Janet from Sussex, brought up the rear. We travelled first along the banks of the Firth of Forth through a pleasant flat country of fields and farms. Spring was slow in coming to Scotland but the snow had gone and I saw the green spears of young grass and the slim brown buds bursting on the silver birches.

We came to Stirling just as the light was fading. A great green-black jagged rock arose out of the plain crowned by the fretted ramparts of a castle. We had drawn up at the side of the road to let an ox-cart lumber by and Richard put his head in at the carriage window.

'The Highlands,' he said and waved his whip to the north. Far in the distance smudged in grey, like clouds against the pale sky, lay the mighty Grampians whose very name is like a gallop of wild horses.

'Do you feel the thrill of it, Miss Gilmour? You should. It was here that Robert the Bruce raised the Lion standard and won the independence of Scotland.'

The independence that Charles Stuart had lost so fatally at Culloden . . . it was unspoken but I seemed to hear it in the irony of his voice. Did he have to remind me that the ancient glory had vanished on that day of bitter defeat?

'There will be other leaders,' I flashed at him.

He shrugged his shoulders. 'I greatly fear the age of heroes is gone for ever.'

It was a gruelling journey. The carriage jolted over the great stone blocks of the military road laid down by General Wade's red-coated soldiers fifty years before. I remembered my father telling me how the Highland chieftains had resented the invasion of their impregnable mountain lands. The inns were mostly poor places and we slept on hard mattresses or bundles of straw. They were sometimes so dirty that we lived on milk and cheese and oatmeal bannocks eked out with delicacies from the provisions which Janet had insisted on carrying with us.

It took eight days to reach Fort William. Once we entered the mountains we were forced to abandon the carriages and take to the ponies. The stout little garrons were sure-footed and tireless but though I would have died rather than admit it, I was so stiff and bruised that at night I could neither rest nor sleep and it was agony to rouse myself at dawn for another day's hard riding. Janet bore it better than I did. She had ridden and hunted since she was a child, not walked the Paris streets, and she raised no objection when her brother pressed on relentlessly.

But I grew used to it and despite my bruised legs and aching back I loved it. Every step of the way was a revelation. My father's dream was coming to life before my eyes. Sometimes we rode through green valleys and sometimes we seemed to be the only living creatures in a savage wilderness shut in by iron-grey mountains, the only sound the icy torrents racing down in sparkling waterfalls, the sough of the wind in the long green grasses or the weird cry of some great bird flying across the loch.

We climbed steep slopes where the pines rose black and menacing, so thick that you could be lost within a minute of entering them. Once when the track was so narrow we had to move in single file, there was a rush of sound and a long drawn-out snarl. Involuntarily I kicked my pony and he leaped forward colliding heavily against Richard.

It jerked an oath out of him. 'Damn you, did you have to do that?' His hand clamped down on my rein checking my pony.

'I'm sorry . . .' I began defensively.

'It doesn't matter,' he said through clenched teeth. 'You needn't be afraid. There are no wild beasts now. That was probably a hunting cat.'

I thought him ill-tempered and boorish and wished I could have given him back some stinging retort but he had already drawn ahead again.

The day we rode through the pass of Glencoe there was a storm. Thunder rolled from one snow-capped peak to another. Lightning tore the sky apart and lit up the haunted glen with a lurid glow. I suppose there is no Scottish child who has not grown up on the tale of that bloody night when the Campbells betrayed the sacred tradition of Highland hospitality, ate and drank with their Macdonald hosts and then rose up at dawn, sword in hand, and slaughtered men, women and children.

Janet had been unusually silent. As we left it behind us, the sun broke through the clouds and a rainbow arched from one side of the road to the other in a glory of pink and gold and green. We were trotting quietly along the track when she said suddenly, 'My grandmother was a Campbell. It makes one feel ashamed, doesn't it?'

It was so unexpected that I had no ready answer. I said at last, 'I imagined you were English through and through.'

She smiled. 'I suppose we are on my mother's side but Margaret Campbell was a very forceful character. She died when I was twelve but I've never forgotten her. She was stern but she could be stimulating too. The whole household went in awe of her. She had an enormous influence on my father. That was how he came to be a colonel in the Black Watch.'

'But that's a Highland regiment surely.'

'Yes, it is, but my grandmother was distant kin of the Duke of Argyll and she insisted. It seemed quite natural for my two brothers to follow suit.'

'Two brothers . . .?'

'Yes. Graham was two years older than Richard and he was actually born in Scotland when my father was stationed up here. I think that was why he always had a special feeling for it and when he was ordered to the garrison at Fort William, he bought the Glenlochy land.'

'No doubt it was easy to buy cheaply at a time like that when so many of the Highlanders were forced to sell,' I said a little bitterly.

She turned to look at me. 'That is true, I suppose. It *was* easy for the English to buy land after Culloden but I don't think Graham felt like that about it. He loved it. He used to write most enthusiastic letters about what he was going to do when he lived there and how he intended to restore the Tige Dubh . . .'

'The Tige Dubh . . .' I said slowly. 'That means the Black House.'

'That's right. Do you know Gaelic?'

'A little. My father taught me.'

'How clever of you. It's only a small place, I believe, used by the Gilmours when they were out hunting.'

'Is your brother still at Fort William?'

'No.' She paused. 'You see he died two years ago.'

'Oh, I didn't know . . . I am sorry . . .'

'It was a great shock for all of us but more than anyone for Richard. They were always very close. I suppose that is why Graham left him the house and lands.'

So that explained the 'damned awkward inheritance.' I would have liked to know more but Janet as if she felt she had said too much suddenly spurred her pony forward and joined her brother. I had a feeling there was something more behind it, something she did not wish to share. I had learned a great deal about her childhood in the English country house, about her dogs, her husband and her disappointment that as yet she had no child, but she could be reserved and she rarely spoke of Richard. It was not for me to question.

We reached Fort William early the following afternoon. It was no more than a huddle of mean houses built around the military garrison but for once the inn was excellent. For the first time we had a comfortable bed and sat down to a well cooked meal of fresh salmon and roasted chicken. We ate bread just out of the oven and there was wine instead of whisky which both Janet and I loathed, so that even Richard relaxed and was quite talkative at supper.

'That was wonderful,' said Janet leaning back with a sigh of pure content and patting her stomach with a most unladylike gesture. 'I've eaten and drunk far too much and I don't care. Now I think I'll go to bed. I feel that I could sleep for a week.'

'Disgusting,' said her brother with an indulgent smile. 'You remind me of a kitten who has fed on cream and is now happily licking her paws. What about you, Marietta?' The name seemed to have slipped out without him noticing it.

'Oh, I don't know,' I said. 'I'll probably follow Janet's example.'

'Well, don't forget. We ought to leave by five o'clock tomorrow morning if we are to reach Glenlochy before nightfall.'

'When do you ever let us forget, brother mine?' said Janet lightly kissing the top of his head. 'You ought to take things more easily. You've been driving yourself too hard.'

I was surprised at the serious note in her voice. Richard had seemed to me to have a constitution of iron. It was only then I noticed how fine drawn he looked and how stiffly he got up almost as if he were afraid to give way to fatigue.

He put his hand on his sister's shoulder. 'Nonsense, my dear. You go to bed. I shall stroll up to the garrison.'

'Don't walk too far. Come on, Marietta. What a blessing it is we haven't got to share our straw bed with the ponies for once!'

I found Jeannie in our bedroom unpacking the small valise which we carried with us since the heavier baggage was strapped to the pack ponies and left unopened until we reached journey's end.

'Oh lordy, lordy, Miss Marietta,' Jeannie straightened her back painfully. 'If I'd known what I do now, nothing would have ever induced me to leave Paris. I don't think there is a single bone in my body that doesn't ache. How I wish I was back in the Rue Chantelle even if it was only scrubbing floors!'

'No, you don't, not really. Remember how you used to

grumble about it? Once we get to Glenlochy, it will be different.'

'Will it? I'm not so sure. I've never seen so many barbarous people and so many dirty hovels in my whole life. Why they even go barefoot,' she went on as if this was the last straw. 'There's not one of them with a pair of shoes to his feet.'

'They're poor,' I said. 'They have to keep them for the kirk on Sundays.'

'If they ever go there,' she said darkly. 'It's my belief they're no better than heathens. Do you know what that maid downstairs said to me when she first saw Mr Wynter? That she'd seen an Englishman like him before and he had the evil eye that can shrivel up the young corn and curse the babe in its mother's womb!'

'What absolute nonsense!' I exclaimed startled.

'That's what I said. Mr Wynter may be stern but he's a fair-minded gentleman and he's looked after us well. But what can you expect from an ignorant creature like that who ties a rowan twig to the milk pail to keep the fairies from curdling it!' went on Jeannie disgustedly.

I smiled. 'Never mind. We're nearly at the end of our journey. We shall be at Glenlochy tomorrow.'

'Thank goodness. I had begun to think we were coming to the end of the world.'

I laughed and stretched my arms wide. 'I like it. I like the mountains and I like the people.'

I suddenly did not want to sleep. I was consumed by a huge restlessness. I took my father's plaid which I had brought with me and held it against my face. It had that lovely peaty scent that always seems to cling to handmade woollen cloth. I stroked it gently remembering the day when my father had put it on for me, belting it round the waist in thick pleats and flinging it across his shoulder like a cloak. It was checked in blue and green with a thin red stripe and faded now from the sun and the many nights it had served as a blanket against wind and rain and heather. It would be cold outside with a fresh wind off the loch. I took it up and threw it around me over my riding dress, tossing it across one shoulder and fastening it with the Sìthen brooch. Jeannie watched me curiously but not even to her could I explain how I felt. At last I was fulfilling what I had sworn to myself when I knelt beside my father on that last night when he lay dying. It was part of him and it delighted me to feel the rough folds against my cheek.

I went down the stairs and out of the door. It was not yet quite dark. I had noticed already that up here in the north the light seemed to linger in a long twilight. I could see the fort with its four angular turrets, the English flag flying and soldiers moving in the courtyard, but I would not go near it. Instead I crossed the track to the edge of the loch and looked over the steel-grey water to the dark shape of the distant hills. Tomorrow we would cross by the ferry and take the road to the sea. Tomorrow I would be at Glenlochy Castle. What would I find there? What would Sir Alasdair say to this grandchild he had never seen? Would I look at them and wonder who had wanted to keep me away? I was filled with excitement and a touch of fear. For the first time I was glad that I would not be entirely alone in the glen, that much as I disliked Richard Wynter and his stern arbitrary manner, he would be there with his sister, steady and reliable, and only a few miles away.

A hand on my shoulder swung me roughly round, a coarse face was thrust close to mine.

'Don't ye know, my lass, that the wearing of the tartan is forbidden?'

Alarmed, scarcely understanding what he said, I struggled to free myself. 'I don't know what you mean. Let me go please,' but his grip only tightened.

'I could bring ye up before the Major, have ye whipped at the cart's tail, you'd not like that, my pretty, would ye now?' gloated the voice. 'But mebbe I won't, mebbe I'll forget for a consideration. What do you say? A bargain's a bargain, eh?' Whisky-laden breath was on my face. A hand tore at the brooch on my shoulder.

I was really frightened then. I cried out and the next moment the soldier was dragged off me and sent reeling back.

'What the devil do you think you're doing, assaulting a lady?' demanded Richard Wynter.

'A lady, is she?' snarled my attacker, touching his split

lip tenderly. 'Then why should she be dressing herself up in one of their heathen plaids?'

'It's no such thing. Pull yourself together, man. You're drunk.'

'Drunk, am I?' repeated the soldier belligerently. 'Not so drunk that I can't ask myself by what right you're giving the orders.' He was advancing with tipsy determination when a gust of wind across the water sent Richard's hat flying from his head. The man uttered a strangled gasp and staggered back with a look of sheer terror on his face. 'God forgive us,' he muttered. 'It's himself come out o' the grave!' I think he would have turned tail and run for his life but Richard seized him by the shoulder.

'What did you say just then?'

'Nothing, nothing,' babbled the soldier. 'Lemme go.'

'Oh yes, you did. What did you mean?' The authoritative voice had its effect. The man straightened himself with an effort.

"Tweren't nothing particular only that just for a minute, I could have sworn . . . I mean I thought . . .'

'Well, what did you think?'

The soldier shuffled his feet, looking away uneasily. 'You standing there, sir, the living image of the Captain . . . well, they did say as he drowned himself and them as do that, they don't lie easy in the earth . . .'

Richard gave a short bark of laughter. 'Well, I'm no ghost. The bruise on your jaw might have told you that. Go on with you, man, get back to your quarters and put more water in your whisky next time or you'll be seeing worse than the dead come back to life.'

The soldier bobbed his head and went running up the road to the fort as if the devil himself was at his heels while Richard looked after him, frowning.

I picked up his hat and held it out to him. 'I must thank you for coming to my rescue. I'm afraid you have hurt yourself. There is blood on your knuckles.'

He looked down at his hand in surprise. 'It's nothing. It so happens that the man was a fool but you ought to be more careful all the same. He was right, you know. The wearing of any kind of Highland dress is strictly forbidden and the penalties are severe.'

I stared at him incredulously. 'I can't believe that even the English would be so harsh, so intolerant.'

'It is the law.' Then he turned to me with his particular quirky smile. 'I don't personally agree with it. It seems to me a degrading way to break a people's spirit but there it is.'

'I see . . . I didn't realize . . .'

'I suppose the plaid belonged to your father.'

'Yes, it did.'

'Well, keep it out of sight until you reach Glenlochy. It should be safe enough there.'

'Even from an Englishman who is also a Campbell?'

'Yes, even from me.' He smiled and put his hand to his mouth sucking his bleeding knuckles. Just for an instant it gave him the endearing look of a small boy caught out in a misdemeanour. It gave me courage to ask a question.

'Mr Wynter, did that soldier think that you were your brother?'

His face changed. The smile disappeared. 'Apparently he did, superstitious idiot. Graham has been dead for two years. How did you know about him?'

'Janet said something . . .'

'My sister talks too much.'

'But she did not tell me that . . . that he . . .'

'He didn't. Graham would never have committed suicide. I am as certain of that as I am of standing here.'

'What did happen?'

Almost without thinking we turned and followed the path along the loch. Richard was looking straight ahead. He did not answer at once and when he did his voice was quiet and without emotion.

'He had a day's leave from his duties and he went to the Tige Dubh as he often did. Later that same night one of his men found his horse wandering on the moor and took it back to the stables. A week later his body was washed up on the beach, cruelly mauled by the rocks but still recognizable.'

'How terrible. Could he have gone swimming and somehow got caught in a current?'

'In full uniform and boots? Graham was not a lunatic.'

'Then what do you think?'

'There was an inquest and the official verdict was suicide. The shock of it nearly killed my father. I was abroad
with the regiment when the news reached me and . . .' but
he did not go on. He turned to me as if suddenly realizing
I was there. 'I don't know why I am burdening you with
our family troubles. It's getting late and as I said we have
an early start. I think perhaps we had better turn back.'

The night was very still. It was cold but with a clean
healthy freshness and the sky blazed with stars. At the
door to the inn Richard paused.

"Will you resent it very much if I offer you a word of
advice?'

'I will try not to.'

His hand touched the plaid where it swung from my
shoulder. 'Don't live too much in the past. It is the future that matters for people just as for countries.'

'What are you trying to tell me?'

'Just that. I think it might be a good thing to remember
when you reach Glenlochy Castle. You know, Marietta,
you remind me of another young woman who came from
France to take up her inheritance, only she was a queen.'

'Well, I'm certainly not that.'

'No, but Mary Queen of Scots had a French mother and
a Scottish father.'

I smiled. 'Who is the romantic now? You should not
compare me with her. She was beautiful.'

'She had red hair and a wilful spirit. She liked to wander in streets at night just as you do and she had courage.'

'Surely you're not paying me a compliment, Mr Wynter?' I said ironically.

'I never say what I don't mean. This last week has not
been easy. You've borne it remarkably well.'

'Better than you expected,' I said demurely. 'Thank you.'

'I only hope that at the end of it you won't suffer the
disillusionment poor Mary did.'

'I'm quite sure I won't. Goodnight, Mr Wynter.'

'Good night.'

He turned into the inn parlour as I went up the stairs.
Jeannie was already in bed and asleep. I undressed slowly, brushing my hair lingeringly and smiling a little to myself at the unexpectedness of Richard Wynter's allusion to

Mary Stuart. I had never thought he noticed anything about me except that I was an unwanted responsibility.

Presently I heard the stairs creak. He must be coming to bed. He knocked at his sister's door and she answered sleepily. I had not been intending to listen but at some time the large upper room must have been divided into the two and the partition wall was thin as paper. There was a murmur of voices. Then I heard Janet say quite clearly, 'I wish you would give it up, Richard.'

'That man tonight,' her brother must have been close to the wall because his voice came through strong and excited. 'There was something behind it, Jan. He was repeating common gossip. It's not suicides that walk. It is men who are murdered . . . it was written on his face only he was afraid to say it.'

'Richard dear, you can't believe someone like that. He was drunk, you said so yourself. Whatever you find out will not help Graham now.'

'It will help me. If Graham did not drown himself and you and I know perfectly well he would never have done such a thing, then he died in some other way and I mean to find out how and why.'

They went on talking but I deliberately moved away and very soon I heard the door open and shut again. Richard must have gone to his own room.

I seemed without any wish of my own to have become involved in a mystery that had nothing to do with me. Did someone resent Graham Wynter, the conquering Englishman who had taken advantage of Highland poverty to buy ancestral Glenlochy land? If they hated enough to have him murdered and his body thrown into the sea, then the ultimate responsibility surely rested with the Gilmours. My grandfather was still Chieftain in spite of everything that had happened, his word would still be law in the remote glens and valleys where his people lived.

I climbed into bed and blew out the candle. It could not be true. I would not believe it. There must be some simple explanation which Richard Wynter, blinded by prejudice, refused to accept. But though I tried to drive it out of my mind, I still found it disturbing.

Chapter Four

ו⁌੭⁊ও⁊ৎ੭

We came to Glenlochy in the late afternoon. I was to see
the sun go down over the sea and gild the distant shapes
of the islands many times. I was to see it in rain and hail
when the wind raged, the lightning lit the sky and the
waves were mountainous, but never with quite the thrill
as on that first day of early spring. The morning had
been cold with brief showers, but by midday sun had
broken through and turned the rain to diamonds on the
bare branches of the trees. We had picked up a guide in
Fort William, a dark-haired brown-faced boy who ran
by Richard's pony holding on to his stirrup leather. Without him we might have wandered there for ever for the
track was barely visible, winding in and out of the valleys.
We were riding past small secret lochs opening out of one
another beside green pastures where the Highland cattle
grazed, slow-moving shaggy monsters turning massive
heads with curving horns and watching us with huge
brown eyes behind a fringe of long hair.

Then the last loch opened out into the sea shining like
grey-blue satin that would soon be turning pink and gold
from the dying sun. The beach stretched white and clean
and empty, jagged with fangs of rock. Behind us towered
the mountain, his majestic head still streaked with snow
amid the green and around him the brown hills gathered
like courtiers around some great king.

The guide was tugging at my rein and pointing ahead.
Glenlochy Castle was on a spit of land jutting out into the
sea, a grey-green mass of jumbled walls and ramparts
with one immense square tower hung with creeper and
bathed in that strange brilliant light that comes sometimes
before darkness falls.

We had reined in our ponies and sat staring at it until

Janet exclaimed, 'Oh how beautiful it is and how I envy you, Marietta! It is the most romantic spot I've ever seen.'

'It's a great deal more than that,' said her brother prosaically. 'Whoever built that had a splendid eye for defence.'

Our guide was babbling something half in Gaelic, half in English.

'What does he say?'

'I think he means that it was once entirely surrounded by water but now a causeway has been built.'

'Thank God for that,' said Richard dryly. 'I thought you might have had to swim. Would you like me to ride across with you? The boy can take Janet up to the Tige Dubh.'

'No, I wouldn't dream of it. It will be getting dark soon and you've still a long way to go.'

'Not so far, I believe, no more than two or three miles up the glen under the shoulder of the mountain. James had better accompany you. He can help unload the baggage and bring the ponies back.'

'Thank you.'

Janet put her gloved hand on mine with a warm friendly pressure. 'All our good wishes go with you, Marietta. You won't forget we are here, will you? I shall be longing to hear about everything. You will come and see us?'

'Of course I will and you must come to me.' I moved nearer so that I could lean over and kiss her cheek. 'You've been so kind, you and your brother. I'm immensely grateful.'

'It has been a pleasure,' said Richard Wynter politely. He took off his hat as Jeannie and I urged the ponies forward followed by James with the baggage. I looked back once. Janet waved, then they turned and went trotting up the glen. I felt suddenly very alone. My heart thudded. The adventure had begun.

We rode along the edge of the beach skirting the rocks. The wind blew salt into my face and the seabirds flashed their white wings above us, diving down to the pools and seaweed left by the receding tide. The sea lapped lazily at the stone causeway. The ponies slithered on the rock and shingle as they climbed up on to it and

I saw then that another track wound inland through a great cleft in the hills opening into a green valley. There were crofts here, low black huts, any number of them. I could smell the tangy scent of peat fires. A child ran barefoot driving a herd of lean goats with shrill cries. Geese hissed at us with outstretched necks and scrawny hens pecked at the thin grass. I turned my pony's head to the iron-bound door beneath the stone portal.

James leaped down, helped Jeannie and I to dismount and then tugged at the bell handle. There was a tall wooden post at one side of the door, seven to eight feet high, with a rusty iron ring fixed at the top.

'What do you suppose that is?' whispered Jeannie fearfully.

'It's the hanging post,' I whispered back.

'You don't mean . . . ?'

'My father told me. In the old days they hung wrongdoers there as a punishment and an example.'

'My God, what have we come to!' muttered Jeannie shuddering.

Then the door swung open. The manservant who stood there staring at us wore what might once have been some sort of livery but the coat was faded, the grubby shirt had no collar and his breeches ended in bare hairy legs thrust into the deerskin shoes they called brogues. He watched me for a moment, then his face broke into a wide grin.

'It's herself. It's the young mistress.' He swung the door back. 'Come ye in. Mac'Ghille Mhoire has been waiting for ye ever since the letter came from Edinburgh. Tam!' he yelled. 'Where in hell have ye got to, ye young imp?'

A boy in ragged breeches and shirt appeared from nowhere and put a rough hand on the baggage.

'Careful, careful!' exclaimed James, his prim English face a study in disgust. 'That's no way to handle a lady's luggage.'

I stayed a moment to thank him for his care of me. He touched his hat politely.

'Glad to be of service, Miss. Don't you worry. I'll see that everything is properly taken care of and carried in for you.'

'Thank you, James. Please take the ponies back to
Mr Wynter with my gratitude.'

I wondered what shocking tale he would carry back to
Rose at the Black House. Then I was being ushered inside.

'If ye'll be pleased to wait, mistress, Kirsty shall take ye
to the Chief.'

The serving man disappeared through some inner door
and I looked about me. This must have been the oldest
part of the castle. The great hall was tall and shadowy,
roofed in timber like the nave of some ancient church.
Pieces of armour and weapons of every kind shared the
walls with hunting trophies, spreading antlers and heads
of huge beasts stuffed and mounted. The furniture was
black oak, enormously heavy and very old and the floor
was stone. No fire blazed in the gigantic hearth and I
shivered as much with cold as nervous excitement.

Kirsty was a rosy-cheeked girl of about sixteen, a mob
cap on her tousled hair, a striped apron over her brown
skirts. She bobbed a curtsey, snapping black eyes examin-
ing me curiously. She led the way to the other end of the
hall beneath a carved minstrel's gallery but before we
could reach it, a woman had come through a hidden
door at the side. In sharp contrast to the others, she
was neatness personified; mouse-colored hair carefully
dressed, plain black dress with small linen collar, shining
buckled shoes.

"I am Mistress Drummond, Sir Alasdair's housekeeper,
Miss Gilmour,' she said quietly. 'It's all right, Kirsty, you
can go back to the kitchen and you had better take Miss
Gilmour's maid with you.'

I saw rebellion in Jeannie's eyes and said hurriedly, 'She
is more companion than maid. Perhaps you would be
kind enough to show her my room so that she can begin
to unpack for me.'

'Certainly if you wish. Did you hear, Kirsty?'

'Aye, ma'am. I did that.'

Jeannie went with her reluctantly. Mrs Drummond's
manner was completely impartial showing neither pleasure
nor resentment at my arrival and yet there was something striking about the pale bony face and a flash in the
brown eyes that made me wonder. Not that I noticed these

things immediately. I was to remember them later. She went ahead of me up a spiral stone staircase until we reached what was obviously a newer part of the castle. Thick matting covered the stone floors, hunting prints hung on the walls and I saw that the windows looked out on to an inner courtyard. Then at the end of a passage she opened a door.

'Miss Gilmour has arrived, sir.'

There are moments in everyone's life that impress themselves indelibly on the memory, not because they are the most important but from a variety of circumstances that gives them a particular significance. If I were to close my eyes now, I would see again that whole scene as clearly as on that first evening. It was a large room, once richly furnished but now wearing a look of faded grandeur. The carpet on the floor was worn bare in places. The magnificent tapestry that covered one wall had dimmed with age, the paint had cracked on a life-size portrait of some earlier chieftain that dominated the room. Logs burned on the hearth and a tall iron candelabra shed its light on the two men who sat on either side of a small table playing chess. I saw the green and white chequered board and the exquisitely carved ivory pieces.

Before I could move or speak two gigantic dogs un-coiled themselves from the hearth and bounded towards me. I shrank back against the doorpost and Sir Alasdair's voice halted them instantly.

'Bran! Wolf! Down, boys!'

The dogs slunk back and watched me from slate grey eyes while their master rose slowly to his feet. How shall I describe my grandfather as I saw him then? He was a very tall man, over six foot and splendid still though he was near to eighty. A hawk-like face carved out of brown wood with a jutting nose, piercing eyes under fierce eyebrows and white hair that fell to his shoulders. He wore a fur-trimmed brocaded dressing-gown hanging open over breeches and waistcoat. It gave him the proud dignity of some ancient king.

He said slowly, 'So . . . you are Marietta.'

'Yes.'

'Come here to me, child.'

He held out his hand and overwhelmed with emotion I

ran across the room. I think I would have fallen at his
feet if he had not caught me in his arms. I was crushed
against him. His moustache pricked my cheeks. I smelled
the masculine scent of tobacco mingled with the wood
smoke from the fire and the fumes of the whisky that
stood at his elbow beside the small silver cup. Then he
held me away from him looking into my face. My bonnet
had tumbled off and one knotted blue-veined hand
touched my hair.

'You have your father's colour. Ian was always the red-
poll among my sons.' He glanced towards the door where
Mrs Drummond still waited. 'You can go,' he said abruptly.

'Very well, but what about supper?'

'Bring it in an hour.'

'As you wish.' Mrs Drummond vanished closing the
door quietly behind her.

'Coll,' said my grandfather, 'move the table aside. We'll
finish the game later.'

'Yes, of course, sir. After supper perhaps.'

'Coll serves as my factor,' said Sir Alasdair with a careless wave of his hand.

'Steward I believe it is called in England but the French
equivalent escapes me. I manage the farms, do the accounts, run the estates and beat the Chief at chess,' said
a pleasant voice with the charming lilt that I had begun
to recognize as so characteristic of the Highlands.

For the first time I was aware of someone other than
my grandfather. I turned to look at him. I held out my
hand and said politely, 'I am delighted to meet you,'
and fell in love instantly and devastatingly.

I know that it sounds ridiculous. I know that in all
sanity no one outside the pages of a romantic novel ever
does such a thing. I was not even immediately aware of
it myself. In the past I had often wondered why my mother, that hard-headed practical Frenchwoman, had fallen
in love with my father, the tall melancholy Highlander
without money or prospects, and now with a startling certainty I knew. It was not that Coll was like my father. His
hair was much darker for one thing. It was more bronze
than red and his eyes were a deep blue in a tanned face.
It was not that he was quite the handsomest young man
I had ever seen though I suppose that was part of it. It was

all those things and more. He was the embodiment of all that I had ever imagined about the Highlands and recklessly, crazily, I lost my heart to a dream.

But I'm racing on. All this only became clear to me afterwards. At that moment I was speechless while he held my hand in his before raising it to his lips with charm and grace. Then he glanced at my grandfather.

'Shall I go too, sir?'

'Aye, do that. Come back to supper and bring Neil with you. Where the devil is the boy anyway?'

Coll shrugged his shoulders. 'I'll find him.'

He smiled at me as he turned to go, a friendly intimate smile as if he were saying, 'I'm glad you've come for the old man's sake,' and I warmed to him. Then he had moved to the door, the two dogs following after him, leaving me alone with my grandfather.

Sir Alasdair let himself drop into his chair, brooding eyes watching me for a moment. Then he said abruptly, 'Why did my son never write to me? Why did he let me go on believing him dead with his brothers?'

'He did write, more than once. When you did not reply, he thought . . .' I paused a little frightened of him.

'Well, what did he think?'

'That you were angry with him, that you rejected him because when he escaped from the prison at Fort William he left his brother Donald to die.'

'Tscha!' he made an impatient gesture. 'Why should I think that? With the English murderers hammering at every door in Scotland, it was each man for himself. I received no letters.' He turned to look at me. 'Was it your mother? Was it the Frenchwoman whom he picked up and married? Was he so ashamed that he could not tell me a child had been born to him, my grandchild?'

'No, no, he was not. She was good to him. He loved her.' It was strange that I who hated my mother so bitterly was now defending her passionately to this fierce proud old man. 'He would have starved but for her. I was a child, but I remember how hard it was for him in Paris at first.'

'It was hard for us all. And so she has sent you to me now he is dead.'

'That isn't true . . .'

'Isn't it? If so, her hopes and yours are doomed to disappointment. There are no pickings here,' he said with extreme bitterness. 'The English have made sure of that.'

'No, you're wrong. You don't understand at all.'

'Do you call me a fool?'

'No, no.' I went to him then falling on my knees beside him. 'My father spoke of you often. He told me of Glenlochy. He made me love it as he did. That's why, when he died, I had to come. I wanted to come more than anything in the world. My mother would have stopped me but I wouldn't let her. Didn't Duncan Cameron tell you when he wrote to you? Didn't he tell you that I brought you this?'

I groped under my cloak and brought out the Sìthen Stone from where I had pinned it to my riding dress. I put it into the old brown hand. The stone in its gold serpent setting shone blood-red in the candlelight. He stared down at it.

'So . . . it has come back and I believed it stolen by some thieving rascal of a redcoat. Do you know about this?'

'My father told me.'

'And named you for it. Ian was always a romantic fool. All nonsense of course,' he smiled grimly. 'There are no faeries in Scotland now nor ever will be again. But sometimes of late years even I have believed that honour and courage went out of Glenlochy on the day my eldest son was killed at Culloden.'

'And now they have come back.'

'The brooch, aye, but for the rest, I wonder. If only I had known . . . Why weren't you a boy, Marietta?' he sighed. ' "It came with a lass and it will go with a lass." Our King Jamie said that when they told him his French wife had borne him a daughter.'

A daughter who had been the unhappy Queen of Scots. I could not help remembering what Richard Wynter had said, 'I hope you'll not find the disillusionment she did', and for an instant a cold wind seemed to whip around me, but it was only the door opening behind us. Mrs Drummond stood on the threshold.

My grandfather looked annoyed. He said harshly, 'What are you wanting now, woman? I told you to bring supper later.'

'Yes, sir, I know, but Miss Gilmour has had a long journey. I thought she would be glad to wash and rest before eating.'

To tell the truth, the last hour had been so momentous that I had forgotten how exhausted I was and how pleasant it would be to dip my face in cool water and shake off the dirt and mud of travel.

'Very well. Go with her, Marietta,' said my grand-father impatiently. 'But come back quickly.'

'Yes, of course.' I bent to kiss his cheek. 'You are not sorry I have come,' I whispered and was reassured by the pressure of his hand and then he pushed me away.

'Get on with you, child.'

I went with Mrs Drummond happily. She led me along passages and up and down bewildering steps until I thought I would never find my way back again. Then she opened a door.

'It has been prepared for you. I'll send someone to fetch you when supper is ready.'

'Thank you.'

I saw that the room was large and well furnished with an old-fashioned four-poster bed but I was too weary to examine it closely. Jeannie had been there because some of my clothes were unpacked and my toilet articles laid out. She must have gone back downstairs and I was glad. I did not want to talk. I knelt by the fire spreading out my hands to the welcome heat before I pulled off my boots to warm my chilled feet.

I stripped off my riding-habit and washed my face and hands. I chose a gown of dark green wool, warm and close-fitting, the elbow-length sleeves and square neck trimmed with frills of cream lace. I brushed my hair until it shone red in the firelight. My mind was a jumble of impressions too early yet to be sorted out. I stared into the mirror. My mother used to be angry with me for not making more of myself. 'That's no way to capture a man,' she would say. Bitterly scornful of her way with lovers I would deliberately become sullen and unresponsive. Now suddenly it was different. I thought of Coll, a young man of whom I knew nothing and yet for whom I was already trying to make myself beautiful. The colour ran up into my cheeks. I pressed my hands against them and turned away quickly, ashamed of my thoughts. I was hunting for a handkerchief when someone knocked at the door.

'Come in, Jeannie,' I called. 'Where on earth did you hide my . . . ?'

'It's not Jeannie.'

I turned round. A boy stood leaning up against the doorpost. He might have been about seventeen. I was conscious of untidy dark hair, a long thin nose, a sullen mouth. Something about the face was oddly familiar though I could not place it.

'I've been told to fetch you to supper,' he said ungraciously.

'Thank you. I'm quite ready.' I snuffed the candles and followed him into the passage.

'Are you Neil?' I asked as we walked side by side.

'Aye, I am,' he shot me a startled glance. 'How did you know that?'

'I heard Sir Alasdair speak of Neil so it was simple deduction,' I said smiling. 'I'm not a witch.'

He stopped dead, glowering at me. 'Are you making fun of me?'

'No, of course I'm not.'

'Everyone else does.' Then he walked on. 'We had better hurry. The Chief doesn't like to be kept waiting.'

I followed this unwilling messenger in silence. Then as we turned a corner and went down a couple of steps, I stumbled and he put out a hand to steady me. I saw him looking up at me, his face pale in the dim light. He said abruptly, 'Why did you come here?'

'Why shouldn't I? Sir Alasdair is my grandfather.'

'I would never have left Paris to come to Glenlochy.'

'Don't you like it here?'

'I hate it and I hate everybody in it,' he said vehemently and then went on so quickly that I had almost to run to keep up with him.

It was strange but the room that I had left only an hour before had somehow become subtly changed. A table had been laid. Silver candelabra and fine glass gleamed on the snowy linen cloth. My grandfather had discarded his dressing-gown and wore a black velvet coat with lace at the throat and wrists. Coll stood on the hearthrug; the leaping flames found red lights in his bronze hair. His blue coat stretched across broad shoulders. Beside him lolled the dogs. They raised their heads lazily as though I were already one of the family and could be safely ignored.

Coll stretched out his hand. 'Come and make friends with them. Are you afraid of dogs?'

'I've not had much experience of splendid creatures like these.'

'You'd not meet with their like in Paris certainly,' he said smiling. 'Bran and Wolf come from an ancient race. Sir Alasdair will tell you they are descended from the deerhounds of Fionn MacCumhaill.'

'And so they are,' said my grandfather. 'A couple were given to one of my ancestors. They've been bred here for over five hundred years.'

I put a hand tentatively on one of the slim grey heads and a cold nose thrust upward into my fingers. 'Who was Fionn MacCumhaill?'

'He was one of our legendary heroes. You'll be hearing plenty about him if you stay with us long.'

'Of course she will stay. She's my granddaughter, isn't she?' said Sir Alasdair irritably. 'Give me your arm, Coll. Where the devil is Fiona? I thought she was supping with us tonight. Ring the bell, Neil. That damned woman Drummond is always late with the food.'

I realized then that with all his apparently splendid physique my grandfather was very frail. Age and rheumatism had sapped his strength and he obviously detested his weakness. He grunted as Coll hauled him to his feet. I would have gone to his other side but at that moment the door opened and a young woman came in. I knew her instantly, the black hair, the dark red gown. She went swiftly as if by right to Sir Alasdair, kissing his cheek and putting her arm through his.

'I'm sorry I'm late, but father is not so well. He has been coughing badly again. I had to see him settled with a hot posset before I came out.'

'Well, well, never mind, my dear. You are here now and that's what is important. I want you to meet my granddaughter. Marietta, my child, this is Fiona McPhail. She is a cousin of sorts through her grandmother.'

She turned to look at me. She had strange eyes. They

were wary and yet oddly searching. I said quickly, 'I believe we have met before.'

For a second I could have sworn she was disconcerted but she replied almost instantly, 'Surely not. I could never have forgotten meeting Mistress Gilmour of Glenlochy.'

Something made me persist. 'I saw you in Edinburgh at the door of a house in the Canongate and afterwards at Mr Cameron's evening party.'

She smiled. 'You saw me? You must have been mistaken. Coll can tell you where I've been for the last fortnight, can't you, Coll?'

'Indeed I can. Over at Armadale on Skye with Angus Macdonald making sheeps' eyes at you, I'll be bound. Everyone has a double so they say.'

'Or else she was in two places at once,' said Neil. 'Fiona is a witch, Miss Gilmour. She flies on a broomstick when she wishes.'

They all laughed as if it were an old joke but all the same there had been real malice in the boy's voice and Fiona's reply was sharp.

'Don't be ridiculous, Neil. You must forgive my brother, Miss Gilmour. He's at the age when he thinks it clever to be impudent.'

Her brother! Of course that was the likeness I had noticed. So it must have been Fiona in Edinburgh . . . or her double.

Then Mrs Drummond came in followed by Kirsty and the manservant, whose name I discovered was Murdo, carrying the supper dishes. They too had been transformed. Murdo's coat was shabby but neat and he wore white stockings and buckled shoes. Kirsty's brown dress was covered by a lace-trimmed apron. We seated ourselves at the table.

I realized many things while we ate the trout caught by Neil as he proudly boasted, followed by roasted kid and drank claret from tall Venetian goblets. I could not help being struck by the contrast between the neglect so apparent on my arrival and the good style, even elegance, with which the supper was served. This must have been how things were once before Culloden, before the English came. There was something pathetic about it that went straight to my heart.

I wondered about Coll too. He was respectful but familiar, not hesitating to give an opinion and even at times contradicting his master without rebuke. He and Fiona spoke together as people do who know one another intimately, so that I felt myself an outsider except that now and again Coll's eyes met mine across the table and I was aware of his interest and admiration.

I noticed also that though my grandfather ate little, his glass was filled again and again. Occasionally he would talk animatedly asking me questions about Paris which he had known well in his youth, and then he would fall silent picking at the food and brooding over his wine.

When we rose from the table, he spoke of the Sîthen Stone. 'Fetch it, Coll. Fiona has never seen it. I had thought it lost but Marietta has brought it back to us.'

'The honour of Glenlochy has returned,' said Coll lightly as he brought it from the cabinet where it had been placed.

Fiona took it in her long thin hands with their pointed nails, the dark hair falling forward hiding her face as she bent over it. 'It's beautiful,' she said quietly. 'My father would say that a blood-red stone like this in a serpent setting has magic powers.'

'What do you mean by magic?' I asked curiously.

She raised her head. Her eyes held mine and I knew that she coveted the stone and envied me because one day it would be mine.

Then my grandfather said carelessly, 'Adam McPhail is not only our minister at the kirk but a scholar too. He could tell you there has always been a great deal of superstitious nonsense attached to stones like these. In my great-grandfather's time it was still used for healing. Water in which the Chieftain had dipped it three times would cure any disease you care to name from an ache in the belly to plague!'

'Did you ever have to do it, grandfather?'

'Once,' he said smiling wryly, 'and I never felt more of a fool. I was young then and had only just succeeded my father as Chieftain. Some wretched woman from the valley went down on her knees begging me to cure her sick child.'

"What happened?"

'The baby recovered. Probably clean well water did it as much good as some filthy concoction from the doctor.'

'We're a long way from medical help here. Our people have their own beliefs and remedies,' said Coll smoothly. 'We might try it again. Set up an apothecary's shop and dispense bottles of faery water for a small fee.'

'If you do, the faery wife will punish you,' said Neil quickly.

'Oh for God sake!' said Coll taking the stone from Fiona and putting it back in its place. 'Where do you get these rubbishy notions from?'

'You like to despise everything I say but it's true,' said Neil defiantly. 'Kat used to say so.'

'Shut up, you idiot.' Fiona gave a quick glance at my grandfather but he was dozing in his chair. 'You know how it upsets him if you talk about Kathryn.' That must be my father's sister, I thought, my Aunt Kat, but before I could ask a question Fiona went on. 'I don't know what is the matter with you tonight, Neil. You'll frighten Miss Gilmour away.'

'Don't worry, I'm not so easily scared,' I said gaily. 'Besides I am named for the faery wife. That's a protection surely.'

'So you are,' said Coll turning to me. 'Marietta . . . a lovely name, and you're wearing green too, the faery colour. I don't think I ever saw it become anyone so well as it becomes you.'

His eyes were on me so that I blushed and could not find words.

'Miss Gilmour puts us all to shame with her fine French gowns,' said Fiona tartly. 'I'm afraid she must find us very frumpish and old-fashioned.'

The touch of spite in her tone made me feel uncomfortable. I said quickly, 'I don't know what you mean,' and was glad to be interrupted by Mrs Drummond who came in with a tray of tea and put it on the table. Fiona rose immediately and then drew back glancing at me.

'Do forgive me. I'm so accustomed to playing hostess . . . I did not mean to take your place.'

'Please,' I waved my hand. 'I'm a guest. Please go on as you've always done.'

In truth fatigue had begun to catch up with me so that

I seemed to be sitting in a daze, things and people beginning to blur around me. I stood up.

'It's been such an exhausting day. Would you excuse
me, Grandfather, if I went to bed.'

'Of course, my dear.' I went and knelt beside his chair.
He put a hand caressingly on my hair as I leaned forward to kiss his cheek.

'Goodnight, my child. Sleep well. Tomorrow we must
talk.'

Coll was waiting at the door, one of the silver candle-
sticks in his hand. 'I will light you. We don't want you to
lose your way and spend the night in the castle dungeons.'

'Are there dungeons?'

'Plenty, gruesome ones. I will show them to you sometime.'

When we reached my room we found the candles already lighted, the fire burning merrily and Jeannie waiting
for me.

He paused outside the door looking down at me, the
candle flame throwing strange shadows on the handsome
face.

'I'm so happy you have come, Miss Gilmour,' he said
gravely. 'You must already have seen for yourself. Sir
Alasdair is an old man and he has not been well. Your
coming will give him a fresh lease of life.'

'I am glad.'

'This is a sad place and we have many problems. I
hope they will not drive you away.'

'Oh no. I love it already. I think I would like to stay
here for ever.'

'Perhaps.' The blue eyes glittered. He pressed my hand
and then as if on impulse leaned forward and lightly kissed
my cheek. 'Bless you for saying that. Until tomorrow
then.'

Jeannie helped me to undress and went on talking as she
unpinned my hair and brushed it with long slow strokes. I
didn't listen very attentively.

'You never saw such kitchens, Miss Marietta, huge stone
places, enough to give you the shivers, but there was
plenty of food, I'll say that for them. They spoke in that
heathenish tongue of theirs so that I could hardly understand a word but one thing I'm sure of, they don't like

that Mrs Drummond. They think she puts on too many airs, proud as a peacock because she won't eat with them. Has to have a tray sent up to her own room. Mind you, I can understand it, some of those boys eat like pigs.'

I said a little wearily, 'It's bound to be strange at first. Go to bed now, Jeannie. Where are you sleeping?'

'I'm to share a room with that Kirsty and I don't much fancy it.' She wrinkled her nose and I laughed and gave her a little push.

'Go on with you. You know you like company. You'll be as thick as thieves in no time. You can come and tell me all the gossip.'

She giggled and said goodnight. I climbed into the big bed and found that Jeannie had put in a hot brick wrapped in flannel to warm the sheets. I lay watching the glow of the firelight. It seemed a very long time since we had ridden from Fort William that morning. I wondered what Janet and Richard had found at the Tige Dubh. Chaotic impressions of my grandfather and Coll, of Fiona McPhail and Neil mingled with magic and witches to dance before my eyes as I drowsed into sleep.

It was a laugh that roused me, a woman's laugh, happy, excited, filled with content. I heard my mother laugh like that after an hour with one of her lovers, a laugh that always ended in smothering kisses. Then a door shut and there was silence. There were a dozen explanations and I don't know why I lay there quivering and for the first time that day remembered the slip of paper that had been intended to keep me away.

Had it come from one of those I had met that evening? And if so, why? There seemed no reason why my coming should threaten them in any way. Then I laughed at my foolishness. Determinedly I dismissed it, snuggling down in the bed, burying my head in the pillow. 'Until tomorrow,' Coll had said. I was content to leave it at that.

Chapter Five

❧❦❧

I slept late the next morning, not waking till Jeannie knocked at the door and brought in my breakfast. Sun was streaming in through the latticed window as I sat up still yawning sleepily and she banged the tray down beside the bed with a clatter.

'What time is it?'

'Past ten and you'd better put something around your shoulders, Miss Marietta, if you don't want to catch your death. This room is cold as an iceberg. I'll get that Kirsty to light a fire.'

'No, it doesn't matter. I'm going to get up immediately I've eaten. What have you got for me?'

Jeannie grimaced. 'They're eating porridge in the kitchen, like glue it is, with salt sprinkled on it if you please and not a drop of milk. It stuck in my throat. Not as much as a mouthful could I get down. "That won't do for my lady," I told them and you should have seen that Mrs Drummond glare. If anyone has the evil eye, she has.'

'Don't be silly, Jeannie.' I surveyed the toasted oaten bannock, the boiled egg and the fat black teapot. 'What are you grumbling about? It looks wonderful and I'm starving.'

'Not a crust of white bread to be had in the whole castle and the coffee like mud . . . I've handed out better to the beggars in the Rue Chantelle!'

I laughed at her. 'It's no use regretting new baked brioches and French coffee, we're in the Highlands now,' I said cheerfully and attacked my breakfast with relish.

When Jeannie had taken my tray, I dressed quickly, eager to begin the day, to see more of Glenlochy, perhaps even explore the valley. I was almost ready when I heard a thunderous barking. I crossed the window pushing

56

hard at the stiff casement. It flew open with a jerk and
I nearly fell out. The two dogs came out of some inner
door with a rush, bounding across the courtyard and
through an opening on the other side, followed more
leisurely by Coll. He was in riding clothes and carried his
hat in his hand. The sun shone on his bronze hair. He
looked very handsome indeed and my heart gave a little
thud of excitement and pleasure.

'Good morning,' I called. 'Where have the dogs gone?'

He looked up at me and waved. 'God knows! Hunting
their breakfast probably. Come on down, sleepy head.
It's a lovely morning and I want to show you something.'

'All right, but wait for me. I'm not sure I know the way.'

'Just follow your nose.'

Despite the sun, the wind had blown in fresh and cold.
I snatched up my father's plaid, flung it around me and
went running down the passage. After one or two wrong
turns I came to an opened door and guessed that this
was the way the dogs had gone. Coll came to meet me.

'Did you sleep well?'

'Too well,' I said ruefully. 'I did not mean to be so late.
I think I must have been making up for all the sleep lost
on the journey.'

'No one would think so to look at you. If you'll forgive
me for saying so, you look fresh as a flower this morning,
Miss Gilmour.'

'Oh come, you don't need to say things like that.
You're teasing me.'

'No, indeed.' He paused for a moment looking at me
half smiling. 'You will think me very discourteous but you
see none of us quite knew what to expect . . . and
now . . .'

'And now?'

'How fortunate we are that it turns out to be someone
like you.'

The unguarded admiration in his eyes disconcerted me.
I turned away. 'I only hope that my coming has not
been too much of a shock for my grandfather.'

'Sir Alasdair, like all of us, can only be delighted.'

'Is he up yet? Should I go to him?'

'I am afraid that for the past few months he has kept to his room until midday.'

'Is he sick?'

'No, not sick. Just old and tired.'

The gentleness in his voice went straight to my heart. 'Are you fond of him?'

'He has been good to me,' he said simply.

It seemed to me then that there was an immediate sympathy between us, but it was too sudden, too quick. I was frightened of it. I said shyly, 'You did say you were going to show me something.'

"So I did. Come this way.'

We walked across the courtyard and through a stone arch into what must have been the ground floor chamber of the tower. It smelled dank and very musty. There was a small iron door on the further side. Coll drew back the heavy bolts and lifted his hand to the latch. It swung open. Instantly the wind rushed in from the sea, so strong that it drove me back and he steadied me with an arm around my waist.

'Careful now. Hold on to me. I thought you would be interested. When the castle was surrounded by water, the only entrance for family or visitors or enemies for that matter was by boat and through this door.'

I stared down at the narrow ledge and the steps, green with slime and seaweed, that went straight down to an emerald sea creaming savagely against the black rock.

'It looks terribly dangerous. Was anyone ever drowned?'

'If they were, I never heard of it, but I wouldn't be surprised. It would be an excellent way of getting rid of one's enemies.'

'One push and that would be the end.'

'It's a good thing those barbaric days are over.' He slammed the door and fastened it firmly. 'It's Murdo's job to see that it is kept closed and bolted.'

We went back to the house by an inner door from the tower and came into a carpeted passage. At the end he opened a door into another room, part library, part study. Two of the walls were lined with books, but there were cabinets to hold files and papers and a massive desk.

'This is the estate room where I work,' he said.

I was conscious of a dull roaring sound that seemed

to come from under my feet. 'What is that noise?' I asked curiously.

He smiled. 'You asked about our dungeons. This is one of them. At one time this was not a room at all but part of the ground floor of the old tower.' He rolled back the faded rug. There was a wooden panel let into the stone floor with an iron ring in it. He bent down and shifted it back. Immediately the roar increased. I was looking down a long shaft into darkness. 'It goes down into the rocks under the castle. Somewhere there must be a gap and at high tide the sea rushes in. In the old days the Gilmours were in the habit of throwing their enemies down there and leaving them to drown.'

'Oh how horrible!' I gazed down into the black depths shuddering.

'Oh I don't know. I can think of one or two I wouldn't mind dropping down there.' Just for an instant the handsome face changed and I sensed a hint of ruthlessness beneath the easy charm. Then he smiled, pushed the wooden cover back and replaced the rug.

'Coll,' I said quickly and then pulled myself up short. 'Do forgive me for calling you that but I don't know your other name.'

'I have none, or none to which I have any right,' he said quietly. 'I never knew my father. At school they gave the name of Grant, but please go on calling me Coll. Everyone does.'

'Thank you,' I said a little shyly. 'I was going to ask you how long you had been working for my grandfather.'

'Six years, even since I left the university at St Andrews.'

'I see. What does Neil do?'

'Oh Neil!' He perched himself on a corner of the desk smiling a little wryly. 'He ought to be here now. He is supposed to be my assistant. Don't take too much notice of Neil. He talks an awful lot of nonsense. He is what you would call in Paris an *"enfant terrible."* He ran away when he was fifteen and tried to enlist in the army at Fort William.'

'The English army?' I asked incredulously.

'The Black Watch actually. They are Highland but they fight for King George. I've never seen Sir Alasdair so

angry. He had him hauled back. Mr. McPhail is a saintly
man but he knows nothing at all about boys. His wife is
dead and poor Fiona was at her wit's end to know how to
control her brother, so your grandfather brought him here
to the castle where I'm supposed to teach him good
sense and something about estate management.'

'Which I am sure you do admirably.'

'I try, but it's uphill work.'

A peat fire smouldered on the hearth and the room was
warm. I slipped the plaid from my shoulders and began to
fold it. Coll stretched out his hand to help me with it.

'It's a long time since I have seen the Gilmour weave.'

'I know. It belonged to my father. I nearly got ar-
rested for wearing it in Fort William but Mr Wynter said
he didn't think it would cause trouble to anyone here.'

He stiffened. 'Mr Wynter?'

'Yes. Colonel Richard Wynter. Didn't you know? I travelled from Edinburgh with him and his sister. They have
gone up to the Tige Dubh.'

'Richard Wynter,' he repeated slowly. 'Would he be related to Captain Graham Wynter?'

'He is his brother.'

'So you know already about Captain Wynter?'

'I know that he bought the house and land and left
them to his brother. Didn't Mr Cameron write you about
it in his letter?'

'If he did, Sir Alasdair did not tell me.'

'Does it matter?'

'No, of course not, but there has been no one living at
the Tige Dubh since . . . oh well, never mind, only I
shouldn't mention it to your grandfather if I were you.'

'But I had hoped to visit Mr Wynter's sister and invite
her here.'

'You must do as you wish of course, Miss Gilmour,' he
said gravely, 'but I would beg you to remember that
Glenlochy suffered greatly at the hands of the English after Culloden. Oh, I know the Chief was lucky to be left
in possession of his home but his sons fought against
King George and the fines were crippling. That's why he
sold the land. There is little left and it is a hard fight sometimes to keep alive, both for us and for those who are

dependent on the castle. So you must realize he will not look kindly on English neighbours.'

'Yes, I understand.'

'I'm sure you do.' He gave me his charming smile. 'Now if you will forgive me, I must do some work.'

'Coll, will you tell me about it? About the estates I mean. How they are run? Where the money comes from? I would like to know.'

'Why on earth should a young lady like you want to know such dull details as to how many cattle we have or whether the herring shoals are as good this year as last?'

'But I do. They are important. I'm not joking. I mean what I say. I want to know everything about it.'

He gave me an odd little smile, then touched my nose with one long finger. 'In that case, Miss Sobersides, you shall know all you wish, but there's plenty of time surely.' He sat down behind the desk. 'If you happen to see that young devil Neil lurking anywhere, will you send him back to me with a flea in his ear?'

'I will indeed.' I laughed and left him.

It so happened that I did not see my grandfather until the afternoon. I ate my midday meal alone as Coll and Neil had gone up the valley on some errand to one of the tenant farmers. I had spent the morning with Jeannie finishing my unpacking and familiarizing myself with the castle. It was a huge rambling place of many rooms, some bare and unfurnished and some with the same look of faded grandeur which had struck me in the drawing-room the night before. Twenty years of neglect had tarnished its splendour. When I was mistress, I told myself, things would be different. Perhaps there was more of my mother in me than I ever realized. With all her faults, she had been an excellent housewife. Our house in the Rue Chantelle had been small but it had not lacked comfort or elegance.

'Give Madame a few weeks here,' remarked Jeannie paying an unwonted tribute to a mistress she had disliked, 'and she'd make a show place of this old ruin, money or no money.' And she was right too.

In the early afternoon, as my grandfather had not ap-

peared, I went to his room. The door was ajar. I was just
about to knock when the sound of angry voices stayed my
hand. I heard Sir Alasdair say incisively, 'Damn you,
woman, what more do you want from me? Haven't you
had enough all these years? If you don't like it, you can
go to the devil for all I care! Get out, do you hear? Get
out, for God's sake, and leave me be!'

The next moment Mrs Drummond came through the
door so swiftly that I was forced to step back. The brown
eyes blazed in her pale face.

'Are these French manners,' she said tartly, 'listening at
doors?'

'I was doing nothing of the sort,' I replied indignantly.
'I was coming to ask after my grandfather as I hadn't
seen him all the morning. I thought he might be unwell.'

She stared at me for an instant and then flung the door
wide open. 'He's in there. Go and ask for yourself.' She
swept past me, leaving me so astonished at the abrupt
change from her quiet reserved manner that it was a moment before I collected myself and went in.

My grandfather was still in his dressing-gown. The window had been thrust open as if he needed air. He was
standing leaning up against the sill with his back to me,
breathing heavily. Sun and wind came flooding into the
room.

He said huskily, 'Well, what have you come back for
now?'

'It's me, it's Marietta,' I said hesitantly. 'I came to ask
how you were.'

'Ah Marietta . . .' he turned slowly round and I was
alarmed at the look on his face. He was ashy pale. He held
out a shaking hand and I ran to his side. He let me help
him to a chair and almost fell into it, leaning back with a
sigh of relief, his eyes closed.

I put a cushion under his head. 'Are you all right? Is
there anything I can get for you?'

He kept tight hold of my hand and in a few seconds the
colour crept back into his face. He sat up a little, opening his eyes. They were startlingly blue, as blue as Coll's.

'Don't worry, my dear. I'm an old man and my heart
goes back on me sometimes.' He managed a smile. 'D'you
know what that quack of a doctor told me the last time

he came out from Fort William? "Don't get excited—
don't get angry!" What does any army sawbones like that
know about such things?'

'Did he give you something to take?'

'Aye, he did, a disgusting mixture bitter as gall. I told
Murdo to throw it down the privy. I have something
better.' He leaned forward reaching out for the whisky
that stood on the small table beside the bed but his hand
trembled so much that I took it from him and poured a
little into the silver cup.

'I'm not sure you ought to be taking this,' I said as I
gave it to him.

'Without it I might as well be dead and buried already,' he said grimly and swallowed it at a gulp. I took
the cup from him and his fingers closed round my wrist,
pulling me towards him with surprising strength and
speaking with a queer intensity.

'Tell me, Marietta, what do you think of Coll?'

The question startled me. 'I don't know. I scarcely know
him.'

He released me and let himself sink back in the chair.
'No, of course you don't. Silly of me, but he's a good boy
and he was worked hard . . .'

I knelt beside him anxious only to soothe and comfort.
'If it will please you to hear it, Grandfather, then from
what I have seen of him, I like him very much.'

'Good, good,' he patted my hand. 'I'm glad. Leave me
now. We'll see one another later at supper.'

'Yes, darling.' I kissed his cheek. 'You rest now, have a
little sleep.'

I went quietly from the room. It had been an odd little
incident and yet, when I thought about it, not really so
strange. Wasn't it quite natural that my coming should
seem like a threat to Mrs Drummond's position in the
household and my grandfather was an autocratic old man.
He would not brook any question, any interference in
what he did. As for Coll . . . why shouldn't he have
grown fond of the young man after six years and believing
that he had no living son? I made no attempt to analyse
my own feelings. They were too new, too uncertain. I
only knew that he disturbed me as no other man had
done.

We ate our meal together that night, just the three of us, my grandfather, Coll and I. Neil had gone to spend the evening with his father and sister. I was first in the drawing-room and when Coll came in, he found me gazing up at the portrait. It was easy to see the family likeness to my grandfather . . . the same hawk-like profile under the Highland bonnet with its eagle feathers, though the hair and moustache were the Gilmour red. The dog who lay at his feet might have been Bran or Wolf.

Coll came up beside me. 'That is Donald Ruadh, Donald the Red, twelfth Chieftain of Glenlochy.'

'He had the same name as the one who married the faery wife.'

'Aye, but he was a very different man.' Sir Alasdair had appeared in the doorway. Tonight he leaned heavily on his ebony stick and Coll went at once to his side. 'I'm afraid my great-great-grandfather had no faery wife,' he went on, settling himself in his chair by the hearth. 'I am sorry to say, Marietta, that he was a great rascal.'

'Was he? Why? What did he do?'

'Stole his brother's bride from under his nose for one thing and then murdered him in a duel. He went raiding into Campbell lands and came home with a hundred black cattle. Their descendants breed to this day in our shielings. When Argyll sent his factor to demand their return, he disappeared and was never seen again.'

'Was he murdered too?'

My grandfather shrugged. 'Disposed of, shall we say?'

I wondered if he was one of the poor wretches who had been left to drown at the bottom of the black hole. My father had said once, 'We're a mixed breed, Marietta, heroes, martyrs, cattle thieves and killers. You pay your money and take your choice!' It was odd to think that the same wild blood ran in my veins.

Coll was looking up at the portrait and something about his expression startled me. There was envy as well as admiration in his voice. 'Ruthless he may have been but he knew what he wanted and he went after it caring for nothing and nobody.'

'He certainly did that,' said my grandfather grimly. 'He was said to be the last man in Scotland to perform the *Taghairm.*'

'The what?' I looked from one to the other.

'Shall I tell her about it?' said Coll with a look of mischief.

'It's no more than superstitious nonsense,' remarked my grandfather dryly. 'But it is one of the Glenlochy legends, I suppose.'

'What does *Taghairm* mean?'

'Literally, calling up the devil.'

'But that's ridiculous. You can't mean it.'

'You'd be surprised at what went on in those days. Donald Ruadh was not the heir, you see, he was a second son and he wanted to be sure that one day he would be Chieftain. So he and one or two of his close companions gathered one night in an old barn near the Tige Dubh . . .'

'The Tige Dubh?'

'Yes, that's how it got its name, the Black House.' Coll paused. 'It's extremely gruesome. Are you sure you want to hear?'

But now my curiosity was aroused. 'Of course I do. After all he was my ancestor too.'

'Very well, but don't blame me if it gives you nightmares. They built a blazing fire and proceeded with the magical rites which included among other unpleasant items putting a harmless domestic cat on a spit and roasting it alive . . .'

'Oh no!'

'I told you that you wouldn't like it. Very soon so the tale goes they were joined by a ring of cats, all howling fearfully and glaring at them like demons with their fierce yellow eyes. The fire flared up, the poor scorched creature went on screeching and then suddenly a huge black monster was in the midst of them. They were scared out of their wits, all except Donald Ruadh who had the courage to clamp Satan down with the cross hilt of his sword and hold him captive while he asked his questions and got his promises.'

'Oh how absolutely horrible!'

'Horrible as you say, but all the same and against all odds he did become Chieftain.'

'It's nothing but rubbish, my dear,' said my grandfather testily. 'Don't believe a word of it. I regret to say that

Donald Ruadh was an unpleasant young man with vicious habits.'

'Don't worry,' said Coll lightly, 'we don't do anything like that nowadays.'

'I hope not.'

But I looked up at the portrait with new eyes. There had been a startling realism about the grim little tale that for an instant had seemed to fill the room with evil. Then Kirsty came in with our supper followed by Murdo and it vanished.

Sir Alasdair said with irritation, 'Where is Ailsa Drummond?'

'She has a sick headache, sir. She's away to her bed.'

He grunted and made no comment. It was Coll who showed a surprising interest. 'Is she really ill, Kirsty?'

'Och no, sir, she's just in a bad temper. She'll be right as a trivet in the morning.'

My mother would have boxed her ears for insolence but servants seemed to be far more outspoken in Scotland than they were in Paris.

After we had eaten and were sitting cosily by the fire my grandfather stirred himself. 'I have been thinking, my dear. Now you are here, we must entertain a little. God knows, I've had no heart for it these last few years, but now it is different. You are my heir and our neighbours should meet you.' He smiled leaning back in his chair. 'I remember when I came of age. I was just back from France and I was sent by my father to hunt the deer with the leaders of the clan. They frowned at me because I used my rolled plaid for a pillow. What kind of a weakling was this, they muttered to one another, who could not lay his head on the hard ground as they did!'

'What happened then?'

'They set me up on a great cairn of stones, put my father's sword in my hand and handed me the wassail cup, a quart of claret to be swallowed at one draught and prove my fitness to be their Chief in war and peace.'

'I don't think I could manage that,' I said laughing.

'Of course not, but all the same it is only right that our people should be given the chance to rejoice that Glenlochy will not pass to one of strange blood. What do you say, Coll?'

He was leaning forward, his hand pulling at the ears of one of the dogs, the firelight playing on his face and it struck me that he had a look of my father as he must have been in his youth. For the first time I wondered what secret hid his birth. Then he glanced round at us and the likeness vanished.

'I agree, sir, absolutely. When do you suggest?'

'We're in April now and we must allow a little time. I want Duncan Cameron here for the legalities. Send out invitations, Coll. There are the Macdonalds and the Macleods from Skye, the Farquharsons, the Camerons from Lochaber . . .'

'Let's make it May Day Eve. Then we can have the games in the afternoon, a banquet in the Great Hall, dancing by torchlight.'

'It sounds wonderful. Do you really mean all this for me, Grandfather?'

'Who else? It is your right. If your father had lived, it would have been for him.'

I leaned forward to touch his hand. 'I wish I had been a boy for your sake,' I said softly.

'Fate has a way of kicking us like a football from pillar to post,' he said with a trace of bitterness but his fingers closed over mine.

We had been talking so happily I forgot Coll's warning. I said, 'Grandfather, may I ask friends of my own too?'

'Friends, child? Who do you know in the Highlands?'

'I was telling Coll this morning. I travelled from Edinburgh with Colonel Richard Wynter and his sister, Lady Thorpe. They are at the Tige Dubh.'

'Wynter?' My grandfather sat bolt upright. His hands tightened on the arms of his chair and I was suddenly afraid. But I had begun it and I had to go on though I faltered a little.

'He is the brother of Graham Wynter.'

'No man of the name of Wynter shall enter my house again.'

I shouldn't have argued but I did. 'I know he is English. But the past is over, Grandfather, we should think of the future. Richard has done nothing.'

'Richard?' he thundered at me. 'Richard? What does this mean? Are you intimate with this man?'

'No, of course not.' I had once thought that I wouldn't mind very much if I never saw Richard Wynter again, but now it angered me that he should be spoken of so unjustly. 'He was kind to me, both he and his sister.'

My grandfather hauled himself to his feet. A gale of anger seemed to sweep through him. He said at last in a choked voice, 'Graham Wynter came here to my house. I admitted him, cursed Englishman that he was, he accepted my hospitality and he desecrated it. He brought shame on Glenlochy.'

'Whatever he did, he is dead. You cannot hold it against his brother.'

'The old days are gone for ever. I know that only too well,' he went on as if he had not heard me. 'After Culloden there was little left to a Highland gentleman but his honour and he robbed me even of that.' Angrily he struck his hand against the stone fireplace. 'God damn the English for what they have done to me and mine!'

He was shaking, his face congested and I was frightened at the violence I had provoked.

Coll said quietly, 'Take care, sir. Don't distress yourself so much. It is not worth it.'

'No, you're right. It's done with, forgotten, finished, except for one thing. I will not meet this man nor permit you to do so. You must understand that, Marietta.'

I was going to protest but a quick glance from Coll silenced me. I said nothing and after a moment I felt the old trembling hand touch my cheek gently.

'I don't want to be harsh but I mean this, my dear.'

I turned to him then filled with pity. 'I understand, really I do. I'm sorry to have caused you so much pain.'

'Never mind that now.' He took a deep breath. 'I'm tired. I think I'll go to bed. Call Murdo, will you, Coll?'

When he had gone leaning on the arm of his old servant, Coll came back from the door and stood looking down at me.

'I did warn you, didn't I?'

'Yes, you did. I'm sorry. I didn't mean to upset him so much.'

'He'll get over it.'

'Coll, what did Graham Wynter do?'

He walked away to the hearth before he answered, kick-

ing the logs so that they flared up in a shower of sparks.
'It was an unpleasant business and it is something that
touches the family very closely. Even I didn't know everything. I don't think it is my place to tell you about it.'

'I'll have to know some time.'

He turned to look at me. 'Ask Richard Wynter.'

'You don't know him. If it is a family matter, then he
won't tell me about it either,' I said dryly. 'I think perhaps
I had better go to bed too.'

He came with me and opened the door. 'Do you know
your way now?'

'Yes. I shall not get lost.'

'Good night.'

I turned to go and the pointed toe of my slipper caught
in the worn carpet. I tripped and without quite knowing
how it came about I was in his arms, the handsome face
very close to mine.

I said, 'Coll, please . . .' and he released me immediately.

'I'm sorry. I should not have done that, a nameless nobody and the heiress of Glenlochy.' There was such bitterness in his voice that I was sorry. I reached out and
touched his cheek lightly.

'Don't say that.'

'It's true, isn't it?' He caught at my fingers and kissed
them passionately. 'Is this forbidden too?'

I drew my hand away. 'We've only known one another
for a day and a night.'

'It is enough. You can fall in love in an hour.'

'No,' I said breathlessly. 'No, I'm not listening to you
any longer.'

I went away from him, running down the passage conscious of my hot cheeks and pounding heart and not per-
mitting myself to look back until I reached the safety of
my own room. I went in and slammed the door leaning
back against it. Jeannie was sitting by the bed, her work
basket open, stitching a torn frill on one of my petticoats.

'What's the matter?' she said calmly, biting off the
thread. 'You look as if you were running away from a
ghost.'

'Perhaps I am. The castle is full of them.'

Then I pulled myself together. Ghosts, devils, murders,

what had they to do with Coll and me or our life here? I was glad of Jeannie's plain common sense, the homely task, my own possessions scattered around me. I sat down at my dressing-table and began to unpin my hair, letting Jeannie's soothing chatter flow over me.

Chapter Six

My grandfather's fierce reaction to the very name of Wynter made me the more anxious to go up to the Tige Dubh despite what he had said. I could not help remembering the conversation I had overheard at the inn. Whatever his brother had done, Richard was not going to rest until he had found out what had happened to him and I wondered uneasily if the people of the glen and the valley were as hostile as their Chieftain. These were my people and already I felt I belonged with them but at the same time I liked Janet. Somehow she and her brother ought to be warned. But much as I wanted to, I could not go at once. For three whole days it rained as it can only in the Highlands. A gale blew in from the sea bringing the squalls with it and mountainous waves beat against the rocks with a deafening roar.

One of these drenching mornings I spent with Coll in the study and as he talked to me about the estates, I heard the dull heavy pounding under my feet and thought of those miserable prisoners who must once have crouched there, shivering, waiting for death in the grip of the hungry sea.

'The land has always belonged to the Chieftain,' Coll was saying in answer to my questions, 'but except for a few acres directly around the castle it is leased to the tacksman . . .'

'Tacksman?'

'That is what he is called up here. You have not met George Fergusson yet but you will very soon. He has been away in the Lowlands on cattle business. He is related distantly to your grandfather. He then leases it out to the farmers, the smallholders and so on down to the poorest

71

who own perhaps a cow, a couple of goats and half an acre on which to grow their oats and barley.'

'And do they pay rent?'

'When they can,' he said dryly, 'occasionally in cash, more often in kind. They supply the castle with meat, milk, cheese, eggs, butter, oatmeal. They drive the cattle to the Fairs in the autumn and sell them. Then there are the herrings. They come twice a year if we are lucky. They are salted for winter eating and we sell the barrels where we can or ship them down the coast. Then there is the kelp. Don't you find all this very boring?'

'No, it fascinates me. What is kelp?'

'It's a fertilizer made from seaweed. We are not rich, Miss Marietta, you must have seen that already from the way we live.' He leaned back in his chair, his fingers drumming on the table. 'In the old days before Culloden, the Chieftain was king in his own lands. He provided his own justice, he had the power of life and death. He could lead the men of his clan into battle. Like Donald Ruadh he could act as he pleased and no one could stop him, but the English have robbed us of all that. Now every Highland Chief is subject to the same law as the meanest of his clan.'

'Would you wish those old days back again, Coll?' I asked smiling.

He leaned forward across the desk. The fierce anger in the blue eyes startled me for a moment. 'Isn't it every man's right to act as he likes, to be master of his own fate?' Then he looked away from me. 'I talk like a fool. Who am I to wish for anything? I have not a foot of land to call my own. All I'm sure of is that it cannot go on. There will have to be changes at Glenlochy if we are to survive.'

'What kind of changes?'

'I have ideas, a great many of them, but Sir Alasdair is an old man and obstinate. He will not listen to me,' he said grimly. 'It will be for you to decide, you and your future husband.'

'But I have no future husband.'

'You will have. If you'll pardon me for saying so, no woman could run an estate of this size alone.'

'There is plenty of time surely. My grandfather is not going to die yet.'

'God forbid. I hope he will live for many years, but it must be borne in mind.'

I leaned across the desk. 'If . . . if anything should happen, you will still be here, Coll? You are not thinking of leaving.'

'I shall stay as long as you or Glenlochy need me.'

'Thank you.'

His hand came out and closed over mine. 'I think you know already, Miss Marietta, that you did not need to ask.'

Since that night when he had taken me into his arms, Coll had treated me with a cool courtesy which in some odd way made me feel restless and dissatisfied. I withdrew my hand and tried to thrust the feeling away from me. I got up and went to the window. The wind blew dismal sheets of rain against the glass.

I sighed. 'Does it go on like this for ever?'

'No, it will be over soon. I know the signs.' He came up behind me. 'It is often like this in the spring but when the sun breaks through it can be glorious here on the West Coast. Over on Skye I have known gale, rain, sun and magnificent rainbows all in a single afternoon.'

'I am longing to explore the glen.'

He put his hand on my shoulder. 'Would you like me to come with you when you go?'

I wanted to feel his arms round me again. I had never felt like this about anyone before and the longing made me tremble. I wanted to say, 'Come with me. Show me everything,' but it was too early for such intimacy and I could not take him with me to the Tige Dubh against my grandfather's wishes.

I said, 'I think I would like to go alone.'

'As you wish.' He withdrew his hand. 'As soon as the rains stop, I will have Neil saddle a pony for you.'

'I should be grateful.' I turned to face him. 'You do understand, Coll, don't you? It's just that nothing like this has ever happened to me before.'

He smiled. 'To wander through forest and glen knowing that one day they will all be yours . . . of course I understand perfectly. I envy you.'

It was said simply and I liked him for his honesty. It must be hard to have no family, nothing that is one's own. I had felt like that once with little of Coll's excuse.

The next morning there was one of those dramatic changes of which he had spoken. I woke to a world brilliant with sunshine. Everything seemed new-minted, fresh and luminous with light when I came out of the door and saw Neil wating for me with one of the sturdy little ponies. The two dogs were there too, alert and dignified. Wolf came and pushed his head against my hand in greeting. Neil helped me into the saddle and came across the causeway with me leading the pony by the bridle. He pointed ahead.

'The track goes up the valley,' he said, 'you can't miss it. George Fergusson's house lies a little back on the left.'

'Neil,' I said as casually as I could, 'is it far to the Tige Dubh?'

He looked up at me sharply. 'Why? Are you going there?'

'I don't know. Perhaps.'

'Let me come with you.'

'No, I don't think you should. Sir Alasdair might be angry.'

'I used to go there often . . .'

'When Captain Wynter was alive?'

'Yes. I liked him.'

'Is that why you ran away to Fort William?'

'Yes. He talked to me a lot about the army and the Black Watch but he never tried to persuade me, you mustn't think that. It was only afterwards that I didn't want to stay here.' He paused and then went on with a rush. 'You see, I knew he was going to die. It was horrible.'

'But he drowned himself.'

'No, he didn't. I'm sure he didn't,' he said fiercely.

'But . . . even if it was an accident . . . how could you know?'

'I did, Marietta, really I did. I tried to warn him, but he wouldn't listen.'

'You tried to warn him?'

'Yes, but he only smiled. No one ever listens to me but sometimes I do know. I wish I didn't.'

I stared at him. 'You mean you know what is going to happen?'

'Only sometimes . . . very rarely. It just comes but I never know when or why. I don't like it. It makes me feel sick, but I can't stop it. That's why I . . .' and then he stopped.

I knew what he meant. It was the *taibhseachd*, the second sight, that strange uncanny power that my father had told me about once. I had always believed it to be superstitious nonsense, something seen by foolish old women, not a young boy like Neil. 'Don't take any notice of him,' Coll had said, and yet now he was looking at me, his face intent and unhappy, and if ever there was truth in a pair of hazel eyes, it was there clear and plain.

He said, 'You're not laughing at me, are you? Not like Coll and Fiona.'

'No, Neil, I'm not laughing. I know what you mean. It is the *taibhseachd*.'

'You know Gaelic?'

'A little. Neil, how do I get to the Tige Dubh?'

'You go up the glen as far as the kirk. Beyond the churchyard there is a track that climbs up the side of the mountain. It is very steep but it will lead you down again. It is quicker through the woods but you might lose your way. Are you sure I can't come with you?'

'Not this time. Later perhaps.'

He put a hand on my bridle. 'I like you, Marietta,' he said shyly.

'I like you too, Neil.' Then I spurred my pony and went on up the path and the two dogs went with me.

The track wound up the valley beside a little river. It flowed swiftly swollen by the rain, frothing over rocks and boulders and so clear that I could see the fish among the brown stones of its bed. This must be where Neil caught the trout that we ate for supper. The tide was out that morning and women were toiling up from the beach, long lines of them, carrying huge round baskets of the dripping seaweed on their heads. Coll had said they used it to nourish the soil for their oats and barley as well as boiling it in great vats to make the profitable kelp.

There were crofts scattered everywhere, small and black, built of stone and turf and thatched with brush-

wood. Poor and wretched they looked with square un-
glazed holes for windows; some of them had wooden shutters but mostly they were stuffed with straw and rag
against the wind and rain. Barefoot children stopped to
stare and then dodged away from me when I spoke to
them. Women stood outside their huts watching but saying nothing. Their eyes followed me until I conquered my
shyness and boldly called a greeting in my few words of
Gaelic. The effect was magical. Their faces lit up. They
called out to me in a flow of words I could not understand but there was no mistaking the warmth. I waved
my hand and smiled. A young girl ran out ahead of me
holding up her little girl for me to see.

'Bless her, mistress, she is named for you, Marietta of
Glenlochy.'

The child could not have been more than two years
old; round blue eyes stared solemnly into mine and I
reined in, bending forward to kiss the rosy cheek. These
were my people and I loved them. I had never felt like
this before about anyone. I had a longing to protect, to do
what I could for this close-knit community who were so
dependent on the will of their Chieftain.

I went on up the valley to where I could see a square
substantial house built in dark stone with barns and stables
and in front of it a wooden bridge that spanned the
brook. On it a man waited, hat in hand, flicking his boots
with his riding crop.

He took a step towards me and put his hand on my
pony's mane. 'Good morning, Mistress Gilmour. Coll told
me you would be coming up the valley. I am George
Fergusson.'

I don't know why I took such an instant dislike to him.
He was a strongly built man with a thatch of reddish hair
and curiously light shifting eyes in a face tanned to ma-
hogany. He was well dressed. He spoke excellent English
and his manner was courteous, almost ingratiating. I
acknowledged his greeting and yet I felt uneasy and oddly
enough so did the dogs. They had halted at a little distance, ears cocked, and Bran growled, a low threatening
murmur in his throat. It was ridiculous but I did not even
like the touch of his hand and an absurd line from somewhere or other went dancing through my mind:

By the pricking of my thumbs
Something wicked this way comes ...

I shook myself free of it.

Fergusson was saying, 'Will you come in? I should be honoured to offer you coffee or perhaps you would prefer milk fresh from the cow.'

I knew at once that nothing would induce me to enter his house willingly, but I smiled and thanked him as pleasantly as I could.

'It is most kind of you, another time perhaps, Mr Fergusson, but this morning I want to reach the end of the valley.'

He stood back to let me pass and I was glad to escape, the two dogs bounding joyously ahead of me. Once I looked back and saw him still standing there, watching me, but the sun was shining, I was happy and I told myself sternly not to let my prejudices create something out of nothing.

The river turned and twisted until at the next bend I saw the kirk, a low squat building with a small bell tower and beyond it the mountain rose steeply. Down one side foamed the torrent in a narrow sparkling stream that after the first fierceness smoothed out into the burn that I had been following. Up the bare hillside lay scattered graves, green mounds for the most part and one curious cairn of black rocks piled on top of one another and towering far above me. Although the wind was sharp, it was sheltered here and the sun was hot. I let the hood of my cloak fall back as I stared up at the man-made hillock. There was no sound, only the rushing of the water and the song of the larks overhead. The voice that seemed to come out of the very stones startled me.

'I would know that red hair anywhere. Mistress Gilmour, is it not?' The man who came stepping lightly from behind the great pile was very small, no taller than myself, with skimpy grey hair that blew about in the wind and dressed all in black. 'Fiona told me about you and Neil too. "She is beautiful as the faery wife," he said, the boy is something of a romantic, you know. Welcome to Glenlochy. I am Adam McPhail, Minister of God to these poor souls.'

I gave him my hand. 'Grandfather says you are a great scholar, Mr McPhail, and know all the ancient legends.'

'I know a little. It would take more than one lifetime to know all.' He waved a hand to the cairn. 'I saw you looking at this. It is the burial place of the Gilmours. Every time a member of the family dies, another stone is added and it has been going on for some five hundred years. Perhaps one day it will reach as high as the mountain.'

He was not at all as I had imagined Fiona's father. He was a little gnome of a man with an impish smile and I liked him. We went on talking as we threaded our way through the grassy mounds. 'I never met your father,' he said. 'I came here to Glenlochy a few years after Culloden. My poor wife was kin to the Chief. She died when Neil was born and my Fiona has had the task of looking after us both. It would have been a hard struggle but for the castle. Your grandfather has been a good friend, and Coll too.'

Coll and Fiona. Why had I not thought of it before? I had known instinctively that she did not like me. Was that why? And Coll? She had known him for a long time and I for only a few days but Coll was mine. I was surprised by the fierce possessive instinct that leaped in me, something I had never suspected in myself. Like Donald Ruadh I would fight to get what I desired.

Some distance away across a width of green turf lay a mound with a granite cross at its head. Unlike the others it had been carefully tended. White and purple violets bloomed shyly midst the young grass. There were green spears of daffodils already bursting into flower. There would be hyacinths soon and ivy climbed up the cross. I bent to look more closely. The name was deeply engraved. Graham Wynter and nothing more. I had never thought that Richard's brother would have been buried here so far from his home. I suppose I showed my surprise. Mr McPhail astonished me further.

'It is the English Captain,' he said grimly. 'In days gone by he would have been buried at the cross roads with a stake through his heart.'

'How can you say so cruel a thing?'

'He died by his own will.'

'How do you know? It could have been accident . . . it could even have been murder.'

He gave me an odd long look. 'Have you been talking to Neil? He has too vivid an imagination. I will have to speak to him.'

I didn't want to get the boy into trouble. 'No, it was not Neil. I know Captain Wynter's brother.'

'Ah yes, the brother who is now at the Tige Dubh and is already asking questions. I have yet to meet him. He is a brave man to come here after what his brother did.'

There it was again and this time it made me angry. I said impatiently, 'What is this crime he is said to have committed?'

'So, Mistress Gilmour, you don't know everything. But then it is scarcely a deed of which his brother would boast. When Sir Alasdair was forced to sell part of his land to the Englishman, there were twenty families or so settled on the strath with many sons, fine young men anxious to make their way in the world. They listened to Captain Wynter when he told them of the countries he had seen as a soldier, Canada and America, countries filled with promise where land was cheap for those who would work and make it fruitful. They were country lads who could speak little English and so it was he who arranged the papers for emigration, the ship that would take them across the sea . . . and he sold them into slavery.'

'He sold them?' I repeated incredulously.

'You may well look horrified, but it is the truth I tell you. I saw it for myself. I saw them shackled on the deck of the ship and forced down into the hold. I heard the weeping of the old people on the shore who saw their sons condemned to labour in the Carolinas, never again to know the freedom that was their heritage.'

'I don't believe it,' I said, 'I cannot believe it of any man.'

'I do not lie,' he replied with simple dignity. 'Ask Coll, ask your grandfather. They will tell you of the shame and the grief.'

But I did not need to ask. The answer was there already in Sir Alasdair's bitter reaction to the very name of Wynter and yet . . . I looked down at the flowers at my feet. 'There is someone who still cares for him, someone who does not believe.'

'There is always someone to care even for the worst of us,' he said sombrely, 'and it is true, there was some quality in him . . . so much so that now and again it has made me wonder . . .' he broke off and I saw why. Fiona had appeared at the door of the church. She came swiftly across to us, her voice sharp.

'Father, you should not be out in this wind. I've told you again and again. It will start you coughing.'

'I'm coming, my dear, I'm coming.' There was something pathetic in his eagerness and the apologetic look he gave me. 'I am afraid Fiona is very strict with me and she is right. I am a great trouble to her.'

'Oh, for heaven's sake, Father,' his daughter took his arm. 'You're just out of bed. Mistress Gilmour will understand I am sure.' Those strange eyes of hers were on me with a look I could not fathom. 'My father is frail. If I did not care for him, who would?'

'I am sorry,' I said. 'I did not mean to keep him talking.'

'He easily gets upset. You must not mind all he says.' She was urging him towards the church but ·he broke away from her.

'My health is not good but I am not wandering in my wits, daughter,' he said in mild reproof. 'We shall meet again, Mistress Gilmour, and soon I hope.' He gave me a little bow and walked away alone with a kind of quaint dignity.

Fiona shrugged her shoulders impatiently. 'You see how it is with him. Sometimes he is more trouble than a child. What was he telling you?'

'I asked him about Graham Wynter.'

'The Englishman.' With one pointed toe she kicked contemptuously at the flowers on the grave. 'He is dead and buried.'

'Do you believe he committed suicide?'

'What I believe doesn't matter, does it? It was the official verdict.'

'Neil doesn't think so.'

'Neil would say anything to draw attention to himself. You must not let him worry you, Miss Gilmour.'

'I don't. I like him. Fiona,' I took a step towards her and held out my hand, 'I am so new here. Everything is so strange. I'm bound to make mistakes. Do you think we might be friends?'

'Friends?' She turned to look at me but she did not take my hand. 'Why not? If that's what you wish. Now I must really go and make sure that father is not doing anything foolish.'

I watched her walk away from me towards the church aware that whatever she had said my offer of friendship had been totally rejected. It had been a strange little incident. I could not help wondering what Mr McPhail might have said if Fiona had not interrupted us and cut him short so abruptly. I had meant to ask him to point out the way to the Tige Dubh. Now I was not so sure that I wanted to go there after all and yet I could not believe that Janet or even Richard for that matter could have known what their brother had done . . . or had he? I knew so little and yet somehow there was a nagging doubt. It did not fit, something was missing. Why should Graham Wynter, rich, successful, heir to a grand estate at Laverstoke, behave in such a despicable fashion? What motive had he to sell free men into slavery?

I picked out the path at last. Neil was right. It rose steeply but my pony was strong and surefooted and after a little we began to descend again. I was coming down into another glen with a view across the shining water of the loch and a great stretch of forest that must lie between the two valleys.

The Tige Dubh was built in a small clearing with the woods almost closing in at its back. There was a courtyard with stables for horses and an arched gateway. It was not black at all but a warm grey stone with turrets and pinnacles, a miniature castle, and I thought it enchanting. I rode in under the gateway and Janet must have seen my arrival from the window. She came running to meet me, a huge white apron over her dress, a bright silk scarf tied round her curls. She threw her arms around my neck as soon as I had slipped from the saddle.

'Dear Marietta, how lovely to see you. I've thought about you so much. I'm dying to hear all your news.'

An old man shuffled out of one of the stables and took

my pony while I followed her into the house. The living-room was large with white rough-cast walls hung with hunting trophies. The dark oak furniture was gay with bright-coloured cushions and there were great jars of budding branches that she must have gathered from the forest. Janet stood in the middle of the room laughing.

'Just look at me. My mother would die of shock if she were to see me now receiving visitors dressed like this, but then I'm cook, housemaid, butler all rolled into one.'

'But what has happened?' I exclaimed. 'Are you all on your own? I thought Mr Cameron had arranged it for you. Haven't you any servants?'

'None to speak of except that old man you saw out-side and his wife. They're both about a hundred-and-fifty years old and only speak about six words of English. We converse in dumb show. I've become quite clever at demonstrating how to grill a steak or make a salmon kedgeree. Rose goes about with a face sour as a lemon through there is James of course. He's a miracle. He's been with Richard for years and years. There's nothing he can't do. Thank goodness for Grannie Campbell. She believed that any young woman, whoever she was, should be able to do all the tasks she expected from her servants so I had to learn how to cook and clean, to dust and sew when I was still a child and how I hated it, but it has paid off. Even Richard was surprised. He says that if I go on like this, John will take me on campaign with him next time. Would you like a glass of wine? We found one or two bottles of good Madeira hidden away in the cellar that Graham must have stored there or I have some coffee on the boil on the kitchen fire?'

'Oh, coffee, please. We don't run to that at Glenlochy.'

'I made sure and brought it with us.' She disappeared through some inner door and was back in a few minutes carrying a tray with cups and a silver coffee pot.

'I've told Richard you're here. He is just washing his hands before joining us. He's been chopping wood.'

I stared at her in astonishment. It was the last thing I'd expected of the elegant Richard. 'You're wonderful, Janet. How have you managed to make it all so comfortable? Don't you mind?'

'Not a bit. It's a marvellous change from "doing the

season" which I'm bored to tears with anyway.' She giggled. 'I shall dine out on it for weeks when I go home.
Most of my friends would fall into a fit of the vapours at
the very notion of looking after themselves and their
brother in the wilds like this. What fun I shall have re-
counting all the horrors. They think I'm crazy to come
with Richard anyway. He says it reminds him of Canada
when he and his soldiers had to fend for themselves in
very rough country. I think it's been good for him. He is
looking much better already.'

'Better? Why? Has he been ill?'

She glanced towards the door and went on in a hurried
half whisper. 'I didn't tell you on the way up here. He'd
have been furious with me if I had breathed a word. You
know what men are, proud as peacocks. He can't bear
anyone to think him not as strong as a horse . . . what a
silly comparison that is, horses are the most delicate of
creatures! Anyway poor Richard was wounded in the last
campaign very badly. In the leg you know. It was thought
at first that he'd never walk again without crutches so he
was invalided home and absolutely hated it. But Richard
has a will of iron. He conquered it somehow, rode when
he couldn't walk and though it pains him still, you'd never
guess, would you?'

'No, I had no idea.' I remembered the many occasions
on our journey when I had condemned him for being surly
and out of temper and felt guilty. 'I wish I had realized . . .'

'Ssh, I think he's coming. Don't for heaven's sake
ever let him know I told you. He'd never forgive me.' She
raised her voice as Richard came through the door. 'Now
tell me every single thing about Glenlochy.'

I don't know whether it was because of what Janet had
just said but I found myself looking at Richard with new
eyes. He was dressed as carelessly as any countryman in
breeches and boots with an open-necked white shirt and
leather waistcoat, his dark hair tied back with a ribbon,
and he looked more relaxed and happier than I had ever
seen him. He gave me his particular quirky smile when
he brought me the cup of coffee his sister had poured out.

'Well, your royal highness,' he said teasingly, 'has your
Highland kingdom turned out to be everything you'd
hoped for?'

'Oh yes, that and more.'

'I'm glad,' and we laughed together.

'What's the joke?' asked Janet plaintively looking from him to me.

'Marietta knows, don't you?' he said taking coffee for himself and looking at me over the rim of his cup. 'Go on . . . tell us about it.'

I had not realized how much I had missed the company of people from my own world. I began to tell them of my grandfather, of the castle and the people there, and I suppose in my enthusiasm I said far more than I should have done.

'How absolutely marvellous,' exclaimed Janet. 'Sir Alasdair sounds like someone out of another age.'

'He is, I suppose. He is very old and he still clings to the past.'

'We seem to have heard a great deal about someone called Coll,' remarked Richard lightly, putting down his cup for his sister to refill. 'Is he the Prince Charming in your enchanted kingdom?'

I knew the colour burned in my face and detested myself for it.

Janet said quickly, 'Don't tease her, Richard. I think it is fascinating and I simply can't wait to see you installed as the next Chieftain. Shall we be given an invitation?'

I had forgotten that the question was bound to be asked and it was difficult to know how to answer. Richard took my cup and replied for me.

'I scarcely think that's tactful, Jan,' he said quietly. 'Sir Alasdair may not feel all that friendly towards English strangers.'

'Oh goodness, that's all over and done with years ago,' objected Janet. 'Graham was invited to the castle. I know because he wrote something about it to father in one of his letters.' Then at a quelling glance from Richard, she broke off. 'Anyway it doesn't matter. We shall hear all about it, I expect.'

But suddenly there was an awkwardness between us that I couldn't bridge. I could not help thinking of what Mr McPhail had told me and yet I couldn't bring myself to repeat it to Janet. Graham had been her much loved brother. I got to my feet.

'I said, 'It must be getting late. I think I should be going. They will be expecting me to dinner at the castle.'

We went out into the courtyard where Bran and Wolf waited for me flopped on the stones. Janet was enchanted with them.

'Richard, did you ever see such fabulous dogs? Father would adore them. Do you breed them at the castle? Would your grandfather sell us a puppy?'

'I don't know. Coll says they are descended from the dogs of Fionn MacCumhaill.'

'Who on earth is Fionn Mac . . . whatever it is?'

'Fionn MacCumhaill, or Fingal as we say down south, my ignorant sister, sleeps still on the mountains of Appin with three thousand of his followers around him. Their breath is the wind off the heather and one day when Scotland is in need of them, they will arise again at the call of Fingal's horn.'

'Goodness,' said Janet. 'How do you know all that?'

'I used to listen to the ballads sung by my Highlanders around the camp fires,' said Richard dryly. 'By the way, Marietta, if you take the path through the woods, it will cut off a couple of miles. I'll come with you and point out the way.'

Janet was urgent that I should come and see them again soon and I promised with some inner misgiving when I thought of my grandfather. Then Richard and I left together. We walked in silence for a little while, leading the pony. The trees were still bare of leaves but the buds were breaking and soon the woods would be a wilderness of fern and bracken under the copses of birch and hazel.

I said, 'I admire Janet so much. Not many girls I know would have adapted themselves as well as she has.'

Richard smiled. 'Jan grew up with two elder brothers and was determined to do everything as well as they did.'

'She is devoted to you.'

'Perhaps. I'm very fond of her.'

I had a feeling we were going on talking of trivialities to avoid the real issue and it was Richard who broached it first.

'I could not help noticing your reluctance to answer when Jan spoke of an invitation to your party.'

'You're mistaken.'

'I don't think so. What grudge does Sir Alasdair Gilmour hold against us?'

I said uncomfortably, 'Not against you or Janet? It is your brother.'

We had come to the edge of a little clearing and we stopped. It was very still. Somewhere near I could hear the dogs hunting through the undergrowth.

I said, 'What devilry inspired your brother to sell the young men of the valley into slavery in the Carolinas?'

'What!' The astonishment on his face was so genuine that I knew that whatever he had expected, it had not been this. 'It is impossible. Why in God's name should he do such a thing?'

'It is common knowledge. Mr McPhail who is Minister at the church told me himself and he would not lie.'

'Maybe not, but he could be mistaken,' said Richard fiercely. 'I have always bitterly regretted that my father was too sick to come here and I was out of the country when my brother died. Graham would never have done so vile a thing. Someone for a reason of his own has blackened his name deliberately.'

I thought of George Fergusson and then rejected it. If it was he, then my grandfather and Coll would also be involved and that I would never believe. Richard took me by the shoulders.

'Do you believe it?'

'I don't know. I would not like to think so badly of any man.'

'My God,' he said suddenly, 'that's why the people here are refusing to work for us. I offered them money which they badly need but they mumbled and shook their heads. I thought it was dislike of the English, but it's more than that.' He struck his fist angrily against the trunk of a tree. 'If only I could speak more of their damned language.'

'I can . . . a little.'

'Will you help me? Marietta, will you?'

I hesitated. 'I don't see how I can. My grandfather spoke of your brother with great anger.'

'That means that I can expect nothing from anyone at the castle.'

'No, I'm afraid not.' I thought of the grave so carefully tended. I said, 'Have you been to the churchyard?'

'Jan has.'

'Someone cares for your brother still.'

'Yes, but who?' His dark eyes looked down on me sombrely. 'I warn you, Marietta. I shan't rest until I find out the truth.' Then he relaxed and smiled. 'This is not showing you the way home, is it?' We turned to go and he stayed me with his hand on my arm. A deer had come into the clearing, her coat pale brown, her large trembling ears transparently pink in a shaft of sunlight, and behind her came two fawns. All three stood poised for a moment, quite still, and then with scarce a sound, they vanished.

I drew a deep breath and felt his fingers close on mine. 'Do you ever hunt, Richard?'

'I have done so, but not creatures like that. You cannot kill beauty. It would be murder.'

'I'm glad.'

It was as if for a moment we had shared a magical experience and then it was gone. Richard pointed ahead.

'There is the path directly in front of you. You cannot miss it.' He was still holding my hand and he looked down at me. 'Goodbye for the present and forget what I said. It is not fair to involve you.'

'I am involved already. These are my people.'

'Well, we shall see.' He kissed my fingers lightly and turned back the way he had come. The dogs came rollicking out of the undergrowth and tore down the opposite path. I followed them.

It wound through the trees and was overgrown in places. I had to lead the pony and somewhere I must have gone wrong. I only know that quite suddenly I had come to the edge of a green dell overshadowed by giant firs. In the centre there was a boulder of rock about five feet high stained here and there with green lichen. There were rocks everywhere in this countryside and I don't know why it frightened me so much. Perhaps because everything was so quiet, no sound of bird, no rustle of animals in the undergrowth, no breath of wind in the branches of the trees. Perhaps it was because the dogs had halted one on each side of me and when I touched Wolf's head, I felt him trembling.

I told myself I was being ridiculous. What was there to fear in a squat black stone? I had only to cross the clearing and take the path on the other side but, when I took a step forward, my pony would not budge. He put his head down, pulling back, and it made me angry because it tensed my nerves. I looped the bridle over a branch and boldly crossed to the gaunt black shape. The dogs did not move and Bran whimpered. It was larger than I had thought when I stood beside it and I had the feeling that at some time it had been shaped by human hands. The top dipped into a shallow basin and something was lying in it. My curious fingers groped and closed round something cold and hard. I lifted it out. I was looking at a little doll crudely moulded in clay with nothing remarkable about it except that it had bright red hair and though I had no idea what it was, I knew instantly that it was evil, the thing in my hand, the stone shaped like an altar, the unseen watching eyes that made my flesh crawl. I hurled the doll away from me and ran back down the path I had come dragging the pony after me stumbling over roots and stones with the dogs wildly clamouring at my heels until suddenly I was out of the woods. Panting, half ashamed of my panic, I saw the stream, the crofts and Fiona coming down the path from the castle with George Fergusson walking beside her. They stopped at sight of me.

Fergusson said, 'Are you all right, Mistress Gilmour? You look upset.'

'It is nothing. I lost my way in the forest.'

Fiona said, 'Have you been to the Tige Dubh?'

'Why do you ask?'

'I wondered when I saw you talking to father this morning. The Chief will not be pleased.'

I was angry at her criticism. I said defiantly, 'If necessary I will tell him myself. I see no point in being on bad terms with people who are our near neighbours.'

'The Tige Dubh has not the best of reputations and the woods are no place to wander in alone,' said George Fergusson.

'Why? What harm could come to me on my own land and from my own people?'

'What indeed?' He exchanged a smiling look with Fiona. 'She puts us to shame with her common sense, isn't that so? Our ignorant Highlanders like to believe the forest is haunted by a *Glasteig* who does not care for strangers.'

They were laughing at me. I knew that very well. I said, 'I don't believe in such things and neither does Richard Wynter, and now I must go. I am late. My grandfather will be asking for me.'

They parted so that I went between them and felt their eyes on my back though I did not turn round. They did not realize how much I had learned at my father's knee. Whatever it was that haunted the forest, it was not a harmless friendly brownie like a *Glasteig,* but something human and far more unpleasant. I tried to thrust the memory of the silent glade out of my mind but the charm of the morning had been spoiled.

Chapter Seven

That night I took out the scrap of paper with its grim warning, 'Do not come to Glenlochy,' and stared at it by the light of my candle. It was becoming clear to me that someone had made very sure that neither my father's letters nor mine had reached my grandfather. But who and why? George Fergusson, Fiona, Ailsa Drummond, Coll? I could not see what advantage they would have gained. Surely if there had been no heir, no one of close kin, then the lands would have had to be sold. They might even have been confiscated by the English. But now I was here and nothing could alter that. I made up my mind to forget it. I held the paper to the candle flame and watched it curl into ashes.

Safe in the shelter of my own room, my panic in the wood seemed suddenly absurd. Children made little clay puppets for their games and what more natural than they should give their doll the red hair of the newcomer to the castle. I was letting my imagination run away with me.

The days flew by and I did not go back to the Tige Dubh. I thought of Janet often and of Richard too but if my grandfather were to hear of it, it would only upset him and I did not trust Fiona or George Fergusson to keep silent. In any case every hour seemed occupied with preparations for the grand celebration which my grandfather was planning and in which everyone in the valley was to be involved.

'Highlanders love a party above all things,' laughed Coll when I protested that too much was being spent on a day's entertainment. He took my hand in his. 'It is the first for a very long time and the Chief is so happy. Don't spoil his pleasure. It may be the last time he will

90

ever see the old glory revived and it is all for you, you know.'

Coll threw himself into it heart and soul and I loved him for his eagerness to please Sir Alasdair and his thoughtfulness towards myself. Busy as he was, he still found time to be always there when I needed him. In the long evenings we spent together, he made me conscious of his interest and admiration. I think it pleased my grandfather to see us together and I did not stop to think what might come of it. For the moment just to see him daily was enough.

I wondered sometimes what kind of person they had expected me to be. It seemed to amuse and astonish Coll that I took so much interest in housewifely duties. He came upon me one morning when I was dusting the treasures in the cabinet where the Sìthen Stone lay. There was the massive silver goblet from which the quart of claret was drunk by the heir. I could scarcely lift it and smiled at the thought of myself draining it to the dregs. There was a gold snuff box encrusted with jewels and a fine miniature of a woman, a pale proud face with reddish-bronze hair whose eyes seemed to look directly into mine as if trying to tell me something. I did not hear Coll come until he spoke to me.

'I never realized how much we have missed a woman's hand about the castle,' he said softly.

I looked up at him. 'I thought Fiona came in and out every day.'

'She used to come occasionally, mostly to talk to Neil or bring a message from her father, not to do things like this.' He ran his eyes around the drawing-room. I had made a few small changes already and brought in posies of spring flowers. 'Where did you learn to do all this?'

'I was not brought up to be idle. We weren't rich in Paris, you know. We did not live in grand society. We were very poor to start with and we never at any time had more than two servants.' I smiled ruefully. 'I'm afraid Mrs Drummond does not approve of my interfering ways.'

He smiled. 'She has been here for a long time and so she is a little jealous. Don't be hard on her. Would you like me to speak to her?'

'No, no, Coll, please. That is not the way. I must learn to deal with people myself.'

'So young, so beautiful and yet so wise,' he said lightly.

I was still holding the miniature in my hand and I held it out to him. 'Coll, who is this?'

He took it from me, looking down at it for a moment before he replaced it at the back of the shelf. 'It is your father's sister, your Aunt Kathryn.'

'My Aunt Kat! Of course I remember now. He told me about her. She is the youngest of the family. Where is she?'

'She went away . . . some time ago.'

'Do you mean she is married?'

'Not so far as I know.'

'Then why did she go?'

'She quarrelled with Sir Alasdair. She was always very independent and she had a little money of her own, so one day she left.'

'How strange. Neil spoke of her the first evening I was here and I wondered about her then. He seemed to like her. Will she come back for the party?'

'I don't know.' He paused and then he said quietly, 'Marietta, don't talk about her to your grandfather. It distresses him.'

'Like the Wynters?'

'Yes, like the Wynters.'

There was something evasive about the way he spoke and I thought of what Adam McPhail had told me about the men who had been sold into slavery. It was on the tip of my tongue to ask Coll about it when Neil came in saying that George Fergusson was waiting to see him. Coll excused himself and went out with Neil so it was still a question left unanswered. I wondered how far Richard had got with his enquiries.

My first real brush with Mrs Drummond came the next day. Up to then she had always been her quiet self, treating me with a cool civility, though with the memory of that afternoon when she had come storming out of my grandfather's room, I was very aware of the hidden fires concealed behind the smooth manner of the efficient housekeeper.

That morning I went down to the kitchens with Jeannie.

I had only been there once before and they still appalled me. They were like arched dungeons cut out of the solid rock with a huge fireplace along one side and deep recesses in the opposite wall.

'They used to lock prisoners up in them,' whispered Jeannie, 'and let them starve to death in sight of the food going up to the Chieftain's table.'

'Ssh, they will hear you.'

'It's true. Kirsty told me.'

Well, perhaps they had done savage things once like the prisoners in that hole in the study floor, but now the cells had been turned into larders. Game of all kinds hung from hooks and a huge silver salmon lay on a slab of stone. I smiled and nodded, too shy to speak to the serving girls as they bobbed a respectful curtsey.

In the dairy the milkmaids were scouring out the wooden buckets. I watched as they filled them with cold water and then dropped into them stones heated white-hot in the peat fires so that the water boiled up, scalding and cleansing. I was suddenly aware that Mrs Drummond, silent as always, was standing beside me.

I said, 'Surely there must be easier ways of scalding out the buckets. Wouldn't it be better to use iron cauldrons and put them directly on the fire?'

'And where do you suppose we can buy iron cauldrons up here?' said Mrs Drummond tartly. 'Besides our people are accustomed to the old ways. They do not care for change.'

'But if it would save time and labour . . .'

'New brooms sweep clean, but they can also sweep away good will,' she said acidly. 'When you are mistress here, then of course you may do as you please, but while Sir Alasdair puts his trust in me, I should be glad not to have my authority questioned.'

I saw Jeannie's eyes flash and said hurriedly, 'I had never intended to do any such thing,' and took her away with me before her hot temper made matters worse.

I spent the afternoon in the little garden that lay to the right of the causeway. Stone walls protected it from the sea winds. No one had bothered with it for a long time but under the tangle of weeds, I had found violets and primroses, daffodils too and rose bushes that must have

been planted by my grandmother who had died long before I was born. In a sheltered corner a hawthorn was almost in bloom and I cut long branches of pink buds and
carried them up to the drawing-room. Mrs Drummond
was there already, standing by the hearth.

'Bring in hawthrown and bring in misfortune,' she said
sourly as I began to arrange them in one of the jars.

'I don't believe in such things. How can anything so
lovely be unlucky?' I stood back to admire the effect.
My grandfather's chair was in the way and I moved it to
one side and the table beside it.

'Don't do that,' said Mrs Drummond jealously, coming
across and putting her hand on it. 'Sir Alasdair likes it just
so.'

'He won't mind if I tell him I moved it,' I said gaily.

'You think you can twist him round your little finger,
don't you?' she said, surprising me by the venom in her
voice. 'Everything is sweet as honey, isn't it? It's Miss
Marietta this and Miss Marietta that and we must all
change our ways because Miss Marietta likes it like that!
But you'll find out how different he can be when he is
crossed. He can be savage and cruel too. He'll crush you
just as he has crushed others. There are plenty of things
you don't know.'

'What kind of things, Mrs Drummond?'

'Why should I tell you? Find out for yourself and don't
say I didn't warn you.'

'I can always ask Coll.'

'Coll?' she repeated and stood very still. 'You like Coll,
don't you?'

'Yes. Is there any reason why I shouldn't?'

'No, but I hadn't thought . . .' She came very close to
me, her hand on my arm. 'He has nothing, you know,
nothing at all, except what your grandfather gives him.'

'What does that matter?'

'So it's that way, is it? Are you in love with him, Miss
Marietta? Are you?'

Her breath was hot on my cheek and I pulled myself
away from her. 'You have no right to ask me that.'

'No, maybe not.' She straightened and smiled. 'But he is
handsome, isn't he? He's a man, full of vigour, strong like
Donald Ruadh up there, and Coll can be ruthless too, you

know. If he wants something, he takes it and that's what a woman likes, isn't it, Miss Marietta?'

It was true what she said. He was so gentle and yet I was aware of his power over me whenever he came near me, but I was not going to admit it to her. I said coolly, 'I don't think you should speak to me like that, Mrs Drummond.'

'No, Miss Marietta, I'm sorry. I forgot myself. I'm a servant and servants don't have feelings, do they? I hope you will overlook it.' There was a savage irony in her voice more disturbing than her bitterness, but I ignored it.

'I am sure you have a great deal to do elsewhere, Mrs Drummond. Don't let me keep you here. I will finish tidying the room.'

'Very good,' she gave me her enigmatic smile and went out, quietly closing the door after her.

When she had gone, I stared up at the portrait. I had not noticed it before but there was a faint likeness to Coll. It was odd how it fascinated and repelled me at the same time.

It was a day or two later when I was dressing for the evening that Jeannie came bursting into my room bubbling over with some bit of gossip she had picked up in the kitchens.

'You'll never believe, Miss Marietta,' she said taking the brush out of my hand and beginning to unpin my hair. 'It was that Kirsty who told me. Mind you, she's an ignorant creature who can't read or write but she must have heard it somewhere.'

'Heard what, Jeannie?'

'It took me by surprise, I can tell you . . . will you have your hair loose in curls on your shoulders tonight or shall I pin it up?'

'Oh, I don't mind what you do,' I said in exasperation, 'do for goodness sake go on and tell me what all this is about.'

'Well, she says . . .' and Jeannie paused, brush in hand. 'She says she believes that Mr Coll is your cousin.'

'My cousin? What on earth do you mean? And if he is, why shouldn't Sir Alasdair have told me?'

'Because he's ashamed of it, that's why. Mr Coll is the son, so Kirsty says, of your Uncle Andrew, who was killed at Culloden, only he's a . . . well, they were not married, see. He was brought here when he was six or seven years old, starving and in rags, and his mother begging for Sir Alasdair's help.'

Of course it could be only a tale . . . nothing could be proved . . . and yet it might explain a great deal; my grandfather's interest, his education of the boy, his wish that he should remain at Glenlochy.

'Does Mr Coll know?' I asked.

Jeannie shook her head. 'Kirsty says no. Sir Alasdair refused to acknowledge him as his grandson because he was never sure whether the woman was lying or not.'

'Who was the woman?'

'Kirsty doesn't know. No one knows,' went on Jeannie relishing the drama of her story. 'It all happened before she was born and it seems no one ever saw her. Just one day the boy was there at the castle and being cared for and your grandfather silent as the grave about him.'

'How does Kirsty know all this?'

But that was easily answered. Men and women gossip and tales grow in the telling, garbled, half lies, but there could be truth in it and, if anything, it only increased my sympathy for him. If it was true, then maybe it was only the tragedy at Culloden that had prevented him from inheriting the lands that would now come to me.

The first of the guests to arrive was Angus Macdonald. He came sailing across from Skye in his own boat on the day before the party and I saw him stride up the beach, a tall thin young man followed by his gillie carrying his master's valise on his head Fiona and her father had come to the castle that morning and she had been helping Mrs Drummond prepare the bedrooms for those who would have to stay the night. She went out on the causeway to meet him and presently they came in with Coll and George Fergusson to where I was sitting with my grandfather and Mr McPhail. Angus greeted Sir Alasdair with a pleasing deference and then turned to me, bowing gallantly over my hand before raising it to his lips.

'*Enchanté*, Mademoiselle, the heiress from beyond the seas! We have heard about you already, you know.' He had light dancing eyes and a gay manner. He waved his hand airily. 'When the invitation came, I thought Mac'Ghill Mhoire was sending round the fiery cross calling us to arms once more but this time to do battle for the sake of a beautiful lady.'

I smiled, responding to his mood. 'But I haven't needed anyone to do battle for me.'

'Ah, but you may and when you do, you can count on me as one of your champions.'

Fiona said sharply, 'Don't be absurd, Angus.'

'But I like being absurd. After all, it's all that is left to a Highlander these days, isn't that so, Coll? It's either that or turning ourselves into a dull solid lump of an Englishman like this fellow Richard Wynter up at the Tige Dubh.'

'He's not dull or solid,' I said laughing and then seeing my grandfather frown I quickly changed the subject. 'What is the fiery cross?'

'What *was* the fiery cross you should say, my dear young lady,' put in Mr McPhail. 'When a Highland Chieftain wanted to call his clan together to make war on the English or anyone else for that matter, he sent round two sticks in the shape of a cross, scorched in the fire and dipped in the blood of a newly killed goat. It was passed on from man to man until the whole clan was alerted, and great shame it brought on them more often than not.'

'Well, well, that is all over and done with,' said my grandfather impatiently. 'Marietta, ring for Murdo. Ask him to bring wine for our guests.'

We supped together that evening. We ate fresh salmon and roasted venison and were kept amused by our young guest's absurd chatter.

Once he said, 'Any chance of some hunting while I'm over here, Coll?'

'If you stay on for a few days and the Chief can spare me, we might go up the mountain.'

'You do what you please, my boy,' said my grandfather. 'My hunting days are over I'm afraid.'

'It's a pity not being able to use the Tige Dubh,' went

on Angus. 'What about this Colonel Wynter? Could we persuade him to join us? Do Englishmen hunt?'

'You had better ask Marietta,' said Fiona. 'She can tell you all about the Honourable Richard Wynter. She goes up to the Tige Dubh frequently.'

My grandfather looked across at me sternly. 'Is this true? Have you gone to see this man?'

'I went once to visit him and his sister. I felt it only courteous after their kindness to me to ask if they had all they needed.'

'I thought I made my wishes perfectly clear.'

'I'm sorry, grandfather,' I said steadily, 'but in this instance it seemed right to me. I have not gone there again.'

'I don't like being deceived.'

'I was not deceiving you. If you had asked me, I would have told you.'

I expected an explosion of anger and I waited trembling, but it did not come. Instead there was an awkward little silence and then my grandfather said tartly, 'Well, it's done now but I'd have you know, all of you, that I'm not dead yet. I'm still master in my own house.'

'There is surely no question of that, sir,' said George Fergusson smoothly. 'However there is just one thing that perhaps I ought to mention. This Colonel Wynter has been asking a great number of questions.'

'Questions? About what?'

'His brother's death.'

My grandfather frowned. 'The man drowned himself. There was an inquest. What more does he want to know?'

'Apparently he is not satisfied with the verdict.'

'More fool he,' growled my grandfather. Then suddenly he glared round the table. 'Or was there something more? Something that has been kept from me?' No one spoke and he brought his fist down on the table with an angry thump. 'Answer me, one of you. I don't like being kept waiting.'

'Nothing has been kept from you,' said Coll raising his head, 'nothing at all. You ought to know that. None of our people raised a finger against Graham Wynter though God knows they had reason enough.'

'Very well then. Let the Englishman make what he likes

of it. So far as we are concerned, the matter is over and done with.'

I saw Neil look up as if he would have protested, but Fiona gave him a sharp nudge and he went back to his food. The conversation took another turn and I don't know why I felt so strongly that something unsaid lay behind the smooth answers.

Later that evening at my grandfather's request the harp was brought out from its corner and Fiona sat down beside it, her red skirts spread around her. Angus came to stand near me, bending over to take my hand, flirting a little, and I was amused at his attentions.

Fiona was singing an old ballad with a haunting refrain . . .

> 'My love he was as brave a man
> As ever Scotland bred . . .'

As the charming husky voice echoed around the room Angus whispered, 'She is a beautiful creature, isn't she?'

'Are you in love with her, Mr Macdonald?'

'I wouldn't dare. She's a witch is our Fiona. She weaves magic spells.'

'Now you're being ridiculous.'

'Am I? You had better take care, Miss Gilmour. There are stranger things than that in the Highlands.'

'I believe you are making fun of me.'

He smiled but his eyes were serious. 'Of course I am. I'm talking nonsense as usual. Who would ever want to harm you?'

Who indeed? For an instant I thought of the dark forest and that hateful little image, then I thrust it away from me.

Fiona was still singing:

> 'No woman then or womankind
>   Had ever greater joy
>   Than we two when we lived alone,
>   I and my Gilderoy . . .'

I whispered, 'Who does Fiona enchant with her magic spells, Mr Macdonald?'

'Ah, that would be telling,' he answered teasingly.

I looked curiously around the room. George Fergusson lay back in his chair, listening with half-closed eyes. Coll had his back to her and, as the music died, his head came round to me and his look was a caress. Such a warmth flowed through me that I cared nothing for what others might say or think. Coll was mine.

Chapter Eight

The fickle Highland sun decided to be kind to us. May Day eve was glorious with the freshness of spring still in the air but brilliant with light and warmth. All the morning guests were arriving, some by boat, some on ponies, and as if by unspoken agreement, a great number of them wore their Highland dress and be damned to the consequences. That day my grandfather was like a new man; tall and erect, the eagle feathers in his bonnet, the Sìthen Stone fastening the plaid on his shoulder, walking proudly among his friends with the great dogs at his heels.

After a light luncheon he rested while I and the younger members of the party went out into the sunshine. Everyone in the valley had gathered on the open space beside the stream, men, women, children and babies. Many of them had flung their plaids around their shoulders, faded now or dipped in muddy dye to hide their brave colours from suspicious English eyes. Dirks and swords that had been buried in the earth or hidden in thatch had been brought out and swung from leather belts. There were wrestling bouts and trials of strength, shooting and feats of arms, and all to the music of the pipes, that strange piercing music that belongs to the valleys and mountains and is like no other sound on earth. Fascinated, I watched the sword dancers. The men weaved in and out of the crossed blades on the ground. It was a war dance, a celebration of victory after battle. It grew wilder and wilder. They took up the swords and Coll leaped down amongst them showing off his skill, the steel like quicksilver in his hands.

It was then that I saw Richard. He was standing apart from the villagers watching the swordplay and I

101

realized that Coll had seen him too. He raised his hand and the men lowered their swords, waiting as he walked across to Richard, the crowd moving back to make way for him. With a tight little feeling inside me, I saw him offer his sword, hilt first, and wondered if he was asking him to take part in the mock fighting. I was certain Richard would refuse, but he didn't. He took the proffered weapon. One of the other men tossed another sword to Coll and they strolled back together. There was intense excitement as the men of the clan drew back to make a ring.

Angus was standing beside me. He took my arm. 'Come on,' he said, 'this should be interesting.' He pushed his way to a place in the front.

Coll smiled, kissed the hilt of his sword to me and turned to face Richard. They had discarded their coats and from the first I felt there was something more than just a friendly bout of swordplay on a spring afternoon.

Angus was whispering to me, drawing my attention to feints and parries about which I understood nothing. To me they seemed to be fighting in grim earnest and more than once my heart was in my mouth. There was a moment when Coll brought Richard down on one knee. A sigh of satisfaction ran all around the spectators, but I saw the sweat on his face as he tossed the hair back out of his eyes. I thought of his damaged leg and wanted to call out to them to stop but knew how bitterly he would resent it if I did. Then he was up and they circled round one another again. How it happened, I don't know, but suddenly Richard lunged forward with a flick of the wrist and Coll's sword went spinning out of his hand. It was so unexpected that for an instant no one spoke or moved a muscle.

Then Richard said pleasantly, 'Do you wish to continue or shall we shake hands and call it a draw?'

There was a look of baffled fury on Coll's face. Then he thrust aside the proffered hand and turned his back. For a moment Richard did not move, then he dropped the borrowed sword to the ground, picked up his coat and walked away, the men opening silently before him.

Angus was frowning and I wished Coll had not lost his temper. It was such a silly incident. I was annoyed with him for starting it and still more with Richard for accepting the challenge. I only hoped it would not reach my grandfather's ears.

The piper was playing again and presently there came the moment they were all waiting for. My grandfather had come out on the causeway. He lifted up his hand for silence. He led me forward speaking to his people in their ancient tongue and a great shout arose to my ears so that I felt exalted and at the same time afraid. Richard had once compared me with a queen and for a fleeting moment I felt a little as Mary Stuart must have done when she came from France to her stormy mountainous kingdom. The weight of responsibility was almost too heavy to be borne. I faltered out my few words of Gaelic. They cheered again with a comforting warmth and it was then that there came a sudden interruption. The crowd gathered around us at the end of the causeway parted, and a woman came swiftly towards us. She was tall, her long dark cloak flowed out behind her, the hood fallen back so that the sun lit red lights in her hair and I guessed that it was my Aunt Kathryn.

George Fergusson gave her his hand and she climbed lightly up beside us. 'Well, Father,' she said, 'I'm late but I am here. Did you forget to invite me?'

I thought he would have replied in anger but she was his daughter after all and there were strangers watching with curious eyes. He only said ironically, 'May I remind you, Kathryn, that when you left me, you said you never wanted to see Glenlochy again.'

'So I did, but that was two years ago and I've grown homesick. Odd, isn't it? I never thought I would. But don't let it trouble you, Father, it is not for you or the castle.'

'For what then?'

She shrugged her shoulders. 'Perhaps I was curious. I wanted to see my niece.'

There were murmurs among the guests, some of them were smiling. Angus said, 'Where have you been hiding yourself all this time, Kat?'

'Oh here and there,' she replied lightly and turned to me. 'So you're Ian's daughter and you're like him too. What did he call you?'

'Marietta.'

She smiled. 'The faery wife. Dear Ian, he always lived in a dream, poor boy. How strange to think that all the time we mourned him dead, he lived and married and had a daughter to show for it.'

My grandfather seemed to pull himself together. He said sharply, 'Never mind that now. It's growing cold. It's time to go in. Coll, give me your arm.'

I hated her then because the spring had gone out of his step. He was old and tired again and I guessed at the effort it cost him to keep his dignity and pride at the head of his guests.

Kathryn looked unconcerned. She walked beside me into the house nodding familiarly to some of the people she knew. Inside the castle she took my arm.

'You don't know how extraordinary it feels to be back after all this time.'

I said awkwardly, 'You had better come to my room. Everywhere else is occupied and I have to change my dress.'

'It's like the old days,' she said cheerfully. 'I remember parties when we slept four or five to a bed and liked it. I rode ahead of my baggage. It is still on its way with Duncan Cameron.'

'Did you come with Mr Cameron?'

'Yes. You know that father sent for him. It was he who told me about it. He couldn't get here before. He was kept in Edinburgh on some legal business.'

I went ahead of her down the corridor but when we reached the door, she was there before me and had flung it open.

'So they gave you my old room. That was Ailsa Drummond of course. She always disliked me just as much as I loathed her. How do you manage?'

'I try to be patient.'

'That's more than I ever did.' She crossed to the window and pushed open the casement. 'I can't believe it. It is all so much the same. When something tremendous happens that alters your whole life, you think that everything else must be changed too and it is not. The world goes on its old way and it is only you who can never turn back.'

I did not quite know how to take her. She was neither

friendly nor hostile. It was almost as if I didn't exist as a person at all. She might have been talking to herself. Then suddenly she swung round, the clear eyes were very alive, they were looking me up and down, summing me up.

'Have you ever thought, Marietta, that if Ian had never had a daughter, if you had never been born to your French mother, then all this might have been mine.'

It had never occurred to me. I stared at her dumbly seeing her with new eyes. I could not think of her as Aunt Kat. She was younger than my father. She could not have been more than thirty-seven or eight and, though she was not beautiful, there was something about her proud fine-boned face that you would not easily forget. I said at last, 'Do you mind very much?'

'Mind? Good heavens, no!' She threw back her head and laughed aloud. 'Why should I mind? What would I do with this old ruin? It should be pulled down anyway. It is choked with too many dark memories. Something new should be put in its place.'

'How can you say such a thing?'

'Very easily, my dear. I lived my whole life here and was stifled by it. Just as you will be if you are not careful. I was as much a prisoner as those poor wretches down there in the rock dungeon. Do you know about that?'

'I have seen it.'

'When I was a child, I used to imagine I heard their ghosts crying out in the night especially when my brothers threatened to drop me down there. Not that they ever did of course. Father would have half killed them if they had.' She paused for a moment and then went on more seriously. 'The valley now and the people in it, that's quite different. I used to have dreams about what I'd like to do there.' She came and sat down on the bed. 'I'm going to stay here, you know, whatever father says. I'm going to live in one of the crofts at the top of the glen.'

'But you can't live in a place like that,' I exclaimed.

'Oh yes I can. I have it already. I made sure of that. It's being made habitable for me now. Father won't like it, but he can't drive me out, not his own daughter, and our people like me, they always have. I tried to start a school once. I might do that again unless you have any objections.' She looked up at me and smiled. 'Poor Marietta, you didn't reckon with me, did you? You think I'm half mad, I daresay. I'm not, I just know exactly what I want and this time nobody is going to cheat me out of it. Now, my dear, you had better get dressed. I know father. He's the most impatient man on earth and tonight it is important. You must do him and Glenlochy credit.'

Jeannie had come in looking curiously at the stranger and I said, 'This is Mistress Gilmour, my Aunt Kathryn.'

She bobbed a curtsey. 'Good evening, Miss, is there anything I can get for you?'

'Nothing, thank you. I shall do no more than wash my face.' Kathryn turned to me. 'A Scottish lass, I see, did you bring her with you from France?'

'Her father was a Mackenzie, Aunt Kathryn.'

'Oh not Aunt please. It makes me feel older than God! Your father always called me Kat so you can do the same.'

Jeannie had laid out the green brocade gown with the cream lace and the embroidered petticoat. She had woven a wreath for my hair of ivy leaves and wild flowers and when I was ready, Kathryn stood back looking at me critically.

'You'll do,' she said at last. 'You're a beauty, Marietta. I suppose you know that, any girl would, and you've got good taste or your mother has. By the way, why didn't she come with you?'

'She has married again.'

'And you don't like someone else stepping into your father's shoes, is that it?' she said shrewdly. I made no answer. I had no wish to discuss my mother with her and she didn't press me further. 'I wish there were some of the family jewels for you,' she went on, 'but most of them went to pay the fines and no doubt Coll has laid his greedy hands on the remainder.'

That aroused me. 'What makes you say that?'

She gave me a sharp glance. 'Like that, is it? Beware of Coll, my dear, he is out for what he can get.'

'Why are you so unjust to him? He works hard, he loves Glenlochy.'

She shrugged her shoulders. 'Oh yes, I grant you that, but for what purpose?' She looked down at herself. 'Well,

my riding-dress will have to serve. Come along, we had
better go.'

To enter the great hall of the castle on my grandfather's
arm was a dream come true. The long table had been
laid with silver and glass and behind each chair stood a
tall Highlander with a lighted pine torch in his hand. The
smoke curled up into the high roof and I caught my
breath in wonder. It was a scene of splendour out of the
past. The wine had been poured. The long line of guests
raised their glasses in salute to me before they drank. My
grandfather lifted the silver goblet and I sipped from it
before he drank deep.

'In the old days,' whispered Angus as he drew out my
chair for me, 'we would have flung our glasses over our
shoulders and smashed them, but alas, such luxuries are
things of the past.'

'Think of having to sweep up the broken pieces afterwards,' I whispered back. He chuckled and went to his
own place. The torchbearers circled the table to the wailing music of the piper at their head and marched out of
the hall.

'Thank goodness they've gone,' murmured Kat. 'Every
minute I've been expecting them to set someone's gown on
fire,' and I was angry with her. She was spoiling my dream
by making fun of it.

An old old man had taken their place. He tottered forward, his long white hair reaching to his shoulders. He
carried a small harp. He ran a thin old hand over the
strings and began to sing in a quavering voice that
gained in strength as it went on.

'Who is he?' I whispered and was astonished to see how
moved Kathryn was.

'He is the bard, the story-teller. Torquil was old when
I was a baby and he used to take me on his knee. He
can't read or write but he can repeat every song, every
ballad that has ever come down to us.'

'I hope to God he doesn't sing them all,' murmured
Coll under his breath. 'The poor old devil will never last
out if he does.'

Kathryn shot him a glance of sharp dislike. 'It would

have broken his heart if father had not let him come to-night.'

I don't think I shall ever forget that evening. It lives in my memory still though it was overshadowed by what came afterwards. The old man's voice telling over again of five hundred years of heroic deeds, the moment when he sang of Glenlochy itself. Kat translated the Gaelic for me:

> Rock of my heart! Beloved rock
> Where my childhood was cherished
> Dearer to me is the deep valley behind it
> Than the rich fields and proud castles of the
>   stranger . . .

I saw the tears well up in my grandfather's eyes and roll down his brown cheek before he brushed them away impatiently. I put my hand on his and he turned to smile at me.

After we had eaten and the tables had been cleared, the fiddlers came in and we danced. The young men whispered compliments to me as we met and curtsied and bowed to one another and it must have been very late when a small deputation came respectfully to ask their Chief if he would condescend to join in the merrymaking of his people outside the castle. A lavish supper had been served to them in the courtyard and on the causeway; broth, salmon, beef and oaten bannocks. For once they had eaten and drunk their fill at the castle's expense.

As we came out into the night I saw that great fires had been lit, long spirals of smoke rising up in the dark sky with little groups gathered around them. A chair had been placed for my grandfather and he sat there with some of the older men, a plaid wrapped around his shoulders and I thought, he is enjoying this, it is taking him back to the days of his youth when he was king on his own lands. I bent to kiss him and then went down among the people. Neil had attached himself to me. He was strongly excited as he took my hand.

'Do you know what this night is, Marietta? It is Beltane, the night of witches and magic and these are the fires of Baal.'

'I don't know what you mean.'

'Father says it is a memory of old heathen Gods and the people still keep it up though they have forgotten its meaning.'

There was a knot of young men standing round one of the fires. Coll was there and Fiona in her long red dress. I said curiously, 'What are they doing?'

'They have baked a cake in the fire. Now they are breaking it into pieces and putting them in a basket. One of the pieces is smeared with charcoal and he who draws it is the sacrifice. In the old days he would have been killed to bring strength and prosperity to the clan, but now all he has to do is to leap three times across the fire.'

It was all absurd of course but on this night with the leaping firelight, the torches of broom or heather blazing on top of long poles and flickering over the dark figures, lighting a face here, a red head there, almost anything seemed possible.

There was a burst of laughter and Coll held up the blackened piece of oatcake. 'Jump with me, Marietta,' he said, 'it will bring good fortune,' but quite suddenly I was afraid. The fire flared up and I shrank back. Fiona gave me a fierce glance and seized Coll's hand. Together they leaped across the blazing twigs to wild cheers.

Neil said discontentedly, 'You should have done it, Marietta. Now she will have the luck and not you.'

'Don't be silly. It's only a jest. I don't believe in such things.'

'Fiona does.'

'Foolish boy,' I said lightly touching his cheek. 'You only say that because she is your sister and you are jealous of her.'

'Don't treat me like a child,' he flung away from me petulantly and I let him go. Neil was a strange moody creature and I had not yet learnt the best way to deal with him.

I wandered from group to group. It was strangely warm for early May, one of those freak nights which come sometimes on the West Coast. The stars blazed in the sky, the fires sent up curling smoke and here and there torches still flared casting queer shadows. To me it was a night of enchantment. Some of the women came up to me looking at me with admiration, stroking the silk of my gown, greeting me in their lilting English. Many of them were dancing in circles around the fires and urged me to join them.

To my surprise I caught a glimpse of Janet standing with Richard in the shelter of the trees and went up to her.

She seized my hand. 'Isn't it exciting? I persuaded Richard to bring me. I do hope you don't mind. What a gorgeous creature your Coll is. If it wasn't for John, I would have fallen dead in love with him on the spot.'

'Jan, you're a grown woman not a gushing schoolgirl,' said Richard rather acidly.

'I know. More's the pity,' she flashed back at him. 'Don't take any notice of him, Marietta, he's jealous.'

'Oh for God's sake,' he moved impatiently away.

'Did your brother tell you about this afternoon?' I asked a little maliciously.

'Tell me what?'

'He and Coll fought a mock duel.'

'No, really? How I wish I had seen it. What happened? Did he win or lose?'

'You'd better ask him,' I said and had the satisfaction of seeing Richard look disconcerted for once.

A long procession of dancing figures came weaving in and out of the trees. They seized me by both hands. I waved to Janet and let them take me away with them. I was amused at first. The firelight flickered eerily on grotesque animal masks: a pig, a dog, a bird, a grinning devil. I thought it part of some age-old ritual and let myself be whirled along with them. Someone ahead was playing on a pipe, a haunting catchy little tune that made one want to dance.

At first we were following the stream, then suddenly we plunged into warm soft darkness and I realized that we had entered the forest. I was a little frightened then. I stumbled over a tree root and was jerked to my feet. I tried to pull away and the grip on my hands tightened. Now I was being dragged along against my will and I knew where we were going. I shut my eyes for an instant and when I opened them again, I saw the dark stone squat-

ting in the centre of the dell and panic caught me by
the throat.

The music was louder now, more insistent. We were
dancing round and round the stone and our steps quickened. The air was filled with a musky scent, sweet and
compelling. Something was glowing in the shallow basin.
Blue and green flames leaped upward and in their light a
black shape seemed to rise up, huge and horned like a
deer.

I tried to scream and couldn't. A voice whispered in
my ear, 'Why do you stay here, Marietta? Go, go now before it is too late.'

Was it Fiona? I didn't know and it went on and on,
hardly rising above a whisper and yet clear as doom in my
ears.

'Aren't you afraid? Fires burn, you know, they destroy
and leave no trace.'

Terror gave me strength. I broke out from the magic
ring and ran away from them. I swore I heard laughter
following me, but I was sure of nothing. I ran and ran
heedlessly, sobbing in an agony of fear until I tripped and
would have fallen headlong if someone had not caught me
in his arms.

'Marietta, what is it? What has happened? I've been
looking for you everywhere.'

It was Coll. His clothes smelled of the fire, the queer
spicy scent was all around us but I cared nothing for that,
he was there and I was safe. I leaned against him, hardly knowing what I was gasping out and he stroked my
hair gently, soothingly.

'But it is all nothing,' he said, 'nothing to be afraid of.
Only the villagers indulging in a little play. They do it
every year, but then you wouldn't know.'

'It's a horrible place,' I faltered. 'It's evil, wicked . . .'

'Nonsense. You're imagining what doesn't exist.'

'They were threatening me . . .'

He held me a little away from him tilting up my chin
to look at him. We were on the edge of the trees and
I could see the laughter in his eyes and the smile on the
beautiful mouth.

'Who on earth would want to threaten you?' he said

huskily. 'I must say it now. I cannot keep it in any longer. I love you, Marietta. Oh God, if you knew how much!'

Then he was kissing me and my whole being responded to him. I could not help myself. I must have shown him then how completely I was his and yet after that first passionate embrace he drew away. He said wretchedly, "Tonight of all nights, I should have kept silent. Who am I to dare to speak? A beggar at the feet of a queen.'

I smiled at his extravagance but it chimed with my mood. I said softly, 'A queen can love a beggar . . .'

He swung round to me gripping my shoulders. 'You don't mean it. I'm a fool even to think of it. It's impossible. Your grandfather would never agree . . .'

'Don't let's think of that now.'

'Is it really true? Has it happened to both of us? I tried to tell you. I knew it the moment I saw you in the doorway on that first evening.'

'I too.'

'Oh my dear, my love . . .'

His passionate kisses carried me beyond myself. The emotions of the day, my terror, everything combined. It would have been easy to let passion overwhelm me. All around us on this night there were other lovers locked in each other's arms. It would have been sweet and wonderful to give myself to him, only one thing held me back. The memory of my mother naked in bed with a stranger. I could not yield so easily, not like this, not even with the man I loved.

I whispered, 'Coll, we should go back. My grandfather, our guests, they will be wondering where I am.'

Reluctantly he released me but he drew my arm closely through his as we walked side by side. Everything had changed so much that now I could say what was in my mind.

'Coll, is it true what they say? Are you . . . are you . . .?'

I felt his arm tighten. He stared straight ahead. 'Am I your cousin, grandson of the Chief, that is what you would ask, isn't it?'

'Do you mind? I have heard what they say . . .'

'Of course you have. I don't know, Marietta. I've never known for certain.'

'But your mother . . . ?'

'She had her secrets and she kept them.' He looked down at me. 'Does it matter so much?'

'No,' and in my heart I rejoiced. We always want to give to the man we love and it seemed to me then that I had it in my power to grant him his heart's desire.

The fires were dying down now and the torches flickering out. Tired children had been taken off to bed. Some of the guests had gone back into the castle but my grandfather was still there. As we came up the causeway I saw to my great surprise that Fiona was talking with Richard Wynter. She was urging something on him because I saw him shake his head and attempt to walk away but she caught him by the hand and drew him towards the Chief.

I thought he went reluctantly and I said to Coll, 'She shouldn't do that. It will only distress grandfather. Perhaps she doesn't realize. I had better tell her.'

Coll held me back. 'She knows,' he said. There was a peculiar look on his face almost as if he were pleased and I could not understand it.

'But you told me yourself how he feels about it and the doctor said he should not be upset in any way.'

'Let her do as she pleases, Marietta.'

'No, I don't want everything spoiled, not today of all days.'

I began to run but I was too late. They had already climbed up on the causeway. The moon had risen and in its cold light Richard's face had a greenish pallor with faint dark hollows. He held out his hand.

'I would not intrude on you, sir, but I am acquainted with your granddaughter and we are near neighbours. I would like to offer my good wishes . . .'

He got no further. My grandfather turned round and saw him. His face went a queer grey colour. He said in a strangled voice, 'No, no, it's not possible . . .' He passed a hand over his face. 'God damn you! Must you come back now? Can you never let me be?' He made a wild gesture as if to sweep away the man in front of him and then swayed forward. Richard tried to break his fall but the weight brought him to his knees as I reached him with Coll close behind me. Angus had sprung forward, then the others crowded around us. Fiona was standing staring down at him.

I said fiercely, 'You should not have done that. Didn't you know?'

'What is there to know?' For an instant her eyes blazed at me with a queer look of triumph that made me shiver, then it had gone. She said quietly, 'It's what you wanted, isn't it? I thought to please you.'

'Not like this.' But before I could say anything more Kathryn had come up on the causeway. She brushed me aside. She was intensely practical. Within a few minutes the men had lifted their stricken Chieftain and were carrying him into the house. I would have followed but Richard held me back.

'I am sorry, Marietta. I did not imagine . . .'

'Haven't you done enough? Couldn't you have let him enjoy this one day in peace?'

'Is it shame or guilt that he doesn't dare to look me in the face?'

'How dare you accuse him after what your brother did?'

We were glaring at one another then Richard's anger seemed to die.

'Listen . . . I'll ride to Fort William. I'll fetch the doctor from the garrison there. I know we can't be back till morning but it's the least I can do.'

'You'll have to ride all night.'

'What does that matter?'

'What about Janet?'

'James will take her home. I'll be back, Marietta, as soon as I can.'

He jumped down from the causeway and for the first time I saw him limp as he quickly made his way to the trees where the ponies were tethered. Then I went into the castle and up the stairs to my grandfather's room. He was lying on the bed, banked up with pillows. Coll was there with Fiona and her father. Kathryn was bending over him and on the opposite side of the bed stood Mrs Drummond, her eyes fixed on the sick man's face.

I said fearfully, 'Is he dead?'

'No, of course he isn't. Hurry, Duncan, it is in the blue phial.'

I saw then that Mr Cameron was there too. He must have ridden in during the evening. He was opening a small chest and a faint dry smell of herbs stole through the room. He took out a phial and handed it to Kathryn.

'What are you giving him?' I said fiercely.

'Something to stimulate the heart. We have always had to be our own physicians in the valley. I know something of medicine.'

She poured a few drops from the phial into a spoon and forced it through my grandfather's lips. After a little, while we watched, there was a response. His eyes opened, a trace of colour stole into the ashen face. Mrs Drummond started forward and I saw Coll put a hand on her shoulder.

I said, 'Richard has ridden for the doctor at Fort William.'

'Good, but it will be morning before he is here.' Kathryn's eyes swept around the room. 'You can all go now. I'll sit up with him.'

'No, I will.' Mrs Drummond's fierce whisper startled me. She stood immovable beside the piled pillows and I had the odd feeling that the two women fought for mastery over the unconscious body of my grandfather. Then Coll moved forward.

'Better not,' he said quietly. 'Mistress Gilmour knows what to do. Fiona, would you take Mrs Drummond to her room?'

I said through stiff lips, 'Perhaps you would have a bed prepared for Mr Cameron.'

'Thank you, Miss Marietta.' The lawyer's round rosy face was pinched with fatigue and anxiety. 'I am sorry to be so late. We will talk in the morning.'

'Yes, yes, if you wish. Ask for anything you need.'

He bowed and went out of the room with a backward glance at the still figure on the bed.

When the door closed, I said firmly, 'I shall stay here with you.'

Kathryn smiled at me across the bed. 'And what good could you do? You're young, Marietta, you've no experience of sickness. I've seen my father like this before.'

I did not want to go but Coll put an arm round me, murmuring soothing words, and I leaned against him,

suddenly feeling so weary that it was all I could do to
hold back tears of exhaustion.

He took me to my room and lighted the candles for
me. 'Don't fret, my darling, don't let it make you sad,
not tonight of all nights. He will recover, I am sure of it.
I'll find Jeannie and send her to you.'

'The guests, Coll . . . what ought I to do about them?'

'Leave everything to me.'

He went out and reaction shook me. My legs felt like
jelly. I could scarcely stand. Wearily I swung back the
embroidered bed curtain and stood transfixed, the blood
freezing in my veins. My strangled cry brought Coll running back.

'What is it? What's wrong?'

I pointed with a trembling finger. 'Look at that! Why
do they hate me so much?' On my pillow lay a squat
clay figure with long red hair and an ugly thorn pierced
through its heart.

I had never seen Coll angry before. It rolled up in him,
a volcano of rage that burst through clenched teeth.

'The fools,' he said, 'the God-damned fools! There
was no need for this, no need at all.' He snatched up the
clay image, threw it to the floor and crushed it furiously
under his heel.

There was a savagery about his reaction that drove the
first shock out of my mind. 'Who do you mean? Who has
done it and why?'

His hands were trembling, but with a tremendous effort
he swallowed his rage. He said in a choked voice, 'It's
that damned boy. It's Neil, playing games with things he
doesn't understand, trying to frighten you.'

'Neil?' I repeated. 'Neil! But it can't be. He likes me.'

But Coll wasn't listening to me. 'I'll teach him to play
pranks on you like this.'

'Coll, please don't be hard on him. If it was Neil, then
I'm sure he meant no harm.'

'Of course it was Neil. Sometimes I think he's half out
of his mind. He's got to be taught a lesson once and for
all.' Then his face cleared. He came to me taking my
hand. 'You're not frightened any more, are you? Not
now.'

The fear was still there, not of the loathesome little im-

age but of something else, something intangible, but I
would not show it.

I shook my head. 'No, not any more.'

'I love you.'

'I love you too.'

His kiss was gentle, but when he had gone I looked
down at the crushed shapeless object on the floor and
shivered. I could not bear to touch it. I had no reason to
doubt Coll and yet something inside me refused stubbornly to believe that it was all a silly prank of Neil's. I
thought of the forest, the whispering voices, the sense of
evil, and terror threatened to engulf me again. Could it
be Fiona? Fiona who was my enemy, I was sure of that
now. Why had she brought Richard Wynter to my grandfather knowing his extraordinary likeness to the brother
who had died so mysteriously? Then there was Kat . . .
my Aunt Kathryn who would have inherited everything
but for me. Did she hate me too? I had no ready answers.

Without the comfort of Coll's arms around me, I felt
very alone and though I had no doubt of his love, I could
not still the uncomfortable feeling that he had lied to
me when there had been no necessity. It was long before
I slept that night.

Chapter Nine

I woke late and was immediately anxious about my grandfather. I had meant to share the night watch with Kathryn and was angry with myself for oversleeping but, in the clear light of morning, things have a way of looking very different. My panic of the evening before seemed foolish and exaggerated. I dressed quickly and as I looked in the mirror, I remembered with shivering delight the joy of Coll's kisses and felt happy in spite of everything. How could I doubt him? He belonged to me as I did to him and nothing could destroy that. As soon as I was ready, I went to my grandfather's room. The curtains were drawn and it was very quiet. Kat was not there but Murdo sat beside the bed and the two dogs lay beside him, heads on paws, watching their master with their slate grey eyes.

'How is he?' I whispered.

'He is better and sleeping.'

'Where is Mistress Kathryn?'

'She will be back soon.'

'You shouldn't be here alone.'

'And why should I not? Don't be afraid, Miss Marietta. I will stay with the Chief as long as he needs me.' The old man put his gnarled brown hand on the long thin fingers that lay quiet on the coverlet. 'You do not understand. How should you?' he said with simple dignity. 'But we are foster brothers. The same mother's milk suckled us both. I have served him all the years of my life and, if God wills, I shall serve him in death too.'

'You will call me if there is any change?'

'Of course. You go now and eat your breakfast, little mistress.'

I went in search of Kathryn. On the stairs I met Angus

118

and heard to my relief that many of the guests had risen
early and ridden away leaving kind messages of sympathy. Food had been prepared and was laid out in the
sitting-room. Duncan Cameron was seated at the table.
He rose politely when I came in and I was just about to
ask him if he had seen my aunt when she entered with the
doctor who was protesting volubly at having been roused
at dawn and forced to ride the miles to Glenlochy without even being allowed to wait for a bite of breakfast.
Colonel Richard Wynter, son of Lord Wynter, had obviously used every ounce of influence to persuade the
red-faced choleric little Englishman to turn out of his
warm bed.

'Thank you, no,' he said, irritably, waving aside Kathryn's offer of food. 'Now I am here, I had better see my
patient immediately though there is little enough I can
do for him. I told Sir Alasdair that when I saw him a year
ago. "You must take things quietly," I said to him. "I'll
never live like a vegetable," he roared back at me, "so if
that is all you have to say, you can take yourself off!"'

Kathryn murmured something tactful as she guided
him out of the room. I would have gone with them but
Mr Cameron stopped me.

'Miss Marietta, could I have a word with you?'

'Now?'

'The sooner the better. I think it important.'

'Very well. What is it?'

He put down his napkin, went to the door, opened it
and peered out cautiously before closing it.

'Mr Cameron, is all this necessary?' I said a little impatiently.

'Experience has taught me that one can never be too
careful where money and property are concerned.' He
took me by the arm and drew me to the window speaking
in a low voice. 'You know why I am here?'

'My grandfather did say something about changing his
will.'

"Aye, that is so, and I only hope that he will be strong
enough for it to be carried out within the next day or so.'

'He is sick,' I said, 'and I don't want him to be worried
about anything. There is plenty of time.'

'Perhaps, but don't let us deceive ourselves. A man

with a heart like his can go at any moment and there is something you should know.' He paused for a moment and then said irrelevantly, 'I am glad to see that he has not turned your Aunt Kathryn away. I feared he might.'

'What has that got to do with it?'

He shot me a keen glance. 'Maybe you do not know that two years ago there was a serious quarrel between Sir Alasdair and his daughter. I don't know all the details, only that soon afterwards he came to see me in Edinburgh. It was the last time he made the long journey. What he told me surprised me very much.'

'Why?'

'He wished to make a new will disinheriting his daughter and leaving everything to this young man, Colin Grant, whom he had reason to believe was his grandson, the bastard child of his eldest boy.'

'To Coll?' I exclaimed. 'So it was true after all.'

'True or not, that was what he told me. Of course at that time we knew nothing of you. I tried to dissuade him, thinking of your Aunt Kathryn, but he can be very obstinate when he makes up his mind and nothing would alter his decision. The will was engrossed and duly signed.'

'Does Coll know?'

Mr Cameron shrugged his shoulders. 'Of that I cannot be certain. All I know is that Sir Alasdair swore me to secrecy and I have kept my word, but you see how important it is in your own interests that a new will should be signed as soon as possible. He wrote me of his wishes. It can be prepared very quickly after I have had an opportunity to speak with him.'

'We must wait and see what the doctor says.'

'Aye, I realize that, but I hope it will be soon. I cannot wait here too long. I am a busy man.'

He went back to his half-finished breakfast. I sat down with him but I was not really hungry. My mind was in a turmoil. Did Kathryn know about this will? Did Coll? The unwelcome thought flashed through my mind that if he did, he could be making doubly sure of himself by marrying me and then I rejected it absolutely. It could not be true. I would not believe it. He loved me, I was sure of it. I got up and moved restlessly to the window.

Oh, why did it have to happen like this and spoil everything? Coming here to Glenlochy had been like a dream coming true and now it was tarnished by talk of wills and inheritances. It seemed to me then that the very thought of money changed people. They became selfish and greedy. I remembered two sisters we had known in Paris who had wept night and day when their mother died and fought like wild cats over the few sticks of furniture she had left behind.

Then Kathryn came back with the doctor breaking in on my thoughts and beckoning me to join them. He looked very grave.

'It is as I have told you already. There is little anyone can do for Sir Alasdair and I can say nothing with certainty about the future. Only that he is very frail. The least thing could cause collapse.' He held up the blue phial between two fingers. 'I noticed this beside the bed.' He took out the stopper, sniffed and then poured a drop on his finger and tasted it. He grimaced. 'Foxglove . . . digitalis. You know, Miss Gilmour, that this is strong poison.'

'Of course I know,' said Kathryn impatiently. 'I distilled it myself, but it is also a valuable heart stimulant. I learned about it from my mother who in turn learned it from her mother. We have had to treat ourselves or die in this valley for many years.'

'In that case,' said the doctor with a thin smile, 'why call me in at risk of life and limb? This is extremely dangerous and should only be administered under proper supervision.'

'I know that too. Murdo is reliable. He would die himself before letting any harm come to his Chief.'

'No doubt but mistakes can be made. Remember that I warned you.'

'I may be only a woman and a Scot, but I'm not a fool,' said Kathryn tartly.

I saw the little man bristle with indignation and intervened quickly. 'Thank you for coming. We are greatly obliged to you.'

'Colonel Wynter has a remarkably forceful personality,' he said dryly and accepted a dram of whisky before he left.

'The man's an obstinate ass,' said Kathryn when he had

ridden away. 'All he could think of was letting blood, as if father wasn't weak enough already. I managed to put a stop to that.' She put the blue phial in my hand. 'I will leave it with you, Marietta. Keep it in a safe place and only use it if your grandfather has another severe attack. Give him a few drops as I did last night. The doctor has left an opiate for him. He should sleep all day and I must see to my own affairs. Goodness knows what has happened to my baggage. I will be back this evening unless you send for me.'

For the next three days there was little change in my grandfather's condition. Kathryn came and went. Coll spent morning and afternoon shut up in the estate room. Fiona stayed on at the castle helping Mrs Drummond with the departing guests, and while Murdo ate and rested, I sat with my grandfather. He lay very quietly, his face like a fine brown carving against the white of the pillows, rousing now and again to swallow a few spoonfuls of broth. Once he murmured my name.

'I'm here, grandfather,' I said. I took his hand and kissed his cheek.

Duncan Cameron looked in more than once but I shook my head and he went away again.

It was the evening of the third day when he seemed so much better that I felt free to get out of the house for a little air. It was cool and there had been a shower of rain but the sea wind smelled salt and fresh. I climbed down the causeway and on to the white sand of the beach. The tide was slowly going out and I walked round until I could look up at the rocky promontory on which the castle was built. The green slime and the mounds of seaweed showed me how high the sea rose and I could just see the small iron door which had been the old entrance and the flight of steps which came worn and jagged down the cliff. Below them about twenty feet or so up from the shore there was a dark opening where seabirds flew in and out. I wondered if it was a cave and how far it stretched. Curlews cried over my head, a lonely desolate sound, the wind whipped at my hair and I was just about to walk briskly along the beach when I saw a girl come trudging up from the sea carrying a huge basket on her hip. She put it down and began to pile it with seaweed. A child was with her, a little girl of no more than two years old, running to and fro with the long wet ribbons and pulling out more than she put in.

The girl laughed and pretended to slap her. 'Stop your antics, Etta, or we shall never be done.'

The child dodged away shrieking with laughter and suddenly I recognized them both. It was the young woman who had held her little girl up to me on the first day I had ridden up the valley. I walked quickly across the sand as she struggled to pick up the heavy basket.

'Let me help you. You'll never manage to carry it alone.'

'Och no, Miss Marietta, you'd spoil your fine gown. I'm strong. It's the little one who keeps getting in the way.'

There was a delicacy about the girl's features and her dress, simple though it was, was clean and neat. I said curiously, 'What is your name?'

'Mary Kintyre.' She put out a hand to pull the little girl close to her. 'And this is Marietta.'

'Yes, I remember.'

'I call her Etta.'

We looked at one another for a moment and then I said, 'You shouldn't be carrying heavy baskets like that. Why doesn't your husband help you?'

'He's away over the sea.'

'Is he a soldier?'

'No.'

'You mean he has emigrated?'

'Aye, these two years back. He hasn't even seen his daughter yet.'

There was a sadness in her voice and with a flash of intuition I guessed the truth. 'Was he one of those who were shipped away as . . . as . . .?'

'Aye, like a slave he was with shackles on his wrists, he who had always lived free as a bird.'

In the stress of the last few days I had forgotten about Richard's brother and the mystery surrounding him. I said, 'Mary, what actually happened? Why didn't you realize what he was doing?'

'Captain Graham had been kind. We liked him though he was English. He was not like the others who had come and thought only of what they could steal from us. He loved Glenlochy and the Tige Dubh so we trusted him.' She looked away from me, her eyes on the distant horizon. 'Even now it is hard to believe that he had such a devil within him.'

'But what did he say?' I persisted. 'How did he justify himself?'

She turned back to look at me. 'But surely you know. The ship did not sail until after he had disappeared.'

'What!' I gaped at her in stupefaction. 'But Mr McPhail said he watched from the shore.'

'Och, the Minister!' she said with a shrug of her shoulders. 'He was not there. He had been sick and Fiona kept him to his bed. No, we thought to see Captain Graham that morning but he was not on the shore nor was he at the Tige Dubh. I ran there myself. We thought he had returned to Fort William. But a little later his body was washed up from the sea and they said he had done this wicked thing and had killed himself because he could not live with the sin of it on his conscience.'

'Who said so?'

'Fiona for one. She had always hated Captain Wynter.'

'Why?'

'Have you not seen it already?' said Mary dryly. 'Fiona likes to think she has all men at her beck and call but Captain Graham had no eyes for her.'

'You don't like her.'

'No, I do not, but all the same it is true what I am telling you.'

'But surely it was not just Fiona . . .'

'No, it was Coll and my father who spoke out very bitterly against him.'

'Your father?' I repeated.

'My father is George Fergusson.'

'But Mr Fergusson has a fine house. If you are his daughter . . .'

'Why do I have to live like this? Is that what you are asking? I do not like my father, Miss Marietta, that is one reason, and then he did not like my husband.'

'You mean you married against his wishes?'

'Aye, I did. He thought because he had me tutored, because I could read and write and play the harpsichord, that he could marry me off to a fine gentleman; but grand clothes and a house in Edinburgh do not make up for losing the man you love so I ran away and married my Keith.'

'But it is so hard a life . . .'

'Keith was a farmer and a good one and we had hopes . . .' her voice choked a little but she went on bravely. 'And I will not beg my father for favours. I look after myself and Etta.'

'What about your mother?'

'She is dead long since.'

'Does your father live alone?'

She avoided my eyes. 'He does not lack for company.'

I said impulsively, 'You must be very brave.'

'No, not really. Often I have been frightened but now it will be easier. I am going to work for Mistress Kathryn. Already I have been getting her little house tidy for her.' She looked at me for a moment as if she would have said more. Then she hoisted the basket to her hip and took the child by the hand. 'If you will excuse me, Miss Marietta, I must go. It is time Etta was in bed.'

I watched them walk slowly up the beach towards the valley. Looking back afterwards I think perhaps it was then that the first doubt crept into my mind though I was far from guessing the truth and even if I had, I would have rejected it utterly. The dream that I had cherished for so long was still too precious to me.

The wind blew in cold from the sea and it was time to go back to supper. Hurrying up the stairs I heard voices raised in angry argument. Ailsa Drummond was standing outside my grandfather's room, a tray in her hands, while Murdo stubbornly refused to let her enter.

I broke in on them. 'What is it? What's wrong?'

Mrs Drummond turned to me fiercely, dark eyes smouldering in her pale face. 'The old fool will not allow me to pass. Who should give Sir Alasdair his supper if not me?'

'Mac'Ghille Mhoire gave me his orders. "Keep the woman out," he said and keep her out I will,' said Murdo obstinately.

'I don't believe it,' said Mrs Drummond shrilly. 'He's lying.'

Murdo shrugged his shoulders and grinned maddeningly. I had an idea he was enjoying himself.

'Give me the tray,' I said. 'I'll take it in to him.'

Reluctantly Mrs Drummond gave it up to me. She stalked down the passage muttering.

'Old besom!' mumbled Murdo under his breath as he stood aside to let me go past him.

My grandfather was sitting up in bed looking more alive than he had done since he had been taken ill.

'What the devil was going on out there?' he demanded.

'Nothing,' I said peaceably. 'Mrs Drummond wanted to bring your supper and Murdo wouldn't let her.'

'Interfering bitch,' he muttered. 'I don't want her in here fussing around me.' He looked at the bowl of chicken broth on the tray with disgust. 'Damned slop! I want food not baby's pap.'

'The doctor said . . .'

'Damn the doctor! Never trust an Englishman. What does he know? Don't stand there grinning, Murdo. Where the devil is the whisky? Have you drunk the lot yourself, you old rascal? I wouldn't put it beyond you.'

'Grandfather, listen. You must do as the doctor says if you want to get better. If you're very good, Murdo shall bring you a glass of claret.'

'Don't treat me like a child,' he growled. 'If I'm going to die, then I'll go like a man not like some whimpering brat,' but he was weakening already. Murdo went out grinning and with difficulty I persuaded him to take some of the broth. Then he pushed it aside and said something very strange.

'Marietta, I don't remember much of what happened before . . .' He moved restlessly against his pillows. 'Fiona brought someone to me and . . .'

'That's right, Grandfather. It was Richard Wynter. He came in friendship, he did not mean to distress you.'

'Wynter,' he repeated slowly. 'Richard Wynter, not Graham . . .'

'Graham Wynter is dead, don't you remember?' I said gently.

'Yes, yes,' he muttered impatiently. 'They told me about the evil thing that he had done but that was not the worst. I was too harsh . . . Kathryn was right . . .' He passed a hand over his face as if trying to brush something away from him.

'Grandfather, may I bring Richard Wynter here?' I said eagerly. 'Will you see him?'

'No, no,' he said in strong agitation struggling to sit up and clutching hold of my arm, 'you cannot ask it of me. Never forget, Marietta, never forget that it was the English who murdered my sons and destroyed your father's life. Remember it always.'

I thought only to quiet and comfort him. 'I will, I will. I'll remember.'

Then Murdo came back with the goblet of claret and he drank it quickly, greedily, his blue eyes bright and excited.

'Marietta, is that lawyer fellow still in the castle?'

'Duncan Cameron? Yes, of course he is and asking to see you.'

'Bring him here.'

'Now? Tonight? Wouldn't it be better in the morning? You mustn't tire yourself too much.'

'Perhaps.' He leaned back against the pillows and closed his eyes for a moment. 'Very well. In the morning but don't forget.'

I took the glass out of his hand and his fingers closed around my wrist pulling me close to him.

'I'm not a fool, Marietta, I know I haven't long and there are things you should know, important things.' His voice was thick and I knew he was wearying.

'Yes, dearest, I know, but there's time.'

'Not too much. We all make mistakes, I more than anyone. But I have always tried to do what I could for our people here. Remember that, Marietta.'

'Of course I will.'

'There's Coll too.' His eyes were fixed on me. 'I've not always been fair to him.'

'Don't worry about it now.'

His grip on my wrist tightened. 'Glenlochy must be yours. It is your right but you will help him, Marietta. You will do what you can for him. Promise me.'

'I promise. Would you like me to stay with you this evening?'

'No, my dear.' He lay back smiling at me. 'You don't

want to spend your time sitting beside an old man's sick-bed. Murdo can stay. He and I are used to one another. In the morning we'll talk.'

So I kissed him and rearranged his pillows, and never realized how much I was to regret that I did not remain with him though it would have made little difference if I had. I went to my own room to wash and change for supper and knew at once with a curious certainty that someone had been there in the room before me. It was not that anything was disarranged. It was just that noth-ing was quite as I had left it. It must be Jeannie, I said to myself, and then remembered that she had swept and dusted early that morning. It was then that I thought of the blue phial, the digitalis that Kat had given me for safe keeping. I knew exactly where I had put it. In the little casket in which I kept my few small pieces of jewellery.

I opened the drawer and took it out. The phial was not there. I stared at it. Had I made a mistake and put it else-where? It is the kind of thing one does and forgets, only this time I had been so careful. I searched the rest of the drawer. I flung open another and began to hunt through clean handkerchiefs and shifts. I ran to the bedside table, the candlestick was there, my watch, but no phial and suddenly I was frightened. Without stopping to think I ran along the passage, down the stairs and into the estate room. Coll was there, talking to Mrs Drummond, but I could not stop to wonder why she should be there.

I said, 'Coll, the medicine that Aunt Kat left with me, the digitalis the doctor said was so dangerous, it has gone. I can't find it anywhere.'

He turned to look at me, calm and smiling. 'It must be there. Who would have taken it? Perhaps you've forgot-ten where you put it.'

'No, I haven't. I remember distinctly and it is not there.'

'Perhaps Miss Marietta thinks that one of us has stolen it,' said Mrs Drummond dryly.

I rounded on her angrily. 'It's nothing to laugh at. It's serious. Can't you understand?'

'I'm sorry,' she said. 'Shall I come and help you look for it?'

'No, leave it to me.' Coll put his arm round my shoulders.

'Don't fret. It has probably slipped down somewhere.'

He came back with me and together we searched. I was kneeling on the floor looking through the bottom drawer of the chest when he held it up triumphantly.

'There you are. What did I say? It was caught in a crack between the drawer and the back of the chest. No doubt it rolled out when you took something out of the casket. You had better let me keep it in future.'

I sat back on my heels, feeling foolish, and he came down on one knee beside me putting his arm round my shoulders.

'You're overwrought, my love, and I'm not surprised with all that has happened these last few days. What did you imagine? That one of us would want to poison the Chief? Why on earth would anyone want to do that?'

It sounded so absurd when he put it like that, quietly and reasonably. I leaned against him glad of his strength. He stroked my hair and I felt again the magic of his kisses.

'You're worn out, Marietta, why not let Jeannie bring you supper and go to bed early? You have scarcely had any sleep these last three nights. It will do you good.'

'Yes, perhaps I will.'

'That's right.' He drew me to my feet. 'I've wanted to go to your grandfather, to ask him when we can be married, but we must wait until he is better. Just a little longer and then everything will be wonderful for us both.'

His arms tightened around me. He kissed me with a sudden passion that swept me off my feet. I was dizzy with it and then as suddenly he released me. He said huskily, "I shouldn't have done that but it is so hard to wait.'

It was not until he had gone that I realized he must have taken the phial with him. I stood in the centre of the room still giddy with his kisses and it was not until then that I became aware of the musky perfume, faint but unmistakeable, the perfume Fiona used that I had smelled in the forest. I felt a gust of anger that she should come into my room, looking through my clothes, touching what was mine. I opened the window. Cold clean air rushed in and the scent was gone. Perhaps I had imagined it. The last three days had been so exhausting, it was not surprising that my nerves should be on edge. I was ready to believe almost anything. If I was to go on like this, I would work myself into a fever. When Jeannie brought in my supper I had resolutely put it out of my mind.

Chapter Ten

I made up my mind to go to the Tige Dubh the moment I woke up the next morning. It was not that I had forgotten what my grandfather had said the night before but he had not forbidden me to go, and someone ought to thank Richard for what must have been an exhausting night ride. But more than anything I think it was because I had been shut up in the castle for days and had an immense longing to be free of it if only for a few hours.

Before I left I looked into my grandfather's room. Murdo put his finger on his lips and I did not disturb him. He had seemed so much better and I knew Kathryn would be there during the morning.

'When he wakes, tell him I will be back very soon,' I whispered and went down to the stables intending to ask Tam or one of the boys to saddle a pony for me.

To my surprise I found Neil there sitting on one of the stone mounting blocks staring moodily at nothing. He jumped to his feet as I came up and I said a little tartly, 'Shouldn't you be inside working with Coll?'

'Yes, I suppose so,' he said sullenly. 'Are you going riding?'

'Yes.'

'I'll get the pony for you.' He disappeared into the stable and I followed him.

'I've not seen you for days. Where have you been?'

'At home. Fiona said I should stay with father while she was at the castle.'

'I see.' I wondered if he was awkward with me because of Coll's scolding and I said half jokingly, 'I've been very angry with you, Neil. I thought you liked me.'

'So I do.' He was busying himself with the saddle. 'Why are you angry?'

'I didn't think you of all people would have played such a nasty trick on me. It wasn't very kind, was it, especially when grandfather had been taken ill.'

'What trick?' He turned to look at me, his face so transparently honest, it was difficult to believe he was not genuinely surprised.

'You know perfectly well what I mean. How could you put that horrible little image in my bed and frighten me to death?'

A flush spread over his pale face. 'Oh that! I heard about that but I didn't do it. I swear I didn't. It was not me, Marietta, it was . . .' Then he stopped.

'Then who was it?'

'I don't know.'

'Don't blame someone else, Neil. It just makes it worse.'

'I'm not . . . it was Coll who told you, wasn't it?' he burst out passionately. 'Coll who'd like to be Chieftain, only he won't be ever . . . I've told him over and over again, that's why he hates me.'

'Oh Neil, you're talking nonsense and you know it.'

'And he's trying to make you hate me too . . .' he went on but now I was angry with him.

'Oh never mind. I've forgotten about it already,' I said impatiently. I led the pony outside and he came out after me. He gave me his hand to help me into the saddle and then he stood still, holding the rein, staring up at me.

'Marietta,' he said, 'why didn't you take any notice of what I wrote to you? I told you to keep away from Glenlochy but you came just the same.'

I thought of the scribbled note which I had burned and resolved to forget.

'You do remember?' he went on urgently.

'Yes, I remember. So it was you who wrote it. Why, Neil, why?'

He shifted his feet looking away from me, half scared, half defiant. 'I heard them talking. They didn't want you to come here.'

'Who are they?'

'Mr Fergusson, Fiona, Coll, all of them except the Chief.'

I didn't know whether to believe him or not. Was he telling the truth or was he just trying to make mischief? I jerked the bridle out of his hand. 'Anonymous letters get what they deserve. Why should I take heed of anything so foolish? I destroyed it long ago.'

I spurred the pony all the more eager to get away from him because he had made me uneasy. Perhaps it was true that Coll had not wanted me to come but then he had not known me. Now it was very different. I was not going to let an idle discontented boy spoil my happiness.

It was a morning of silver. The sea, the trees, the purple mountain were all shrouded in thin shreds of mist. I went the long way round following the beach and turning up beside the loch because I did not want to go through the forest. The water was steel grey. It lay still and beautiful. Only the keening cry of the curlews far above my head broke the silence but as I followed the path, the sun broke through in long quivering bars of gold between the veils of mist.

Yellow marsh flowers grew in and out of the reeds at the brink of the water and I was just thinking that I must be near the Tige Dubh when something seemed to flash past in front of me diving from a high rock. At first I thought it was a giant fish, a leaping salmon perhaps or even one of the water kelpies my father used to tell me about. Then to my utter amazement I saw that someone was swimming. Intrigued, I urged my pony nearer the edge and then smiled to myself as I recognized the dark head of Richard Wynter. He was cleaving through the water with long powerful strokes, no doubt imagining himself completely alone. I saw the naked shoulders and knew that in all decency I should have closed my eyes and crept away, but I lingered for a moment amused to have caught him out and in that time he changed his course coming in towards the shore. He saw me and promptly dived under the water, coming up much further away.

I stayed where I was to spare him embarrassment. I dismounted, tethering my pony and kneeling down to pick a few of the flowers. Presently Richard emerged from the shelter of the trees. He must have dressed with remarkable speed and for the first time I saw him in the Black Watch kilt, with a shirt hastily pulled on and a plaid over his shoulder, his bare feet thrust into deerskin brogues. He had always been so completely English, it

was strange how different it made him look. There was
none of the sleek sophistication, none of the slight super-
ciliousness which I had so much disliked when I met him
in Edinburgh. He was the last person on earth that I ever
expected to look awkward but now, towel in hand, his
wet hair dripping on his shirt, he said ruefully, 'I thought
I had the loch to myself.'

'I'm sorry to have disturbed you,' I said trying not to
laugh, 'but isn't it very cold?'

'Yes, it is, but I like it.' Then he smiled a little reluctantly. 'This is a ridiculous situation. It could only happen in the Highlands. I hope you are not shocked.'

'Oh I am . . . to my very soul. You know this is a very
dangerous loch. I remember my father telling me. An *each
uisge* lives in it.'

'And what is an *each uisge?*'

'If you wear the kilt, then you ought to know.'

He looked down at himself. 'Do you disapprove?'

'It wouldn't make any difference if I did, would it?'

'It might.'

There was a look in his eyes I had never seen before. I
said a little hastily, 'An *each uisge* is a water-horse, a
very beautiful creature who wears a harness of gold and
if you think to capture and ride it, then it will carry you
off to the depths of the water and eat you.'

'What a fearful prospect!' he said dryly and made a
futile attempt to rub his soaked hair.

'Give me the towel. Let me do that.'

'Certainly not.'

I tried to snatch it from him and suddenly we were
caught up in a laughing tussle. Then as he swung round
holding it high above his head, I saw the long deeply fur-
rowed purple scar that ran down his thigh to the knee
and could not prevent a little exclamation.

His eyes followed mine and the laughter died. He said,
'Revolting, isn't it?'

'No, it's not that at all. It must have been agony when
it happened.' I remembered all that his sister had said, his
fight against pain and disablement, and moved by an impulse of sympathy I leaned forward and touched it very
gently. I felt him shiver and thought quickly that someone

at some time had made him suffer because of it. I said,
'Does it hurt now?'

'Not so often these days. It comes and goes like an old
man with gout. I think we had better go to the house.
Janet will have some coffee ready. She usually does when
I have been swimming.'

As we walked side by side along the path he enquired
politely after my grandfather and I thanked him for using
his influence at Fort William and fetching the doctor so
promptly.

'Grandfather did not mean to be insulting that night,' I
went on. 'He was disturbed by your likeness to your
brother.'

'I guessed that when I thought about it afterwards.' He
turned to look at me. 'I shouldn't have said what I did
either. I apologize.'

'It doesn't matter. What was it that Fiona said to you?'

'She told me your grandfather had asked to speak with
me.'

It could be true and yet somehow I doubted it. We
went on in silence for a little before Richard said quietly,
'I took good note of your handsome Coll. Have you quite
lost your heart to him?'

'You shouldn't ask a question like that.'

'Shouldn't I? Well, I do have a special interest after
all. I feel a responsibility for you. He manages Sir Alasdair's estates very efficiently from all accounts.'

Something about the way he said it jarred on me. I
said, 'And he will continue to do so for a very long time I
hope.'

'As your husband, Marietta?'

'Richard please . . .'

'So it is true.' He paused before he said, 'Does your
grandfather know?'

'Nothing is settled. It is too soon.'

'Much too soon . . . only a few weeks.' He gave me
his quirky smile. 'The young Queen Mary from over the
sea—do you remember? She fell in love and married in
haste . . . disastrously.'

'What does it matter what she did? Richard, you are being unfair to Coll and me.'

'I'm sorry. I shouldn't tease you, should I? Jan would say it is all pure jealousy,' he went on lightly.

'Jealousy?'

'Of course. With those looks of his what young woman could resist him?'

I looked up at him walking beside me. 'Is that what made you join him in the swordplay?'

'He presented me with a challenge, Scotland against England. I couldn't let that go by, could I?'

'I wish you had.'

'Why? Because he didn't like being beaten?'

But I didn't have to reply because we were already at the house. Janet came running out to meet us and with her came Angus Macdonald.

'No doubt you're surprised to see me here,' he said grinning at me. 'I find the castle a little oppressive just now, besides I can't resist the charms of Miss Janet.'

'Lady Thorpe to you,' said Janet but she was smiling at his impertinence.

'I beg your pardon. I cannot believe you are married. No husband should go off and leave so pretty a wife alone in the wilderness.'

'But then I'm not alone. I have Richard to protect me from the wicked wiles of young men like you and Marietta knows how stern he can be, don't you, Marietta?'

'Not so stern this morning. She caught me naked and defenceless swimming in the loch,' said Richard lightly.

'Did she indeed?' Angus looked from me to Richard and grinned. 'Coll might have something to say about that.'

By this time we were in the house and a prim disapproving Rose brought the coffee. I think if she had her way she would have whisked her mistress out of this barbarous country and back to civilization in Sussex. I caught Janet's eye and giggled. I'd been living so intensely the last week, it was good to be lighthearted and laugh once again.

We drank the coffee and Richard got up to fetch glasses and a fat black bottle. 'Will you take a glass of Madeira with us? I am afraid I can't swallow your Highland whisky at eleven o'clock in the morning.'

'That's your weak English stomach. A dram sets a man up for the day. Now Madeira always reminds me of funerals,' said Angus irrepressibly. He accepted a glass and brought one to me. 'Tell me, Marietta, what will you do when the old man goes at last? Sell up Glenlochy and go back to Paris?'

'Why on earth should I want to sell?'

'Why not? I'd sell Armadale if I wasn't a younger son. You'd not lack for a buyer these days. Why, even Richard here might take it off your hands, or come to that, you could lease it to him, then he could send all the crofters packing, bring in flocks of sheep and make a fortune. It's happening already up in Ross and over in Skye.'

I looked from him to Richard. The latter's face was inscrutable. Had they been discussing such an outrageous idea? Angus was such a tease. I was never sure whether he was serious or joking.

'I would never do that, never,' I said at last. 'The valley belongs to the people. Their families have lived here for hundreds of years. It would break their hearts to be turned off.'

'Needs must when the devil drives,' he went on lightly. 'I remember Coll was speaking of it not so long ago, only of course he could never persuade Sir Alasdair to agree. But after he is gone . . .'

'Coll said that? But he does not feel like that at all. He loves Glenlochy as much as I do. You must be mistaken.'

'Probably,' Angus shrugged his shoulders. 'You know me, in one ear and out the other. Perhaps it was Fiona. She hates the valley, poor girl, longs for Edinburgh, balls and bright lights, but there she is, stuck in the glen with her tiresome old father and no chance of escape.'

It was Fiona of course, not Coll. Angus had got it muddled as usual. I said suddenly, angrily, 'Fiona is not my grandfather's heir and neither is Coll.'

Angus gave me a queer look and it was Richard who changed the subject. He put down his glass and went to a chest in a corner of the room.

'I've something to show you, Marietta. It turned up a couple of days ago in one of the stone barns at the back of the house. I thought they might make good stables if they were repaired so I had them cleaned out. We found this.'

He was holding out a Highland claymore, the sword blade notched and blackened. 'It has the Gilmour badge engraved on it, do you see? A crowned cat, isn't that right?'

'Yes, it is.' I took the sword with an odd reluctance that I couldn't explain.

'God knows how long it had been there but the queer thing is that we found it hidden in a great heap of charred wood and ashes and, buried beneath it, the mummified bodies of several animals we took to be cats.'

'Oh no,' exclaimed Janet, 'how absolutely horrible! You never told me that. The poor creatures must have been burned alive.'

'Not necessarily, my dear, they could have been accidentally trapped, but it was rather gruesome, I must admit. The strange thing was that old Lachlan went the colour of putty and refused point blank to finish the job. I had to do it myself.'

'And ended up looking like a chimney sweep,' said Janet laughing.

'Dashed peculiar it was. What do you think, Angus?'

'God knows,' he said with a certain reluctance. 'You should ask Mr McPhail. He is an expert on old Highland customs. Some of them, I'm afraid, are pretty nasty and some simply silly. Over in Armadale we have an old lady who swears she can foretell the future by reading the blade bone of a sheep.'

'Really? How?' asked Janet curiously.

They went on talking but I didn't listen. I was hearing Coll tell again the story of the *Taghairm* with that extraordinary living realism. Was it merely the legend of Donald Ruadh or was it his own experience? Had he called up the devil to find out whether he would be Chieftain in place of the girl from over the sea whose coming he had tried to prevent? The idea was so vile, so unbelievable that I couldn't bear to think of it. The sword fell out of my hands with a clatter and they turned to look at me.

"Is anything wrong?' asked Janet.

'No, of course not, but I think I should be going. I don't like to leave my grandfather for too long.'

'Yes, I understand, but are you sure you're all right?' She had come solicitously to my side but all I wanted was to go now before they began to question.

Angus had sprung to his feet. 'I will ride back with you.'

I would rather have been alone but could find no excuse to escape his company. I was reluctant to take the sword but when Janet wrapped it up and gave it to me, there was no reason why I should not accept it.

Richard came out into the courtyard when the ponies were brought round. He gave me his hand to help me into the saddle. 'Don't let what Angus said about Coll worry you,' he said quietly, 'there may be nothing in it.'

'I know there isn't,' I said quickly. 'It is all nonsense.'

Angus chatted of this and that as we made our way back to the castle and I answered at random. Commonsense kept telling me I was being foolish. An old sword had been found amongst a pile of rubbish. Was that surprising up here in the Highlands where men had hunted wild animals and fought one another for centuries? And yet I could not rid myself of a creeping doubt, a dark tide of something uncanny, something evil, that seemed to be coming closer and closer despite my steady refusal to accept it.

The fitful sun had vanished by the time we reached the sands. Heavy dark clouds surged in from the sea. I quickened my pace. When we climbed up on to the causeway I sensed that something was wrong. The big oaken door was open but no one was about in the great hall. I slid out of the saddle, threw the reins to Angus and went in and up the stairs to my grandfather's room.

They were all there, Coll, Fiona, Mrs Drummond, Kathryn, even Neil, Mr McPhail on his knees by the bed and my grandfather lying very still, the pillows removed, the windows thrust wide open to allow the departing spirit to wing its way to freedom.

They all turned to look at me as I stood in the doorway. Then Kathryn came quickly towards me putting an arm around my shoulders.

'We didn't know where you had gone. It happened very quickly.'

We had known it could come at any moment and yet it was still unexpected. I felt grief rise up in me, a bitter regret that I had not stayed with him, a sense of guilt that while I laughed and jested with Richard on the banks of the loch, he had died alone.

Kathryn was saying, 'The doctor has been sent for though it is quite useless. I shall stay with him until he comes.'

'No, I shall stay,' said Mrs Drummond. 'It is my right.'

Kathryn looked at her and for the first time I saw the naked dislike on her face. 'You may once have shared my father's bed and God knows how bitterly he regretted it, but I am still his daughter.'

'The daughter he disinherited,' said Mrs Drummond, her voice venomous and deadly, 'the daughter he drove from his house like the whore she is . . .'

'In that case there are two of us, aren't there?'

'And now you've come creeping back for what you can get . . .'

Kathryn threw up her head proudly, 'I asked nothing from him while he was alive and I ask nothing now.'

Hatred crackled between the two women and it jarred on me unbearably. 'Be quiet,' I said. 'He's dead. Isn't that enough?'

'And who are you to say what should be done?' said Mrs Drummond, her voice rising shrilly. 'There are others here with a greater claim than yours . . .'

'Shame on you, woman!' roared Mr McPhail rising to his feet. 'Shame on you both! It is not seemly to wrangle in the presence of death.'

'You old fool, what do you know about anything?' sneered Mrs Drummond.

'For God's sake, hold your tongue. This is not the time or place,' exclaimed Coll and suddenly everyone was screaming at one another. It was as if my grandfather's death had released pent-up feelings, ancient malice, old spite that had smouldered beneath the surface. They were snarling at one another like wild animals. I wanted to silence them but the words stuck in my throat.

Then a cold sharp voice cut across their wrangling. 'If you want to tear one another to shreds, then have the decency to do it elsewhere.'

Duncan Cameron had come into the room. The little

plump lawyer had suddenly acquired a dignity and authority that I had never suspected.

'By what right . . .?' exclaimed Coll.

'By every right,' he said quietly. 'I am the trustee and executor of Sir Alasdair's will.'

'What will is this?' interrupted Coll.

'You shall hear when the time comes but until after the funeral, I am in charge here. I suggest, Colin Grant, that you carry on with what needs to be done.'

They were all staring at him as if they wondered what lay behind the shrewd brown eyes and I remembered what my grandfather had said and how he had asked me to fetch the lawyer to him.

There was silence for a moment, then Mr McPhail took the lead. 'He is right. Come, Fiona, Neil . . . I will be at hand if you want me, Miss Marietta,' and he touched Mrs Drummond on the arm. She went with him reluctantly, only Coll lingered and would have spoken with me but I shook my head. I longed desperately to find comfort in him but just then my feelings were too mixed so he only pressed my hand and went after the others.

It was not until then that I saw Murdo crouched by the head of the bed, tears running unheeded down his wrinkled cheeks, the two dogs huddled against him. They seemed the only ones who mourned for him with no thought of gain for themselves.

'Leave them there,' whispered Kathryn, 'it is kinder. They will get over it in their own way.'

The next few days passed in a kind of dream. The doctor came and went. Certain formalities had to be completed. Papers were signed. Messages had to be sent. The guests who had come to the party were invited to the funeral. Coll dealt with everything with the help of George Fergusson. He seemed to be continually at the castle, soft-spoken and ingratiating whenever I met him so that if possible I disliked him more than ever. I could not bring myself to question Kathryn about the accusations she and Ailsa Drummond had hurled at one another. I still found it hard to believe that this strange woman with her ruined beauty had been my grandfather's mistress and yet it explained so much. Her familiarity, the demands she made on him, even his harshness.

The old sword Richard had given me still lay in my room. I could not bring myself to talk to Coll about it yet found myself keeping away from him during these days, until one morning he deliberately sought me out.

'What is it, darling? Why are you so cold to me?'

We were in the passage outside my room and I longed to relax against him, to let his kisses carry me away from the wretchedness of grief and regret and yet I could not.

I said, 'Coll, I want to show you something.'

'What is it?'

He stood in the doorway while I went to my chest and took the sword out of its wrapping. I put it into his hands.

He stared down at it for a long moment before he said, 'It looks like one of the ancient weapons from the great hall. What on earth are you doing with it?'

'Richard found it in one of the barns at the Tige Dubh.'

'Richard?' he said quickly, angrily. 'Is that where you were on the morning your grandfather died? I might have known.'

'Is there any reason why I should not visit him and his sister?'

'Yes, every reason. I don't like him and neither should you. I won't have you running to meet him whenever you feel like it.'

The gust of his anger took me by surprise and touched me to the quick. 'In matters like these I please myself. You must leave me free, Coll, to do as I think best. You are not my master yet.'

'I'll not have it, do you hear? That damned arrogant Englishman with his wealth parading himself in the valley, asking questions, stirring up trouble.'

'Why do you say that? What trouble?'

'There was none until he created it with his meddling.'

'I don't understand what you mean.'

Then he quietened. 'I'm sorry, dearest. I shouldn't have lost my temper. I'm jealous, I suppose.'

It was odd that he should use that word and Richard too. 'You have no need to be.'

'I know. Oh, to hell with him! Why are we quarrelling

like this all over nothing? What did he tell you about the sword?'

It suddenly didn't seem so important after all. 'Only that he found it in a heap of rubbish and beneath it were the burned bodies of some poor cats.'

'Cats!' Then he laughed. 'Oh my God! And you thought it was the *Taghairm*.'

'Coll, you didn't . . . you couldn't . . .'

He went on laughing. 'Of course not. We're living in the year 1770 not in the middle ages. What on earth put such an idea into your little head?'

'I'm sorry. It was silly of me, but I couldn't help remembering.' In my relief I let him take me into his arms and yet for some reason his kisses did not give me the same delight as they had done before and I struggled to free myself.

He said, 'What has happened to you? Don't you love me any more?'

'It's not that. It's just that . . . with grandfather lying dead, it does not seem decent.'

He smiled. 'So many foolish scruples. I shall have to teach you differently when we are married.'

'Are we going to be married?'

'I thought it was understood.'

'I wish we had been able to speak of it to grandfather.'

He moved impatiently. 'We're all a little on edge but this will be over soon. Now I'm going to take the sword back to where it belongs. It's all forgotten, isn't it?'

'All forgotten.'

'Good.'

He touched my cheek tenderly and went away from me, but it was not completely forgotten.

I had a terrifying dream that night. I was walking along a track in some dark place and Coll was ahead of me. I could see him quite clearly but I could not reach him and I was in deadly danger. I called but he did not turn and behind me voices laughed and whispered, like an echo insistent, menacing but with no substance, and all around me was the sweet spicy smell of the forest.

I tried to run and my legs were paralysed as they are in nightmares. I was wading through something thick and heavy and suddenly before me gaped a black pit. I tried to stop myself and couldn't. I stepped into it and went down a long shaft into the dizzying darkness. I was screaming and yet there was no sound. Then I woke up, gripping the sheet, sweating and trembling and that sickly scent still thick in my nostrils.

I lay shaking until gradually the moonlight picked out the pale frame of the window, my clothes chest, the mirror, and a sweet relief flooded through me.

Chapter Eleven

They buried my grandfather at sunset. The leading man of the clan came to speak to me that morning. He was tall and brown-faced with greying hair. He stood just inside the door clutching his hat in both hands.

'I am Hamish Kintyre, Mistress Gilmour,' he said in his slow stilted English.

'Kintyre?' I repeated. 'Then is Mary Kintyre your daughter-in-law?'

'Aye, Mary is wed to my Keith, but I am not wishing to speak of that now. It is about the Chief. Maybe you do not yet know our ways, young mistress, but we have no need of any carriage to take him up the valley. It is by the hands of his people and shoulder high that Mac'Ghille Mhoire should be carried to his resting place.'

There was a touching sincerity in his manner. I said, 'You must do as you think right.'

Four of the men carried the coffin, others standing by to take their place when they tired as they had done in centuries past. He was their Chieftain, the father of his people, and even though sometimes he had dealt harshly with them, they loved and honoured him.

The long procession wound up the glen, the torchlight falling on eagle feather and faded tartan. I had no mourning and I've always hated black so I wore a white dress under my father's plaid, the Sìthen Stone on my shoulder and walked hand in hand with Aunt Kat. Heavy black clouds rolled across the sky when we reached the slopes of the mountain and lightning flashed as Mr McPhail read the prayers. There was thunder when Coll helped me to lift the black stone and it was placed on the great cairn while the piper played a lament so sad and so sweet that the tears choked in my throat.

The flaring torches lit Richard's face for an instant. He was standing apart from the others, near to the grave of his brother, and I was glad he had come. I would have gone to him but Coll held me back.

He said fiercely, 'He should have had the decency to keep away.'

'He means well, Coll. Now grandfather is dead, we should forget the past.'

'No, never.'

'Why? Are you afraid to meet him?'

'Damn him! Why do you say that?'

I could not understand his anger. I broke away from him and crossed to Richard.

'It was kind of you to come.'

'Jan wanted me to tell you how sorry we are. If there is anything we can do . . .'

'Thank you.'

'I mean it, Marietta.' He had taken my hand in both of his and then Coll was beside us.

'Marietta, come. They are waiting for you.'

He took my arm, swinging me roughly away and I saw the astonishment on Richard's face.

'Did you need to behave so boorishly?' I exclaimed.

'Your grandfather scarcely buried and yet you can smile at the Englishman!'

I felt the reproach and rebelled against it. Coll had stopped for a moment to look down at me.

'I love you, Marietta, haven't you realized that yet? Even to see you glance at another man makes my blood boil.'

Then the rain came down so blindingly, it was a race to get back to Glenlochy before the whole company was soaked to the skin. Food and drink had been set out in the great hall and in the kitchens and outhouses for all those who wanted it. I should not have known what to do if it had not been for Kathryn. She moved from one to the other, taking me with her. Many of them were men she had known from childhood. They did not say what they thought but I read it in their eyes. The great days must be gone indeed when five hundred years of inheritance come to a puny girl. Then Kat put her arm around me and drew me away.

'We can leave them now. They won't want us. Most of them will make a night of it. You mustn't mind, Marietta. It is the custom. There will be sore heads in the morning I have no doubt. After tomorrow when we know how we stand, we must talk, my dear. It is time we got to know one another.'

'I would like that.'

I went to bed early weary with the long day but there were stirrings in the castle all night and I slept restlessly. Jeannie brought my breakfast on a tray and sat on my bed while I ate.

'Did you hear them last night, Miss Marietta? Drinking and singing they were down there till all hours. You'd have thought it was St Bartholomew's Fair instead of that poor old gentleman being laid to rest. And Mr Coll! I stuck my head in once to see what was going on and there he was on the table . . . dancing!'

'Dancing?' I repeated amused at her scandalized tone.

'Aye, drunk he was and dancing one of their outlandish jigs, and them all lifting their glasses to him. Disgraceful, I call it.'

'It's just their way. It doesn't mean anything,' I said and wondered how many of them in the great hall and up the valleys were already toasting him as the heir in their secret hearts. I felt tired and out of sorts, thinking of what the morning would bring and dreading it a little. Duncan Cameron had asked everyone to be in the drawing-room at eleven o'clock and I was not sure what was to come out of it or even what I wanted to hear.

I went down as soon as I was dressed and found myself alone. The room seemed strange without my grandfather. The portrait was there with its brooding look, the dogs on the hearth, the silver drinking cup beside the whisky, the table still set out for chess; only the tall chair was empty. Then Mr Cameron came bustling in, greeting me courteously, and then the others one by one. Murdo stood just inside the door, Hamish Kintyre beside him with the men from the clan crowding behind. Mrs Drummond came last. She was very pale and gaunt in her severe black dress, looking at no one and taking her place at the back of the room. Coll stood on the hearth rug, tall, handsome, completely master of himself. If he had been drunk last night as Jeannie said, he showed no sign of it.

Mr Cameron unfolded the crackling parchment and began to read. At first I scarcely listened. The formal language rolled above my head, certain small bequests to friends, books from his library to Mr McPhail, a legacy for Murdo, nothing at all about Kat, then suddenly it was there, the lands, the castle, the house in Edinburgh—'all my property whatsoever and wheresoever I leave and bequeath absolutely to my granddaughter, Marietta Gilmour, with the proviso that she should keep in her employment the young man known as Colin Grant who has served me well . . .'

And so it went on. I glanced at Coll but his face betrayed no bitterness, no anger, only a great sadness. I wanted to go and put my hand in his. I wanted to say, 'My grandfather has been cruelly unfair but he trusted me to act for him and I can make it up to you. What is mine shall be yours.'

The interruption came from Mrs Drummond with a violence that startled me. She had risen to her feet.

'It's a lie,' she said in a queer strangled voice. 'It must be a lie. He never made that will, he never signed it.' She came across the room and faced Mr Cameron across the table. 'He was sick . . . he was not in his right mind . . .'

'I assure you, my good woman,' said the lawyer calmly, 'Sir Alasdair was in complete possession of his faculties. He sent for me secretly, very late it was on the night before he died. It was signed and witnessed there and then.'

'I won't believe it, never, never.'

'Ask Angus Macdonald. He will tell you himself. He was one of those who witnessed the Chief's signature. What further proof do you require?'

'You've concocted it between you, you and that chit of a girl. He promised me,' her voice had risen to a shrill scream and I saw Coll start forward. 'He promised me over and over again that he would do it and he did.' She grabbed Coll by the arm pulling him forward. 'Here is his true heir, my son . . . a Gilmour though the name was denied to him . . . he promised me I tell you . . .'

But now Coll had taken her in his arms, quietening

her. 'Hush, Mother, it is no use. The Chief had his own way of doing things. You ought to know that by now.'

'Damn him!' she sobbed, 'damn him for a liar and a cheat!' She collapsed against him weeping.

I stared at them. It was so obvious I could not imagine why I had not known it before. She was Coll's mother and all these years she must have played this game of house-keeper to please a proud old man who had only half believed her story and had given with one hand and taken with the other.

She was quieter now and Coll put her gently into the chair by the hearth.

'May I continue?' said Mr Cameron dryly.

'Please go on.'

'There is not much more.' He read the last details in his precise voice and then folded the document carefully. 'I am afraid I must now return to Edinburgh,' he said turning to me. 'My business will not permit me to stay longer, but I will see that all legal matters are carried out and you can call on my services at any time.'

'Thank you. I am grateful for all you have done, Mr Cameron.'

It was then that I acted foolishly, recklessly, carried away on the spur of the moment, moved by love and pity for the young man who had lost everything because of me, who stood there proud still but bitterly humiliated in front of everyone by the woman who was his mother. I got to my feet looking around at them all.

'I know I am the stranger among you and that you may well have resented my coming. I had hoped so much that grandfather and I would have had a longer time to know one another, time in which I would have grown closer to everyone at Glenlochy. But there is something I would like to tell you,' I looked at Coll trembling a lit-tle, 'something we both wish to tell you.'

But he did not move. 'No, Marietta,' he said steadily. 'I know what you are going to say but I cannot accept it, not now.'

Any doubt that I may have had of him crumbled away in that instant. I said impetuously, 'But you must. It is what grandfather wanted.'

'Marietta, think carefully. Do you really wish for this? Are you sure?'

'Quite sure.'

'Very well.' He raised his head proudly. 'I fell in love with Marietta the first moment she came through that door. But who was I to speak of my love? It was only when I knew she felt the same that I dared to tell it to her. She has promised to become my wife.'

I don't know what I had expected but certainly not the utter silence that greeted our announcement. Mr McPhail stared at the floor, the men in the doorway shuffled their feet, no one moved or spoke till Duncan Cameron said in his dry way, 'In that case I must offer you both my congratulations. Doubtless there will now be other arrangements you will wish me to make. I can only repeat I shall be at your service when you need me.'

He bowed to me and the company, then picked up his papers and went briskly from the room. The men gathered in the doorway followed after him. George Fergusson leaned against the doorpost, an odd little smile on his face. I wondered what he was thinking.

Coll came to me then. 'You've taken them by surprise, including me. I don't know what to say.'

'There is no need to say anything. I know that grandfather would be pleased.'

'You have made me the happiest man on earth.' He kissed my hand tenderly.

Mr McPhail said, 'Come, Fiona, Neil . . .'

But Fiona did not move immediately, those queer eyes of hers were fixed not on me but on Coll. 'I congratulate you. You've got what you wanted. I hope it contents you,' and she went swiftly from the room taking her father and brother with her.

Mrs Drummond was staring at me, her ravaged face still blotched with tears. Then she got up and walked straight past me out of the room.

Coll said quickly, 'You mustn't mind. She is not herself. She was really fond of the Chief, you know.'

'Why didn't you tell me she was your mother?'

'He did not wish it and neither did she. It was part of the bargain,' he said bitterly. 'My education and upbringing for her silence . . . and the sharing of his bed.'

'Poor Coll.'

'Not poor any longer. Forgive me, darling, but I ought to go to her.'

'Of course, but come back soon.'

I watched him go and thought I was left alone. I had forgotten Kathryn hidden in the window embrasure. Now she came out.

'You fool, Marietta,' she said slowly, 'you fool! Do you realize what you've done?'

'Perfectly. I have righted a wrong. If it had not been for me, Coll would have inherited everything.'

'Never. Father did that only because he was angry with me. He would have changed his mind whether you had come or not.'

'Are you angry because he gave you nothing?'

She looked at me with contempt. 'How little you know me.'

'I'm sorry. I shouldn't have said that.'

'Do you love him?'

'Yes, yes,' I said fervently. 'It is true what he said. I knew it from the moment I came here. He means everything to me. He wants to do great things here and so do I.'

'You really believe that?'

'Yes.'

'So much the worse for you.'

'What do you mean?'

'Never mind. Perhaps I am wrong. I hope for your sake that I am. I do wish you well, Marietta, believe me I do with all my heart.'

I went to her then. 'Why don't you come here? Live at the castle?'

'Coll would not like that.'

'He will if I ask him.'

She gave me an odd look. 'No, I prefer my independence. I shall stay in my little croft. He will not drive me out of that. If ever you need help, you know where to come.'

'Why should I need help?' I said proudly.

'Everyone does at some time or another.'

Then she kissed my cheek and went out leaving me alone at last except for the dogs. I went and sat in grandfather's chair. A queen come from over the sea to take possession of her kingdom, that was what Richard had said, and now I would share it with the man I had chosen for myself. Wolf laid his head on my knee and the blue eyes of Donald Ruadh looked down at me with quizzical amusement. He had got what he wanted and so had Coll and so had I. At least I thought I had.

Chapter Twelve

ᕦ⊙ᕤ

It seems strange to say it but during the first weeks after grandfather's death though I mourned for him, yet I was radiantly happy. It was not just that I who had possessed nothing was suddenly mistress of a vast estate. I did not think of it in those terms. I was conscious of the responsibility and very eager to make a success of it. It was a heady experience but I feared to make mistakes. I was willing to let Coll be my teacher, constantly beside me to guide and explain and I left everything in his hands. I did suggest once that his mothar should now take her proper place in the household but he shook his head.

'She won't do it. She prefers to remain as she is.'

So I said nothing more and was secretly glad of it. She was a strange woman and try as I would, I could not like her. I did my best to be civil and left it at that.

My days were full. I explored every inch of the castle with Jeannie filled with a zeal for improvement. I examined old embroidery designs and embarked ambitiously on a set of chair covers to replace the shabby tapestries. I began to make plans for the gardens. I visited some of the crofters and was shocked by the pitiful poverty in which some of them lived, sharing their smoke-darkened room with their animals. I had never known anything like this before and I was touched by their welcome. They would shyly offer me a place by the fire. They would fetch their babies and bring me milk and cakes out of their scanty store.

The one thing I did not do was to visit Kathryn or invite her to visit the castle. I had taken her place in the house she had known all her life. It was an awkward situation particularly when I knew she did not like Coll. I was relieved when I met Mary Kintyre one day and she told me that Kathryn had gone away for a few weeks so that the decision could be postponed.

When did the slow and painful process of disillusionment begin? It is difficult to say exactly because at first I would not heed it but I think it was on a morning in June when I was carrying some blankets to an old couple who had nothing but a bed of brushwood covered with rags and I met Fiona.

'Lady Bountiful!' she remarked with a touch of scorn. 'I would not have thought that was your style at all or Coll's.'

'Why not? He agrees with me that we should do what we can for our people and I understand their needs better than he does.'

'Really! Is that all you and he talk about during the long summer evenings?'

She leaned against the rail of the little bridge looking flamingly beautiful. I knew exactly what she implied. Though Mrs Drummond was there in the castle with us, though Jeannie sometimes sat with us helping me with my tapestry frame, Coll and I were often alone together. Convention would have been outraged but I had never cared much about that and here, in this remote place, it did not seem important.

'There's a great deal to discuss,' I said defensively. 'We are to be married in August.'

'I'm surprised it is not sooner. I always thought Coll a most impatient man. How he must have changed!'

'Perhaps you don't know him as well as you think you do,' I retorted.

Her eyes flashed at me. 'You are very sure of yourself.'

'Yes, I am. You see I love him.'

'And does he love you?'

'Why do you say that?'

'What an innocent you are!' and disconcertingly she began to laugh.

I said quickly, angrily, 'Don't do that!'

'Why shouldn't I laugh if it amuses me? I wish you luck, Marietta. I would not take Glenlochy as a gift.'

I watched her walk away from me and thought she is jealous. Whatever she says, she would be glad to be in my place. But all the same I knew she was right about one thing. In some ways Coll had changed even in this short time and sometimes I had found it disturbing. He was more masterful, more sure of himself as if for the first time he felt independent, freed from all restraints.

I didn't usually interrupt Coll at his work, but that morning when I returned to the castle I went into the estate room before going upstairs. Hamish Kintyre was there and he was vigorously protesting about something, banging his fist on the desk, his stern dark face aflame with anger. They spoke in Gaelic so that I understood little and he broke off when I came in. Coll dismissed him with a wave of his hand. He stood his ground for a moment, then he nodded curtly to me and strode out of the room.

'What was all that about?' I asked in some surprise.

'Nothing that need worry you,' said Coll shortly.

'He was saying something about rent, I understood that much,' I persisted. 'Is it that he cannot pay?'

'It is not he alone, it is all of them. He brought a petition,' he said impatiently. 'Now the Chief is dead, they are full of complaints. What the hell do they want from me?'

'How do you mean?'

He glanced at me, drumming his fingers on the table. 'The fact is that I have had to raise their rents if we are to live and he says they starve already.'

'I think perhaps they do. It has horrified me to see how some of them live. Coll, don't you think you should have spoken to me first before making any changes?'

'My dear girl, do I run this place for you or don't I?'

'Of course you do, but it is my responsibility and I owe it to grandfather to do all I can for our people. He spoke to me about it more than once. I think I should have been consulted.'

'Do you have to remind me that I'm a pauper marrying an heiress?' he said savagely.

'That's unfair, Coll. I've never even hinted at such a thing. It's only that I think I have a right to know.'

He got up moving restlessly around the table. 'I'll have to remember that in future, won't I? Please, Miss Gilmour, may I give orders for this to be done, or that, or something else? Or will it change when I am your husband? Will you graciously permit me to be master then?'

The bitterness in his voice hurt me. 'You know perfect-ly well that is not what I meant.'

He came behind me then, swiftly repentant, sliding his arms round my waist and kissing the nape of my neck. 'I'm sorry, really I am. I wish we could be married to-morrow.'

'It's not long, only two months.'

He turned me round to face him. 'Two months are a lifetime when you are in love. Let's go up to the kirk tomorrow. Mr McPhail will oblige us, I am sure.'

I smiled a little thinking him like an impatient boy. 'It's too soon. We don't want people saying we had to marry.'

'What the devil does it matter to us what they say?' He began to kiss me with a passion that both stirred and frightened me. His hand tugged at the lace of my dress, he kissed my neck and then my breast. I felt my head swimming and struggled to free myself.

'No, Coll, please. Please no.'

'Why should we wait?' he murmured huskily. 'I want you, Marietta, I want you now, this minute, more and more every day.'

I moved away from him. I felt as if I were being rushed into something for which I was not yet ready. I said, 'It wouldn't be right . . .'

'Right! Don't be such a little prude. Who is to say what is right or wrong for people like us!'

I might have yielded, I don't know. When he held me in his arms, it was as if I was under enchantment, I seemed to forget everything else. It was the dogs that in-terrupted us. They came bounding into the room, bark-ing hysterically and chasing one of the household cats, followed by Neil laughing at their antics.

'What the hell do you think you're doing? Can't you keep control over those damned brutes?' exploded Coll.

Neil looked from him to me grinning. 'I'm sorry. I didn't know Marietta was here.'

I hastily turned my back rearranging my dress and try-ing hard to recover myself. It pulled me up short. It made me realize what an extraordinary position I was in and how inexperienced I was. I had a feeling of being trapped. Coll wanted to dominate me so completely and I hated to lose my independence. Much as I disliked my mother, for the first time in my life I would have been glad of her practical advice and her astringent company.

It was about a week later that I woke up to one of those marvellous mornings that are rare in the Highlands but, when they do come, have a light and glory like nowhere else on earth. Coll was busy. Jeannie was occupied somewhere in the kitchens and I could not bear to remain in the castle. I wanted to be out walking in the fragrant air. I made up my mind to go in search of seals.

'This is the season for them,' Murdo had said only the day before when I stood at the window hearing their strange barking cry and watching their round human-looking heads bobbing in the sea.

I walked along the hard white sand with the salt wind in my hair, waving to the seaweed gatherers and watching the birds swoop down and up again with their sharp keening cry. After about a mile I came to where the loch widens out into the sea. There, to my surprise, I saw Richard Wynter, his small boat hitched up against the bank while he patiently tried to disentangle the snarls in his fishing line. I had not seen him since the funeral and I thought he looked tanned and well as if the Highland air suited him.

'Good morning,' I said gaily. 'Why don't you let me do that? I'm good at unravelling knots.'

He looked up at me and smiled. 'Your fingers are smaller than mine, it is true.' He relinquished part of the line to me and I sat down beside him on the rock.

'What are you doing so far from the castle on this lovely morning?' he said.

'Hunting for seals and not finding any.'

He pointed to where we could see the green and grey of a small rocky island. 'That is the place for them. It's uninhabited so they like it, I'm told. I'm going to row across there in a few minutes.'

'It does look inviting. Why isn't Jan with you?'

'She hates boats. The sea is smooth as glass. Want to come? I can guarantee you won't be seasick.'

I hesitated. 'I'm not sure that I should.'

'Don't you trust me?'

'It's not that.' I didn't quite know what held me back. I had an odd feeling that if I went, I would be taking a step into something of which I was uncertain.

He put the unravelled line together and got to his feet. 'Are you afraid that Coll won't approve?'

And that decided me. 'No, of course not. I'll come.'

'Good.'

He helped me into the boat, put the line in and his fishing basket and began to pull out across the sunlit water with long powerful strokes of the oars.

The island was larger than it looked, part grey rock, part low wooded scrub and he was right about the seals. After we had beached the boat, we walked up the sands. Richard spread his plaid and we sat on it to watch. Presently they came, dozens of them, quite unafraid, gambolling and playing games in and out of the surf. There were babies too, with round dark eyes, their fur coats white and silky. One came so near I could have put out a hand and touched it.

'They're so human, aren't they? It's easy to believe the old legends.'

'You won't catch me out this time,' he said lazily. 'I know all about seals. They are "King's children under enchantment." They come out of the sea on midsummer nights shedding their fur coats and dancing in the moonlight. Isn't there a clan up north that claims to be descended from a seal maiden?'

I laughed. 'So they say. Coll tells me there are so many of them that they have seal hunts sometimes. I don't know how anyone can kill them. They're so trusting.'

'Some people would do a great deal for easy money and their skins are valuable.'

I turned to look at him. 'Could you shoot that baby there?'

He sat up with his hands round his knees. 'I have been a soldier, Marietta, and for a soldier, it is often kill or be killed. I have done my share of it but it has had the effect of making me dislike killing for its own sake. Oh I'm quite practical. I shoot a buck sometimes; Jan likes venison or a rabbit for the pot. I net salmon and there are trout in that basket, but I'm not a hunter.' He smiled ruefully. 'My father is a great rider to hounds. He keeps his own pack and he despises me for a sentimentalist.'

'I don't.'

'You'd better not let Coll hear you say that. All Highland gentlemen are hunters to a man.'

I did not want to discuss Coll with him and we sat there so long watching the antics of the seals that we grew hungry. Richard coaxed a fire from twigs and dry branches and grilled the trout from his fishing basket on a forked stick. One fell in the fire and we laughed over it.

'I'm afraid I'm not as expert as my soldiers were on campaign,' he said spearing another fish. We bent over it together, burning our fingers, but in the end we succeeded. The skin might be scorched and blackened but the fish inside was delicious eaten with a couple of bannocks pulled out of his pack.

'Jan puts them in. She's always afraid I shall starve to death if she is not with me,' he said laughing.

It was odd, I thought, watching the lean dark face as he dug a hole and buried the remnants of our meal, how easy I felt with the man I had disliked so much.

I said suddenly, 'I never had a brother.'

He went on patting down the sand. 'Is that how you think of me?'

'I'd like to. Do you mind?'

'I suppose I should say I'm honoured,' he said a little dryly.

'Richard, how old are you?'

He turned to look at me, dark brows raised. 'What an odd question. I am thirty-one if you really want to know.'

I flushed. 'It was impertinent of me to ask but I was thinking of something.'

'What were you thinking?'

'That you ought to be married.'

'That's what my father tells me,' he said as he wiped his fingers on his handkerchief. 'I was engaged once.'

'What happened?'

'She didn't like the idea of marrying a cripple.'

'But you're not.'

'I was up to a few months ago.'

'I'm sorry.'

'I'm not. I think perhaps I had a fortunate escape.'

'That sounds very cynical.'

'Perhaps. Experience hurts but you learn from it.' He was staring straight in front of him. 'The last time I saw her was in Paris. I went to the church to see her married.'

'Did she know you were there?'

'Oh yes. I think she was rather pleased. It must have given her a feeling of triumph—the rejected lover who couldn't keep away.' He spoke with an acute bitterness. 'I came straight from France to Scotland.'

'That's when I saw you first . . . on the ship.'

'And I you. A little red-haired girl fighting valiantly against seasickness.'

'I thought you looked very lonely.'

'I used to watch you battling with the wind and the rain, marching bravely round the deck when most of the passengers were prostrate in their cabins.'

'It smelled so horrible down there.'

He smiled and leaned back watching the waves as they creamed along the shore. Then he said quietly, 'I'm afraid my brother and I are not very lucky people.'

I sat up. 'Are you still troubled about what happened to him? George Fergusson said you had been making enquiries in the valley.'

'Yes, I have, but with very little result. You think I have an obsession about it, don't you, so does Jan. But I do have a reason. I'd like to tell you something, Marietta, if you can bear to listen.' He paused a moment tracing a pattern on the sand with one long finger before he went on.

'My brother wrote me a letter which I didn't receive until after his death. In it he told me that he had fallen in love. "She's the most marvellous person in the world," he wrote. "There are problems but I'm sure I'll win her in the end." Does that sound like a man who is about to take his own life?'

'Who was she?'

'He didn't say. Perhaps he thought it best. So many letters got into the wrong hands, but there is not much choice in the valley, is there?'

'Perhaps it was someone at Fort William.'

'No, she lived here. I'm certain of it.' He turned to look at me. 'I've thought about it a lot these past weeks and I've asked questions, but so many of them don't understand English or pretend they don't if it suits them. There is your Aunt Kathryn.'

'Kat! But she would have been years older!'

'What's that got to do with falling in love?'

'Have you asked her?'

'Not yet. It's not easy when you don't know what happened.' I thought of what my grandfather had said. 'He robbed me of my honour' and of the insult Mrs Drummond had hurled at Kat, but I didn't like to speak of it. If Graham and Kat had been lovers, then Richard must find it out for himself.

'What are you going to do?'

'I've not decided. She is living not far from the Tige Dubh but I have only seen her once on the night your grandfather was taken ill. I can scarcely walk in and say, "Was it you who drove my brother to his death?" '

'Oh, no, I'm sure that's not true. It was an accident, it must have been. He could have been caught by the tide, they are dangerous and he was a stranger. He could have gone out in a boat like you and been caught in a squall.'

'Perhaps,' but Richard still looked unconvinced. Then he got to his feet with an exclamation. 'We're forgetting the time. It's late. We should be getting back.'

But we had reckoned without the weather. In our sheltered spot among the rocks we had not noticed the wind that chopped up the channel between the island and the mainland. Richard looked across the water doubtfully.

'I daren't risk it with the tide race against us. The pull could drag us out to sea. If we wait until it turns, it will be easier. The flow will carry us in.'

The sun had vanished and it began to blow cold. He picked up the plaid and wrapped it around my shoulders.

'We can shelter from the wind in one of the clefts between the rocks.'

It was one of those sudden squalls that break over the mountains on the West Coast. We flattened ourselves inside the narrow opening and despite the plaid I shivered in my thin dress.

'What a fool I am not to have seen this coming and taken you back before. I only hope you won't take cold.'

Richard put an arm round me holding me against him. The day had darkened so much I could scarcely see his face. After a little he said, 'Jan tells me you are to be married.'

'In August.'

'So soon.'

'There's no reason to wait. I have written to my mother.'

'Will she be coming to stay with you?'

'I can't see her making the journey from Paris just for my sake. She has never cared for me very much.'

'I see. Have you no other friends?'

'Not here.'

'I hope you don't still regard me as the enemy?'

'No, of course not.' And it was true. When I was with him, it was impossible to remember what my grandfather had said and how much I had once hated the English.

'I'm glad.'

I saw the gleam in his eyes as he turned his head. Then he kissed me gently but firmly. For an instant I found an intense pleasure in the touch of his lips and then I drew back shocked at myself. I'm like my mother after all, I thought, engaged to one man and enjoying the kisses of another. His arm tightened around me. I knew I was trembling.

I said, 'Richard, don't please.'

He released me at once. 'I'm sorry. Have I offended you? You have adopted me as a brother after all.'

The lightness of his tone drove away my embarrassment. We spoke of other things and it must have been about half an hour later that Richard put out his head.

'I think we can try our luck. There's a break in the sky and the rain has almost stopped.'

Everything dripped with water but the worst of the wind had gone as suddenly as it had arisen. Richard pushed out the boat and despite the strong pull of the sea, the turning tide carried us towards the mainland. But it took much longer than when we had come and it was late evening by the time Richard rowed along the shore and tied up at the little stone jetty belonging to the castle. He helped me out and walked with me up to the causeway. I slipped the plaid from my shoulders.

'Thank you for a lovely day,' I said and moved by an impulse of affection stood on tiptoe to kiss his cheek. 'Give my love to Jan.'

'I will.'

He waited while I climbed up on the causeway. Halfway across it, the door was flung open and Coll stood on the threshold.

'So there you are,' he said with a note of anger in his voice. 'Where on earth have you been? I have been half out of my mind all day wondering what had happened to you.'

'I'm sorry, Coll. I hadn't intended to be out so long but I met Richard. We've been watching the seals on the island and forgot the time. Then the storm delayed us.'

'Richard?' he repeated fiercely. 'Richard, did you say? I might have known.' He pushed me roughly aside and strode down the causeway. 'Well, Colonel Wynter, what the hell have you to say for yourself?'

Richard had begun to walk away. Now he stopped and came slowly back. 'I see no need to explain myself to you.'

'Oh yes, you will.' Coll leaped down. They were facing one another, two angry young men, and I was suddenly afraid.

I said, 'Coll . . . please . . .'

'Be quiet, Marietta, this is my affair.' He took a step nearer Richard. 'How dare you come sneaking around here where you are not welcome, persuading my future wife to go with you to God knows where. Why? For what reason?'

'Hadn't you better ask her that?' said Richard coldly. 'It was a harmless picnic, nothing more.'

'A picnic? Alone, just the two of you? Are you asking me to believe that? Were you planning to seduce her?'

'You'll take that back.'

'I'll take nothing back.' Suddenly Coll seemed to lose all self-control. 'You damned English, you think you can carry everything before you! You steal our lands, our honour, our women and we can do nothing, but this time it is different.' Deliberately he raised his hand and struck Richard across the face.

With the mark plain to see on his cheek, Richard said thickly, 'I could kill you for that, but I won't. Not for your sake but hers. You can think yourself lucky.' He turned and would have walked away but Coll went after him, seizing him by the shoulder and swinging him round.

'Coward!' he sneered. 'Coward like your brother, full of fine words and hiding behind a woman's skirt!'

For an instant Richard stood poised, then his fist shot out and Coll reeled backwards. He hit his head as he fell and was momentarily stunned. I ran to him then, falling on my knees beside him.

Richard was shaking with anger. 'He shouldn't have said what he did about my brother . . .'

'Go, Richard, please go.'

Coll was struggling to his feet, blood trickling from his mouth. 'You'll pay for this, by God you will!'

Richard looked at him for a moment. 'When and how you like,' he said curtly and walked quickly away towards the boat.

Coll was staring after him and something in his expression frightened me. I said, 'What are you going to do?'

'Teach him a lesson, make him eat humble pie,' he muttered through clenched teeth. Then he turned to me, cupping my face in his two hands. 'Listen, Marietta, I've told you before, you're mine, you belong to me, do you hear? I'll not share you with anyone.'

'But, Coll, there is no question of such a thing. Richard cares nothing for me.'

'Oh yes he does. Do you think I'm blind? Do you think I don't see how he looks at you?' He dabbed at his bleeding mouth with his handkerchief. 'Do you know what Donald Ruadh did when another man dared to lay a finger on the woman he wanted? He challenged him to a duel. They fought in the tower there with the shaft open and the sea roaring beneath them. One false step from either of them and it was death on the rocks below.'

'Oh how savage!'

'Savage perhaps but very satisfying.' Then he smiled grimly. 'Don't be afraid. I'm not going to do anything like that. There are other ways of getting even with the Honourable Richard Wynter.'

'How?'

'Never you mind.'

'You'll not challenge him?'

There had been duels in Paris. Young men who killed one another in the Bois de Boulogne for a trifling point of honour that mattered nothing.

'A duel?' he said slowly. 'I would like that. He'd not beat me a second time, I promise you that.'

'Oh Coll, no please. It is so unnecessary, so foolish. Forget it. I promise I'll not see him again if that is what you want.'

'And go on resenting me because of it. No, there are other ways.' He took me by the arm. 'Come along, Marietta, supper is waiting and I'm hungry.'

We went into the castle together and while we ate he said nothing more about it, talking of trivial matters. Afterwards he said, 'You must excuse me, my dear. I've some business to discuss with Fergusson.'

'What business?'

'Nothing for you to worry about.'

I watched him go down the causeway and along the track with his swinging stride and could not shake off a feeling of uneasiness. Light lingers late in the Highlands in June and it was not yet dark. I don't know what it was that impelled me to go down to the estate room. It was darker there, hanging strands of ivy draped the windows. I must have it cut back some day, I thought. I rolled back the rug and took hold of the iron ring in the wooden cover. It was heavier than I had expected but as I shifted it half back, the roar of the sea seemed to fill the room. I stared down into the black hole, seeing nothing, fascinated and yet shuddering, wondering if the man with whom Donald Ruadh had fought his duel had made the fatal slip and gone to his death in the swirling water below.

'What are you doing here?'

The voice startled me and I spun round but it was only Ailsa Drummond standing in the doorway, a candle in her hand.

'Nothing,' I stammered feeling foolishly caught out like a child stealing jam. 'I was curious, that's all.'

'Curious about what?' She came into the room putting the candlestick on the table.

'Nothing important. An old tale Coll was telling me.'

'What old tale?'

But I did not answer. I was still staring into the dark depths. 'Did anyone ever escape from down there?'

'Not that I ever heard of. We had better replace the cover. It is dangerous. If I had my way, it would have been nailed down long since.'

We pushed it back into position and replaced the rug. When we stood up, she put a hand on my arm.

'You do love Coll, don't you?'

'Yes, of course.' I moved away. I never liked her touching me.

'Then don't ask too many questions. Don't probe into what doesn't concern you.'

'What on earth do you mean?'

'Exactly what I say. You may be sorry if you do.'

'I don't understand you. Coll tells me everything.'

'Yes, I know, only . . .' she paused and looked around her. 'I've always hated this room.'

She annoyed me with her mysteries. I said briskly, 'It is gloomy. I shall change it when we are married. I'm going back upstairs. Would you ask Jeannie to bring lights?'

She was herself again, calm and enigmatic as usual. 'Yes, of course, Marietta.'

When I went to the drawing-room, the eyes of Donald Ruadh looked down at me cynically out of the shadows. For an instant the resemblance to Coll seemed startling, then I took myself severely to task. It was absurd, I told myself. It was Ailsa Drummond who liked to create drama out of nothing, and yet when Jeannie brought the candles, I came to a sudden decision. I would ask Coll to have the portrait removed to some other room in the castle, anywhere so long as I did not have to see it every day.

Chapter Thirteen

A few days later a letter came from my mother. The mail boats were often unreliable. She had received the first note I had sent from Glenlochy at the same time as the second telling her of my grandfather's death and my engagement to Coll. She wrote in her usual sarcastic strain.

'Now you've achieved your heart's desire, I'm sure I hope you will be happy. It wouldn't be my choice, a castle miles from anywhere and surrounded by savages, but you're of age, my dear, you can go to the devil in your own way, I suppose. But why marry in such a hurry? Has your handsome Highlander taken advantage of you, as they say? Surely not, you were always far too much of a prude, or is there nothing more amusing to do in that gloomy Glenlochy? And why pick on a man without a sou or even a name to call his own? It is not your place to make up for your grandfather's mistakes . . . what was wrong with the Englishman you mention? I've heard of Lord Wynter. His son is a woman-hater so Henri tells me. There was some scandal about a broken engagement, but men like that are always the first to fall flat on their faces if you're clever and you're not my daughter for nothing, but no, Marietta the romantic has to throw herself away on a penniless fortune-hunter! Once a fool, always a fool, I used to say that about your father . . .

'Henri sends his love. I am going to have trouble with that one but I'm fond of him. We'll not come to the wedding, the very thought of that tiresome journey turns my stomach. Why couldn't you have brought the young man to Paris? Ah well, *chacun à son goût*, I suppose. Tell me what you need most in that God-forsaken castle of yours and I'll try to get it for you. . . .'

How like my mother to sneer at Coll! She had no feeling for the past. It was all self with her. Angrily I threw
the letter into the fire and then perversely would have
rescued it when it was too late. I didn't care whether she
came or not and yet in a way her company would have
been a stimulus and a challenge and just then I was feeling very much alone.

I still did not know what had happened between Coll
and Richard and in the circumstances I could not go to
the Tige Dubh and provoke further trouble. It was odd
but the quarrel had had the very opposite effect to what
Coll had intended. I was thinking more of Richard than
ever before. I began to look back, to remember little
things that had meant nothing at the time and to wonder
what the girl was like who had jilted him for such a
paltry reason. What a fool she must have been. If I loved
a man like that . . . then I pulled myself up. What on
earth was I thinking about? I did not love Richard and
he wouldn't thank me for feeling sorry for him. How exactly like my mother to make fun of me for not throwing
myself at him. She would have fastened like a leech
on a title and a fortune and not given in till both were
hers. I despised her for it. I tried to put all thought of
Richard out of my mind but despite my resolution there
were times when I caught myself remembering the moment when he had kissed me and wondering if he still
loved the girl who had hurt him so cruelly by flaunting
her marriage to another man.

It was towards the end of June when the herrings came.
I was awakened very early one morning by Jeannie in
a great state of excitement. She put the tray by my bed
and pulled back the curtains so that light flooded into the
room.

'They are here,' she exclaimed, 'thousands of them.
Everybody is on the beach and they have all gone from
the castle, Murdo, Kirsty, the boys, even Mr Coll . . .'

'Who have come? What on earth are you talking about?'

'The herrings, Miss Marietta.'

'Herrings?' And then I remembered. The fishing boats
went out all the year, winter and summer, but the

great shoals of herrings that come swimming up the sea
lochs were capricious. Some years they never came to
Glenlochy at all, so when they did it was a time for rejoic-
ing; it meant feasting, it meant that even the poorest
could salt a barrel for the winter, it meant that the fear
of starvation was postponed for another year.

I dressed quickly, putting on my oldest gown, tying a
scarf over my hair and running down to the beach with
Jeannie. It was an unforgettable sight. The sea was a heaving mass of fish, an amazing brilliance of colour in the
sunshine, diamond, sapphire and emerald. Gulls swooped
and screamed, gannets plunged down in a white flash,
diving under the waves and soaring up again with their
silver prey. A long line of men were wading out into
the surf with great nets, dragging in the jostling, leaping, slippery multitude to where the women waited, pil-
ing them into baskets and carrying them up the beach.
They were laughing, singing, shouting like children
exulting in the harvest of the sea.

At one moment during the morning I found myself
standing beside Hamish Kintyre. He was naked to the
waist, sweat pouring down his brown face. He smelled of
the fish, his arms shining with iridescent scales.

'How long does it last?' I shouted to him above the
roar of the surf.

'A day and a night, two days perhaps, if we're lucky.
Stand back, Mistress Gilmour, or you will be splashed.'

'It doesn't matter. Will it mean food for everyone during the winter?'

He paused a moment, wiping his face with a filthy rag
from his pocket. 'Aye, if we're fortunate,' he said in his
lilting stilted English, 'and if we are here to eat it.'

'What do you mean?'

'I think you know very well what I mean,' he said and
there was a sternness in the look he gave me. 'In your
grandfather's time we'd not have been driven from our
homes.'

'Nor will you be in mine,' I answered him.

He stared in front of him. 'You're a stranger, Mistress
Marietta, and you're young and beautiful. It's the way of
things that you should want fine gowns, rich possessions, but you should think sometimes of the men and

women of the valley who've served you and yours . . . didn't we fight and bleed at Bannockburn, at Flodden, at Culloden?' he went on with a sudden fierceness. 'Have ye no pity in your heart for us?'

'I don't understand, Mr Kintyre. Why should you say that? What have I done?'

He gave me a long meaning look. 'Maybe I speak when I should keep silent, but it is not easy. *Gille Ghille is measa na'n diobhul!*'

'What does that mean?' I said in exasperation.

'The servant of the servant is worse than the devil!' he said bitterly and plunged back into the sea with the rest of his team of men.

'The servant of the servant' . . . that must mean George Fergusson. I couldn't understand it. I had already spoken to Coll and he had promised that no one should suffer through me. I remembered Mary saying that her father-in-law was a man whose proud spirit had always made him rebellious against those in authority, a man who fiercely upheld the rights of his fellow clansmen and had done so all through the years even arguing with my grandfather. I would speak to Coll again. I would speak to George Fergusson myself. I would make sure.

Jeannie and I went back to the castle for the midday meal but Coll did not come with us. I had only caught glimpses of him during the morning. The herrings straight out of the sea and grilled were delicious. I had never cared for them before but these were like no fish I had ever tasted in Paris.

My dress was already soaked almost to my knees, everything about me reeked of fish, but I went out again because I could not keep away. There was something barbaric, something primitive about that day. Up in the stone huts the women were gutting the fish ready for the barrels, singing as they worked with a rhythmic swing of the knife. The pile of entrails grew and the gulls fought over it screaming.

I wondered once if Richard and Janet had come down to watch, but the crowd was so great on the beach, it was impossible to be certain. Late in the afternoon I saw Mr McPhail watching his flock benevolently and he waved to me.

'A strange sight and a wonderful one,' he said. 'The Lord provides out of His abundance.'

I was walking towards the castle when I noticed Fiona. She was sitting on one of the rocks singing softly to herself. The wind had torn the pins from her hair and it blew around in a black silken cloud. She was again the girl I had seen outside the house in the Canongate. She stopped singing immediately I dropped down on the rock beside her.

'Fiona, may I ask you something personal?'

'If you wish.'

'I don't want to pry but it was you I saw in Edinburgh when I first came to Scotland, wasn't it?'

She turned to look at me with those strange eyes whose colour I could never determine. 'Yes, it was,' she said simply.

'I knew it was. Why did you deny it?'

'Oh that,' she smiled, a little secret amused smile. 'Coll had loaned me the key of the house but without Sir Alasdair's permission. I did not want him to be blamed because of me.'

'I see. Did you go there to meet somebody?'

She laughed, a full-throated rich laugh that reminded me of something though I couldn't place it. 'You are very persistent, Marietta.' She was in an odd teasing mood. 'You will not give me away.'

'No, I swear it.'

'Well then,' she swung one slim foot under the red flowered skirt of her gown, 'the answer is yes.' She gave me a quick sly look. 'Are you shocked?'

In a way I was. After all she was the daughter of the minister. I said, 'Who is he?'

'You surely don't expect me to tell you that?' She got to her feet and stretched lazily. I was aware of that strong sweet perfume, seductive and alluring, that clung about her. Then she turned to me. 'You'll keep my little secret, won't you, Marietta? Now I must go. I think I should take father home before he catches a chill.'

I was almost sure she had been amusing herself at my expense and yet she had said nothing to which I could object. I went slowly back to the castle to strip off my soiled dress and wash away the smell of the fish. My hair was

sticky with salt from the sea so Jeannie brought up buckets
of water and I washed that too. It was still damp when I
went down to the drawing-room. From the windows I
could see the beach. Dusk was falling but the fish still came
heaving in and the water looked as if it was on fire,
luminous with a sort of phosphorescent glow. They were
working by torchlight. Fires burned on the sand and had
been lighted even up in the hills.

I heard the door open and guessed that it was Coll.
He came up behind me, his hand touched my hair.

'It curls like a baby's when it is damp and smells sweet
as a flower.'

I turned to him but he backed away from me laughing.

'Don't touch me, I'm filthy and reek like an ancient
fishery. I'm going down to the courtyard to strip off and
get under the pump. Do you see the fires out there? It's
midsummer eve. What with that and the herrings, they will
be eating, drinking and dancing all night.'

The excitement of the day had made me restless. I said,
'Can we go out and join them?'

'No,' he said quickly, 'no, my dear, you wouldn't enjoy
it.'

'Why wouldn't I?'

'Oh, for heaven's sake, Marietta, they won't want you
there spoiling the fun. Most of them will be drunk before
the night is over.'

'Will you go?'

'For a while. They will expect it. I shall not stay long.'

But the time passed and he did not come back. I sat at
my tapestry and could not concentrate on it. At last I
stabbed in my needle and left it. I felt very lonely. Even
Jeannie had gone out with Kirsty. No doubt Mrs Drummond was somewhere in the castle but it was not her
company I wanted. I could hear the sound of music, the
wailing of the pipes, shouts and laughter. Fires twinkled
everywhere, burning like trapped stars scattered here and
there over the hills.

As so often when one is alone, doubts nagged at me.
There was Hamish Kintyre, something would have to be
done about him. I was worried about Richard. The very
fact that Coll had been silent about him only made me
more anxious. I wondered if there was any truth in Fiona's

strange confession. Then suddenly without warning a memory stabbed me. The very first night I spent in the castle and a woman's laugh, warm, happy, sensual, just as Fiona had laughed that afternoon when she spoke of her lover. It brought me to my feet. Why had Coll been so insistent that I should not go out with him? Hardly stopping to think, I snatched up a shawl and ran down into the hall and out on to the causeway. I was a fool to let him go from me.

Fires still burned on the beach but there were few people around them. The music was far off now. They must have gone further up the glen. It was very late, past midnight. A huge moon blazed in a black velvet sky and it was almost light as day. I stopped, irresolute, realizing how crazy it was to go in search of Coll. He could be anywhere. Reluctantly I turned back to the castle and it was then that I saw Neil. He was leaning against a tree, his face very white and a curious blank stare in his eyes. He looked so strange that I paused beside him.

'Neil, what is it?'

He did not move or even seem to hear me. He said in a low excited voice, 'It is on fire. The castle . . . it is on fire . . .'

'You're dreaming,' I said a little impatiently. 'It's the bonfires on the beach, that's all.'

He put out a hand and gripped my wrist so hard that it hurt. 'The flames . . . can't you see them? They're destroying it. There'll be nothing left but ashes and I'm glad, I'm glad . . .' Then suddenly he went limp. He turned to look at me with a sick terror in his eyes.

I said urgently, 'What's the matter, Neil? Are you ill? You'd better come inside with me.'

'No, no, I can't . . . Coll would be angry.'

'Coll? Why?'

'Because I tried to stop them, you see, I did try to stop them . . .'

'Stop what? What are you talking about?' I took hold of his arm trying to shake some sense into him. 'Neil, you must tell me.'

'It was Richard Wynter . . . it was horrible, horrible . . .' he broke away from me and went running down the beach like a madman.

All the frets and anxieties of the last few hours seemed

to knot together inside me. It was a warm night. Moonlight silvered the sea, beauty was all around me and yet something evil seemed to stretch out its hand and touch me so that I felt chilled. I had an irrational desire to run to the Tige Dubh, to hammer on the door, to hear Richard's cool English voice, a little amused, asking why on earth I had come disturbing them at this unearthly hour. I conquered myself with an effort. Neil could have been talking nonsense, exaggerating as usual. I went back to the castle, but not to sleep. It was past three when at last I went up to my room. Coll had still not returned. Restlessness got me up again soon after six. When I went downstairs, no one was about even in the kitchens. Sleeping off the effects of last night's fun, I thought sourly, as I went out into the walled garden.

During the last few weeks I had spent some time there nearly every day clearing the beds and had been rewarded by seeing the straggling roses bloom and unsuspected flowers raise their heads, glad to be free of the clogging weeds.

It was there that Jeannie came to me. 'I've been looking for you everywhere,' she said accusingly. 'Mr Wynter's servant brought you a note. He was very insistent that you should have it at once.'

All the worry of the night surged back in full force. I tore it open. It was very brief. 'Richard has been badly hurt. Please come.'

'Is James still here?'

'No, he galloped off. He said he was going to Fort William.'

If Janet had sent for the doctor, then it must be serious. I said, 'Tell Tam to saddle a pony for me. I'm going to the Tige Dubh.'

'What has happened?'

'Never mind that now. Be quick, Jeannie, please.'

I changed into my riding dress and pulled on my boots. Before I left, I went down to the estate room but Coll was not there and neither was Neil. I went by the shortest route taking the track through the forest, thinking only of Richard. Was it an accident . . . or was it something worse? Did a dark spirit of revenge still lurk in the valley against the English, against the brother of Graham Wynter who had sold their sons and brothers into slavery? Is that what Neil had meant last night? It was possible and yet I did not quite believe it.

Rose opened the door to me at the Tige Dubh, looking pale and shocked. Then Janet came running down the stairs and threw herself into my arms.

'Oh Marietta, I'm so glad you're here.'

'I came as soon as I got your message. What has happened to Richard?'

'He won't tell me. He keeps saying it is nothing, that he had a fall in the forest and lost his way, but stupid things like that don't happen to Richard and why should he go out in the middle of the night? James knows, I'm sure of it, but if Richard forbade him to speak, then he wouldn't say a word. I don't know what to do for the best.'

She looked so distracted, I took her hands and made her sit down. 'Now tell me quietly. Has he been badly injured?'

Her hands tightened on mine. 'I'm not sure. You see he is always up early and when he didn't come to breakfast, I went up. He didn't want me to go into his room and when I did, he practically ordered me out. Oh Marietta, I was so frightened. James must have bandaged his head but there was blood all over it and he was so feverish. I knew he was in terrible pain and I sent James for the doctor without telling him.' She looked at me with wide terrified eyes. 'Do you think that someone attacked him?'

'I don't know.' It was then that I made up my mind. 'Listen, Jan, I'm going to fetch my Aunt Kat.'

She stared at me and I remembered that they had never met. Richard must have kept his thoughts about Kat to himself. Janet was hardly even aware of Kathryn Gilmour.

She said, 'What can she do?'

'She is clever with medicines. She did more for my grandfather than the doctor. You stay with your brother. I'll go for her now.'

I knew that Kathryn had returned to the valley and Mary Kintyre had told me where the cottage was. There was a path that led up from the church. At the foot of the waterfall the stream took a bend and within it lay a small green glen. It was quicker to go on foot but it was a steep climb and I was hot and breathless when I reached the waterfall and searched distractedly for the path. I might not have found it at all if I had not heard the childish laughter. With the roar of the torrent behind me, I saw the grassy dell, the sturdy thatched croft and the two children, little Etta Kintyre and a small dark-haired boy of about the same age. They were struggling over the possession of a toy cart and as I watched the girl suddenly let go and the boy tumbled over backwards into the grass shrieking at the top of a powerful pair of lungs. Mary came running from the house, picking him up and scolding Etta. She did not see me until I was almost beside them, then she looked up in astonishment.

'Why, Miss Marietta, what are you doing here?'

'Is my aunt there, Mary?'

'Aye, she is that.' She kissed the small boy on the top of his head and then put him down. 'All better, Robbie. Now play nicely, the pair of you, not fighting like little animals.' She turned to me. 'Come this way, Miss Marietta.'

Kat was at the door before I reached it and I knew at once that I was right to come. There was something calm and reassuring about the fine-boned face and the clear eyes. A swift thought raced through me that I had been a fool not to come before, to let prejudice blind me to someone who might have been my friend.

I said at once, 'Richard Wynter has been hurt and his sister is very anxious about him. Will you come?'

'Hurt? In what way?'

'Why do you ask?'

'I had better know what to bring. Do I need bandages, salves?'

'I think you might. Please hurry, Kat, please.'

'Very well. Wait a moment.' She disappeared inside and was back almost immediately in a long hooded cape with the medicine chest under her arm.

'Take care of the children, Mary, I'm not sure how long I'll be away.'

'Aye, ma'am, of course.'

The small boy made a dive at her burying his head in her skirts. She touched his dark hair lovingly.

'Stay with Mary, Robert, there's a good boy.'

He set up a howl but Mary lifted him in her arms, soothing him, as we went down the path and began to climb down the steep slope. We had negotiated the worst of the track before she spoke.

'Go on, Marietta, I can see your question in your face.'

'I was wondering about the little boy. Have you adopted him?'

She paused for a moment and there was a hint of laughter in her eyes. 'It would be easy to hide behind that lie but why should I? I am not ashamed. No, I didn't adopt him. He is mine, all mine.'

'Yours?'

'Yes, mine, and now tell me about Richard Wynter. What has he been doing with himself?'

'I don't know yet. I think perhaps it is what others have done to him.'

She looked at me sharply. 'What makes you say that?'

'It was something Neil said last night . . .'

'I wouldn't put too much trust in anything Neil tells you.'

'I know.' I hesitated because I didn't want to speak about the quarrel between Coll and Richard and by this time we were in sight of the Tige Dubh so I said nothing. At any other time and if it had not been so serious I think I might have been amused at Richard's fierce resistance to being fussed over by women. He struggled to sit up in the bed when Kat went into the room, his eyes fever-bright, his dark hair tousled and blood seeping through the bandage round his head.

'What the devil are you doing here? Where is James? He can do anything that's necessary.'

'That's hardly polite, Colonel Wynter,' Kat said brusquely, 'when Marietta and I have come here to help you. James may be an excellent servant but he really doesn't know how to treat injuries like these.'

She was unwrapping the bandage as she spoke and I drew a quick breath at the raw ugly place on his forehead reaching up into his hair.

Kat said calmly, 'Bring me the bowl of water and the lint.'

Janet had gone very white. She was shaking and I thought she would faint. I took the basin out of her trembling hands. 'Wait downstairs,' I whispered and she went quickly from the room.

Richard had closed his eyes against the pain. Kat

swabbed and cleansed and dressed his head with skilful fingers.

'Someone did their best to kill you, do you realize that?'

'It was when I tried to free the dog,' he muttered, 'they came up behind me . . .'

We exchanged a look, then Kat said briskly, 'And that wasn't the worst of it, was it? Now let me see the rest of you.'

Richard's eyes were open now. He shivered, one hand gripping the blanket that covered him. 'No. Leave me alone. I'm perfectly all right. They will heal well enough.'

'Don't be a fool. Marietta won't faint, you know. Do you want to die of blood poisoning? Believe me, I know what I'm talking about.'

He tried to prevent her, but she pushed aside his hands. The sheet that James must have wrapped around him was horribly stained with blood. Kat gently turned it aside and I bit back the shocked exclamation. He might have been savaged by wild beasts. I saw the scratches, the claw marks, the long deep furrows on his back. The sight turned me sick. They must have tied him up before they lashed him with a horse whip. Kat said nothing. She worked with quick gentle fingers, cleansing and then smearing on salves. Then she said, 'Help me, Marietta,' and together we wound the light bandage around his chest. I felt his rapid breathing and when I met his eyes, he closed them as if he could not bear to see me. He lay back, looking white and exhausted.

'There, that's done,' said Kat. 'I'm sorry if it was painful. I'm afraid it will go on hurting for a few days more but you will recover.'

'Thank you,' he said grudgingly and I thought, he hates us both because we've seen what must have been a bitter humiliation to a man of his proud spirit.

'Don't distress yourself,' Kat was looking down at him with a little smile. 'I've seen men in worse plight than yours. Now we'll leave you in peace. Try to sleep.'

She put her salves and liniments together and went out of the room but I lingered for a moment looking down at Richard. The shock and the horror were still with me and something else, something that stirred deep within me. I was shaken by a helpless rage against the devils who had tortured him so cruelly. I bent down and gently touched his cheek.

'I'm sorry, Richard, desperately sorry.'

His eyes opened. He moved his head so that he could kiss my fingers. It was absurd but I wanted passionately to kneel beside him, put my arms round him, comfort him. I went quickly away, frightened of what was happening to me. Outside the door I paused trying to still the pounding of my heart. It was a minute or two before I could steady myself to go quietly downstairs.

Janet was huddled in one of the chairs, her face buried in her hands. She looked up as I came in, tears in her eyes. 'I'm so ashamed of myself. I can't bear the sight of blood. It's so stupid but I've always been like this. I don't mind anything else. It's just the blood.'

'I've been telling her. It's nothing to be upset about,' said Kat cheerfully. 'There are men who fight like heroes and faint when they cut their finger. Now don't worry too much about your brother. Most of his injuries are superficial. They'll heal. What he needs is to forget it for a while.' She took a phial from her little chest. 'Give him a few drops of this.'

'Richard hates drugs.'

'Because of that leg of his?'

'Yes.'

'Then don't tell him. It's only a tincture of opium. Give it to him in a glass of wine and if necessary, repeat it. He badly needs to sleep.'

'I'm very grateful to you.'

'No need to be.' She picked up her cloak and swung it around her. 'We're a long way from doctors. I do what I can. If you want me, you know where I am.'

'I'll come tomorrow,' I whispered kissing Janet's cheek. She clung to me for a moment. 'Would you like me to send Jeannie to stay with you?'

'No, I shall be all right. I don't want to be a nuisance.'

'Don't be silly.' I gave her a quick hug.

Outside Kat said quietly, 'She has been delicately brought up. It's a good thing she didn't see the worst of it.'

'You guessed, didn't you? Why, Kat? Who could have attacked him so brutally?'

'I'm not sure. Old hatreds don't die, you know, they live

on in places like this and they take strange forms. Hamish
Kintyre was very bitter about what happened to his son.'

'But Hamish is a good man.'

'Yes.' She looked at me oddly. 'But there are others.'

'Will Richard really be all right?'

'Oh yes. He is strong and healthy . . . but how is he going to feel about it? Most men would want revenge for a
humiliating ordeal of that kind. Will he, Marietta?'

'I don't know.' How well did I know Richard? How well
did I really know Coll? I kept thinking of the quarrel between them.

'When Graham Wynter died,' Kat went on, 'the soldiers
came here. They asked questions, some of them were
brutal, and yet they learned nothing. When anyone in the
valley is under suspicion, then the whole clan closes up.
They would never betray their own. You must understand
that.'

'Yes.'

'If Colonel Wynter makes a formal complaint, then the
English will come here again. It has happened elsewhere
in the Highlands. I sometimes think it is only our isolation
out here that has protected us in the past. If they cannot
make an arrest, then they may burn the crofts, evict our
people from the valley. Everyone would suffer for the sake
of the few. Would you want that to happen?'

'No, of course not.'

'Then do nothing about it, not yet. Wait a little. And if
the worst comes to worst, try and persuade Colonel Wynter. I think he might listen to you. Now I must go back to
Mary and the children.'

I watched her walk quickly up the path before I
turned my pony homeward. My thoughts were going round
and round in turmoil. I was sure of only one thing. I must
find out the truth whatever Kat said.

When I got back to the castle, they were already at
supper; Coll and his mother, Fiona and Neil with George
Fergusson. They sat there, calmly eating and drinking, as
if nothing had happened and it made me furiously angry.

Coll rose as I came into the room. 'We were down on the
shore watching the last of the herrings brought in so I
invited them back to supper. Whatever happened to you,
Marietta? We've been anxious about you.'

'I might ask what happened to you last night?' I said tartly. I looked round at them. 'Don't you know? Don't any of you know?'

'Know what? What are you talking about?'

'Richard Wynter was assaulted last night, savagely beaten, very nearly murdered, in our own woods, on Glenlochy land.'

If I thought to surprise something out of them, I was mistaken. They turned to me with blank astonished faces, only Coll showed a flash of anger.

'So that's where you have been all day, at the Tige Dubh. I thought you promised me . . .'

'What do promises matter when something happens like this. I had a message from his sister. She is nearly out of her mind . . .' Remembering my shock and my horror, it was suddenly too much for me. I began to tremble. I tried to speak and my throat closed up.

Coll came to me at once. 'You're over-wrought, dearest. You've been doing too much.'

Fiona had risen. She moved towards me and I said fiercely, 'Don't touch me,' and Coll waved her back.

'Leave her to me. Come along, Marietta.' He put his arm round my shoulders. He was leading me from the room and I went with him.

In my bedroom he said, 'Now, tell me quietly, what is all this?'

I could not stop myself. It all poured out in one long stream of distress and reproach and he took me by the shoulders, his face tense and angry, shaking me into silence.

'Are you accusing me?'

'I don't know, Coll, I don't know. You hated him. You said so. You wanted to get even with him for what he did to you.'

'And you thought I'd stoop to something like this? Is that what you think of me? Are you in love with this man? Are you, Marietta? Does he mean so much to you?'

'No, no, I swear it. It's not that at all, but what am I to think?' Anger and wretchedness were forcing the words out of me. 'I was so happy here and now it is all spoiled. Hamish Kintyre accused me of driving the people out of their homes. Why should he say that when it is not true?

And then this terrible thing happens to Richard. Ever since I came, I have brought nothing but trouble.'

My voice was breaking in spite of myself and Coll sat beside me on the bed, pulling me close to him. 'I told you before, don't you remember? Hamish Kintyre is a trouble-maker, a disappoined man with a grievance. You don't understand how things are here. Why can't you leave it all to me? Don't you trust me?'

'You know I do,' but the old magic was not working. I could not yield to the charm of his voice, the sweetness of his caress. I stiffened against him. 'I still want to know who was responsible for this attack on Richard.'

His mouth was against my hair. 'What did he tell you about it?'

'Nothing. He was in too much pain. It was horrible, Coll, horrible. He had been flogged with a whip.'

'Will he recover?'

'Kat says so.'

'Kat?' his arms around me tightened.

'I took her to see him.'

'Why?'

'There was no one else.'

His hands caressed me. He murmured, 'Don't worry, sweetheart. Leave it to me. I'll tell Fergusson to start an enquiry.'

I sat up, pulling myself away. 'Coll, I don't like him. Must he stay here? Can't we dismiss him?'

'Just like that?' He smiled. 'But he is good at his work. Besides he has a claim, you know. He is a cousin of the Chief.'

'I don't care. I don't want him here. Please, Coll, please . . .'

'Ssh . . . now don't get excited all over again. You will make yourself ill. It will be different when we are married. You will see.'

He drew me back against him. He undid the top of my blouse. His hand was cool on my breast. He was kissing me with passion.

I pushed him away from me. 'No, Coll, please don't. Leave me alone.'

'What's wrong?'

'Nothing.' I got up and moved to the dressing-table.

'Would you ask Jeannie to bring me some milk? I don't want anything else.'

'All right, my pet. If you're sure that's all you need.'

'Yes, it is,' I said steadily. 'Goodnight, Coll.'

He went reluctantly and when the door closed behind him, I stared at myself in the mirror, at my hair blown into rats'-tails, my eyes in dark hollows, my lips bruised from his kisses. Already the spell was fading. It was Richard of whom I was thinking, Richard and that strange new tenderness that had gripped me at the sight of his pain and humiliation. I tried to dismiss it, but it was there inside me and for the very first time I admitted that my mother could be right. Marietta the romantic . . . had I been a fool? Was it true that I had fallen in love with a man who didn't really exist? Had I lost my heart to a dream?

Chapter Fourteen

When I woke up the next morning, I knew I had to go back to the Tige Dubh. Too much had been left unsaid but I had an uneasy feeling that Coll would prevent me if he could. I made up my mind to walk instead of taking the pony. In that way I could slip out of the castle unnoticed. It was a cool blustery morning with little scurries of rain so I pulled on thick boots and wore my long hooded cape.

Jeannie was making my bed and tidying the room. She looked at me disapprovingly. 'You oughtn't to be going off on your own like that, Miss Marietta. It isn't right. You don't know who might be hiding in those woods.'

So they had been gossiping about Richard already in the kitchens. I said, 'Don't be silly. Why should anyone want to attack me?'

She suddenly turned, looking at me entreatingly, the duster still in her hand. 'Must we stay here, Miss Marietta? Can't we just pack up and go back to the Rue Chantelle? I know Madame was not always easy to live with, but she is your mother after all and Monsieur Henri could be kind even if he did give me a sly pinch when he came creeping up behind me on the stairs.'

I had to smile at her. 'Why, Jeannie, I thought you liked it here.'

'Aye, I did after that first day, but it's not like it was. I know you're going to marry Mr Coll, but it's been different somehow ever since the old gentleman passed away. It's as if something went out of the castle with him and I don't like what's taken its place.'

'Oh come now, Jeannie, it's not like you to be fanciful. Nothing has changed, nothing at all.' But I knew she was right. I had been wilfully blinding myself but it was there.

I had been living in a fool's paradise ever since grandfather died. My first joy, my first wonderful feeling of home-coming to the lovely valley my father had remembered with so poignant a longing had vanished.

It was a long walk and the rain was now coming down heavily. I stepped out sturdily but it was nearly midday before I reached the Tige Dubh. The door was open. I went straight into the living-room and was startled to see Richard standing by the window. When he turned I saw how pale he looked but flogging or not he held himself stiffly erect and he was impeccably shaved.

I said at once, 'You should not be out of bed.'

'Why not? I had six months flat on my back once. It is not an experience I am eager to repeat.'

'Oh Richard!' I exclaimed. 'Why do you have to drive yourself all the time?'

'That's what Jan tells me.'

'I don't know what Kat will say . . .'

'We shall soon know. I've sent James to ask if she will be good enough to come here as soon as she can.'

'Why?'

'I think you know why.'

'Because of your brother?'

'Yes.' Then he took a step towards me. 'What am I thinking about? It's so good of you to come through all this rain. You must be soaked. Let me take your cloak.'

'Certainly not. I can take it off perfectly well myself. Where is Janet?'

'She will be down in a moment.'

'What did the doctor say?'

'He didn't come.'

'Didn't come? What do you mean?'

'James returned without him. He is away from the garrison, up in the hills somewhere.'

'Thank goodness for my Aunt Kat,' I said a little dryly.

'Yes, indeed. I owe her a great deal and you too.' He paused. 'I have an uneasy recollection of behaving very badly yesterday.'

I met his eyes and looked away. I could not help remembering the cruel marks of the whip on his naked back. I said awkwardly, 'It was understandable. You were in great pain. Are you sure you're really better?'

For the first time that morning he gave me his little quirky smile. 'It hurts like hell, but it will pass.'

'I've been worrying about you all night.'

'Have you, Marietta? Why?'

His eyes were on my face. For an instant a warm wave of sympathy flowed between us. 'Because . . . because . . .'

'Because what?'

I don't know what I might have said but then we were interrupted. Janet came running down the stairs. Rose opened the door and Kathryn came in, holding the hand of the little dark-haired boy. He hung back shyly hiding his face in his mother's skirt. She gave him a little push.

'Go along, Robert. Go and greet your Uncle Richard.'

None of us moved or spoke for a second, then Janet gave a little gasp and Richard dropped stiffly on one knee and held out his hand.

'I am pleased to meet you, Robert,' he said gravely.

The child took one or two uncertain steps towards him, then quickly put his hands behind his back, looking up at his mother and bursting into a babble of incomprehensible words.

Kathryn laughed. 'I am afraid he speaks Gaelic or English just as he feels like it. That meant, "Is he going to give me something?" I am sorry to say your nephew is a greedy little boy.'

Richard smiled and got to his feet. 'I seem to remember that my brother always managed to get the largest slice of the cake.'

Janet said in a trembling voice, 'Graham's son . . . but it can't be . . . I don't understand . . .' Bewildered, she looked from Kat to her brother.

He said brusquely, 'Now don't cry over him, Jan.' He turned to Kat. 'Will you tell us about it?'

'Is there anything more you need to know?'

'Yes, a great deal.'

'Very well then, I suppose I must, but first, what about you? I left you very sick yesterday. I don't know as you should be on your feet like this, Colonel Wynter.'

'Richard,' he corrected, 'I am Graham's brother, remember, and you do not need to worry about me. I am an old campaigner, and thanks to you, I'm as good as new, or almost.'

She smiled a little. 'It's quite extraordinary. You are so like Graham,' then she let herself drop on to the stool in the window, pulling the child against her. He sucked his small fist, too shy to do more than stare at us with large round grey eyes.

Kathryn looked down at her hands loosely clasped in her lap. 'When your brother first came here, I hated him as I hated all the English. I was fifteen when my brothers were killed at Culloden. For twenty years Cumberland's men had ravaged through the Highlands, robbing, burning, murdering. My father was in desperate straits. The harvest had failed, the herrings had not come for two years. He had to find money to buy food if his people were not to die of starvation during the winter and here was a stranger, rich and eager to buy. So Graham was invited to the castle and treated with courtesy and he came more than once. He was different from the others . . . Oh, I can guess what you are thinking,' she threw up her head with a proud gesture, 'you can laugh if you wish. I was thirty-five, resigned to the life of an old maid, caring for my father, looking after our people. Have you any idea what life had been like here? No money for visits to Edinburgh, no parties, no balls, no visitors, not even a new dress— only father and his mistress and Coll. Of course it was ridiculous, I saw that myself all too clearly, but all the same it happened. I fell in love . . . and so did he . . .'

'Did he ask you to marry him?'

'Yes, he did. At first I said no, over and over again. I was five years older than he, but he wouldn't listen . . .'

'I know,' said Richard gently. 'She is the most marvellous person in the world, that is what he wrote to me.'

'Did he?' Kathryn flushed like a young girl. 'It was hopeless from the start. You never saw father in a rage, did you, Marietta?'

'Only once, when he spoke of him.'

'The Gilmour temper could be terrifying. For him the English could never be anything but the enemy who had murdered his sons. He raved at Graham and me. He forbade him to come to the castle. He talked about his Highland honour . . . I know it was shameless of me but what did I care for honour?' she went on with a flash of defiance. 'Graham begged me to go away with him at

once, but how could I live with him at Fort William where
everyone knew me. I would not shame him or my father.
His period of service up here ended at Christmas. I said
we would wait until then. So I came here secretly whenever I could . . .'

'Then what happened?' I whispered.

'I became pregnant. Stupid, wasn't it? It was something
I had never reckoned with. When it was certain, I was
wildly happy and terrified too. Ailsa Drummond had always hated me just as I did her. She guessed what had
happened and she told my father. We had a terrible quarrel, screaming at one another like lunatics, saying horrible unforgiveable things. At one moment I thought he
would kill me or lock me up somewhere—it's not un-
known in families like ours, you know—but he didn't. I
walked out of the castle and came here. It was a day
or two before Graham could come and when he did, he
was very upset about something he had found out.'

'Did you tell him about the child?'

'No. I wish I had. It might have made a difference. I
don't know.'

'Was it about the ship and the young men he was helping to emigrate?'

'Yes. He had been responsible for that. He was sympa-
thetic towards their plight, trapped here with no future.
He had done what he could but the shipmaster spoke
little English, he could not do it alone. George Fergusson
had been interpreting for him. He did not tell me of it
that evening, only that he had to see my father. He had
to tell him what was being done in his name, so that it
could be stopped in time. After that he would take me
away. He wanted me to go to your parents at Laverstoke.
We sat here in this very room and talked about it before
he went to the castle. I never saw him again. A few days
later his body was washed up from the sea.'

'Did they kill him?' whispered Richard grimly.

'I don't know, I don't know. There was no mark on
him, no wound, nothing.'

The tears were running freely down Janet's face but
Kat sat dry-eyed, very still and quiet, only I saw how her
hand tightened on little Robert's shoulder so that he
turned to look up at her in surprise.

Richard leaned forward. 'When the English investigated his death, did they question your father?'

'Yes, of course. He swore that Graham never came near the castle that night and Coll and the servants said the same.'

'And what about you?'

For an instant Kathryn's composure was shaken, then she went on steadily. 'I knew that someone had lied but what could I say? That I was his mistress? What fine sport they would have got out of bullying the Captain's Scottish whore! My father had kept silent about me. I couldn't bring shame on him or Graham. He was dead but there was his child. I wanted only to go away.'

Richard said quietly, 'It must have taken great courage. My brother wanted to take you to Laverstoke. Will you allow me to do so?'

'One day perhaps, but only if your father wishes it.'

'He will, you can be sure of that. Graham was always very dear to him.'

Kathryn stood up. 'I think perhaps I had better go now, but before I do, I would like to know what you intend to do.'

'Do? About what?'

'Have you forgotten that the night before last you were savagely attacked?'

'Oh that!' Richard's eyes turned to me. 'I think I know the reason for that. It's not myself I am concerned about. It's my brother. I want to know who killed him and why.'

'But it's all over and done with . . .'

'He went to the castle and never returned.'

'It was not my father. Do you know nothing of Highland traditions, of Highland honour? He had been a guest in his house, he had eaten his bread, that if nothing else would have made him sacred whatever he might have done.'

'All very fine and noble, but Sir Alasdair could have ordered others to do what he scorned to do himself.'

'Oh no,' I exclaimed. 'You're wrong. How can you say such a vile thing?'

'Your grandfather is dead, Marietta, nothing of this can affect him now,' said Richard steadily. He turned to Kathryn. 'Don't you want to know who murdered the man

you loved, the father of your child? Who are you protecting?'

'Don't you understand anything?' said Kathryn passionately. 'I'm not protecting any one person, but the
people of this valley are my people, their blood is my
blood. They have suffered enough. I'll not see them destroyed for something that happened two years ago, that
could have been an accident. Marietta, you tell him. You
feel as I do.'

I knew then that much as Kathryn had loved Graham
Wynter, she would still fight for those she had grown up
with, the men and women who were part of her heritage.
Richard was the brother of the man she loved, but he
was still the enemy and I was torn between the two. I
shared her feeling. Hadn't I felt the same about my father and resented my mother because she attacked what
he loved and believed in? . . . and yet I understood Richard too and knew that the fierce love he had for his
dead brother would not let him rest. It would drive him
to any extreme to discover the truth.

It was the child who interrupted us. In our passionate
argument we had forgotten him and he suddenly let out a
howl of rage. It broke the tension.

Janet went down on her knees putting her arms round
him. 'Poor little boy, he's hungry,' she murmured re-
proachfully.

'He's always hungry,' said Kathryn, 'and Mary will be
wondering why I am so long.'

'Let me say this before you go,' said Richard quietly.
'I'll make sure no harm comes to you or him, but I must
do what I think is right.'

'Perhaps Marietta can make you see that there is right
and right and there are different ways of looking at it,'
she said dryly picking up the child.

Janet gave us a quick glance before she said, 'May I
walk with you, Kathryn? I'd like to see where you live.
Do you mind, Richard?'

'No, of course not, but better take James with you. I
don't like the thought of you walking back alone.'

She wrinkled her nose at him. 'Who is making the fuss
now? I won't be long. Look after him for me, Marietta.'

Janet was so simple, so uncomplicated. I knew that

most of what we had been saying had gone over her head. She longed only to talk to Kathryn about her brother.

I said, 'I think I had better go too.'

'Not for a moment. There is something I want to say to you.'

'You are not fit. Won't another time do?'

'No, it won't.' Richard went to the table holding up the bottle of Madeira with a little smile. 'Will you drink with me or are you too angry?'

'Why should I be angry?'

He didn't answer but poured two glasses and brought one to me.

I said, 'It will go straight to my head.'

'Mine too probably. Never mind. Perhaps it will help.'

I sipped the rich sweet wine and nibbled the biscuit he offered me, waiting for him to speak. He was standing with his back to the smouldering peat fire, his face stern and dark. He was once again the man I had known in Edinburgh, the Englishman, the enemy, not the gay companion with whom I had watched the seals and grilled trout over a picnic fire.

He said abruptly, 'I shall have to take Janet back to Laverstoke.'

'You are leaving Glenlochy?'

'I am not running away but what else can I do after this? I don't want anything to happen to her. With her husband away she is my responsibility.'

'I am sorry.' A few minutes before I had been angry at his harsh criticism of my grandfather. Now the prospect of the Tige Dubh lying empty and deserted made me feel desperately lonely.

He finished the wine in his glass and put it down carefully on the table before he spoke again. 'I hadn't intended to tell you but there is something that I think you ought to know.'

'What is it?'

'Are you aware that Coll sent me a challenge?'

A little cold chill crept up my spine. 'A challenge to a duel?'

'Yes. Oh, you needn't be afraid for him. I returned it unanswered. I was sorely tempted to take it up but I found I was unwilling to fight over such a triviality. It should never have happened. It was my fault. I lost my temper.' He paused and then went on in the same dry level tone. 'The night before last I went out of the house because I heard an animal crying out in pain and I thought it might be an old half blind bitch that belongs to Lachlan. She is in the habit of roaming off if the stable door is open. I followed the sound into the forest. She had been cruelly tied, her feet lashed together and she was moaning pitifully. I knelt down to free her and then they were on me. There were a great number of them and they dragged me to a clearing. There were only torches but I could see quite clearly . . .'

'A great black stone and men and women wearing fantastic heads of animals . . .'

'Yes,' he sounded astonished. 'You know?'

'I saw them on the night grandfather was taken ill. It means nothing, just an old custom hanging on from pagan times so Mr McPhail tells me,' I said as lightly as I could.

'A very unpleasant custom if I may say so,' he said grimly. 'I don't want to talk about it only that at the moment when they tied me to the pillar I saw the hand of the man who held the whip. He was wearing a very unusual ring. I saw it quite clearly in the torchlight, two intertwined snakes and some sort of animal in the centre, a cat, I believe.'

My grandfather's ring. Last time I had seen it was upon his finger as he lay in the coffin. I got to my feet. 'Why are you telling me this? Do you think this was a way of getting even with you because you refused that challenge? Are you accusing Coll?'

'Did I mention his name?'

'No, but that is whom you meant.'

'You defend him very passionately. Does he wear a ring like that?'

'No, of course not.'

'But it is the Gilmour seal?'

'Yes, yes it is,' I said reluctantly.

'I did not imagine it, Marietta. Who else would wear it?' He paused and when I didn't answer, he went on. 'Believe me, it hasn't been easy for me to say this, but you did tell me you thought of me as a brother and it is a brother's duty to offer advice . . .'

'Advice about what?'

'Marietta, you have pledged yourself to marry a man whom you scarcely know. You've been here so short a time. Wait a little.'

Against all reason I bitterly resented the cool dispassionate voice tearing my dream to shreds. 'Thank you, but I know perfectly well what I'm doing.'

'I don't think you do. Marietta, please listen to me. It is important. I've been making enquiries . . .'

'I know you have. It has caused nothing but trouble. You will be saying next that it was Coll who murdered your brother.'

'I have said nothing of the kind, but why will no one answer my questions? What has he to hide?'

'Nothing, because there is nothing. Kathryn is right. It's all your own invention. If that is all you have to tell me, I think I had better go.'

'It is not all. There is something else.'

'I don't want to know.'

'You can please yourself but I think you should. It is in a letter from Duncan Cameron.'

That brought me up short. 'Why should Mr Cameron be writing to you?'

'We have had business dealings. You may not remember but I did say once that I was interested in the price your grandfather was asking for the house in Edinburgh.'

'Why?'

'I don't think the reason concerns us now,' he went on coldly. 'In any case circumstances have changed. Mr Cameron wrote to me about this matter and he mentioned something else that has surprised and shocked him very much especially in view of what you have always been at such pains to impress on me.'

'I don't know what you mean.'

'Don't you? Does Highland honour have nothing to say about a young woman who is willing to lease her very considerable estates to men who intend to evict the inhabitants within three months and turn the whole valley over to the very profitable rearing of sheep?'

'What!' I stared at him astonished, thinking I must be dreaming.

He went to a small desk in the corner and took out a letter. 'Do you want to read it for yourself?'

'What does he say?'

He turned the pages until he found the passage. 'Here it is. "I am surprised that so soon after her grandfather's death Miss Gilmour is willing to lease her lands to the highest bidder. There are plenty to pay the price demanded but I find it tragic, especially after Sir Alasdair resisted the temptation for so long, maintaining to the last that he owed it to his people to keep their homes intact for them as long as humanly possible. Of course it will give her a fine income, far more than can be expected from the rents these unhappy people can afford to pay but the Chief trusted his granddaughter and it seems to me another sign of the degeneracy of our times here in Scotland that our young people are willing to betray their trust for the sake of gold and idle pleasure . . ." I fear that Mr Cameron is somewhat of a Puritan in his views.'

'It's not true. It can't be true.'

'I am afraid it is. He would hardly have gone ahead without authorization from you.'

I thought wildly of all those documents I had signed after grandfather died, believing in Coll, taking his word for what they contained, not going through them as carefully as I should have done. Could it have been one of those? I was angry with myself and perversely even more angry with Richard.

I said, 'And you believed it of course. You thought that was the kind of person I was, a lying cheat, coming here only for what she could grab from a sick old man . . .'

He folded the letter carefully. 'I learned some time ago not to trust what any woman said to me.'

'You think I'm like the girl who jilted you. If you were as cynical with her as you are with me, I'm not surprised. A woman wants a man who trusts her, who loves her, not a cold-hearted critic always finding fault . . .'

He caught me by the wrists, holding me in a grip of iron. 'What else am I to believe? Are you such a fool that you sign papers without even looking at them? That you let a handsome face and pretty manners blind you so completely to what is going on around you?'

'Let me go.'

He released me so suddenly that I staggered backwards.

'Oh God,' he said with a bitter disgust. 'It's I who am the fool, but I thought better of you, I thought . . . oh what the hell does it matter what I thought? Go ahead, do what you like, marry your handsome Coll, sell the land, sell the poor wretches, see them driven into starvation if that's what you want, only don't for God's sake come bleating to me about the love you have for your people, that their blood is your blood, because I know better. You're like all the rest, thinking only of yourself, selfish to the bone!'

'I'm not staying to hear any more. Believe what you like, I don't care. Go! Get out of Glenlochy! You have no place here. My grandfather made the greatest mistake of his life when he sold his land to your brother who repaid him by seducing his daughter and selling his kin into shameful slavery. Isn't that worse? If my grandfather did have him murdered, then it was no more than he deserved!'

I knew I was shouting in a frenzy of rage and misery. I saw Richard's appalled face and then I had gone out of the house. I was running down the track, my tears mingling with the rain, careless of the mud under my feet, and mingled with my distress, a certainty that it was my own fault, that I had no one else to blame and that my anger with Richard was because he was right. I had been a fool and I was too proud to own it, too proud to admit that I had let myself be deceived, my Gilmour blood raging against Richard because he had seen what was happening so much more clearly than I had done. I would show him. I would prove that I was not a liar and a cheat, make him apologize, come crawling . . . then I pulled up short. That was what Coll had said and then he . . . no, I would not believe it. He could not have behaved so despicably . . . there must be some other explanation.

All the long way home I tried to fight it out with myself, but nothing took away the plain fact that Coll had deceived me, he had lied to me over and over again and I might never have known about it until it was too late.

It was early evening when I got back to the castle and everything was quiet. My feet were soaked through, my gown splashed with mud to the knees. I went to my room to wash and change and pull myself together for what would no doubt be a battle. Kirsty came hammering at my door saying that supper was ready and I realized that I had taken nothing all day but the biscuit and wine that Richard had given me.

It was an eerie sensation to walk into the room and see last night's company seated around the table almost as if they had never moved since the evening before. I paused in the doorway and Coll looked up, my handsome Coll whom I loved so well. What were the blue eyes hiding from me?

'Where have you been?' he said gaily. 'We have missed you.'

I took my place at the head of the table and glanced around at them. 'You must forgive me but I was not aware that I had invited guests.'

Coll looked startled, 'Marietta, my dear . . .'

Fiona interrupted him. 'You didn't give us an opportunity to explain last night,' she said sweetly, 'and you've not been in the house all day. We have been having trouble at home. Water has been seeping into the downstairs rooms for some time now and it is beginning to affect father's health. You wouldn't know about it of course. You have been here so short a time. Coll was kind enough to ask us to stay here while the problem is dealt with.'

Neil kept his eyes fixed on his plate. Ailsa Drummond who so rarely sat with us was crumbling a piece of bread. Mr McPhail looked up awkwardly.

'I hope we're not inconveniencing you, Miss Marietta. If so,' he looked helplessly at Fiona, 'we can return home at once.'

'I wouldn't dream of it. I would not want you to make yourself ill because of me. The castle is large enough.' I looked across at Coll. 'Only I would have preferred to have been asked first.'

'It was a sudden decision. I only discovered what a state the house was in this morning. You're so generous, dearest, I knew you would have been the first to suggest it.'

'And what about you, Mr Fergusson?' I said dryly. 'Is your house uninhabitable too?'

He laughed. 'You will have your joke, Miss Gilmour. I'm not staying here. But Coll and I have been hard at work all day and he suggested that I should stay for supper. There's a good deal of business just now, you know.'

'What kind of business?'

'Legal matters connected with Sir Alasdair's will, all dry-as-dust, not at all interesting to lovely young ladies like yourself.'

'You wouldn't be thinking of selling my land or leasing it, would you?'

His eyes flickered to Coll and then he smiled as if I were a foolish child. 'What an idea! Certainly not.'

I was tempted to come out with it there and then, throw it in their faces and then changed my mind. I would give Coll the chance to explain in private.

'And then of course there has been this affair of Mr Wynter,' he went on. 'Coll told me how upset you were at his little accident. How is he, by the way?'

'It was not an accident. It was a deliberate assault on him. I am glad to say he is recovering but very angry.'

'Naturally. I have been making enquiries already.'

'And finding out nothing, I suppose.'

He shrugged his shoulders. 'It is never easy.'

I would have liked to say, I don't like you, Mr Fergusson. I think you're a rogue and a liar and probably worse. Take a week's notice and go, but you cannot do that to a man whose ancestors have served yours for generations, who however distant is still kin to you.

Instead I said, 'He is our close neighbour. I feel a responsibility.'

'Is he going to make trouble?' asked Coll.

'What would you do if he did?'

'We have dealt with the English before, my dear, we can always do it again.'

'How? by murder?'

'You're in a very odd mood tonight, darling. Is something wrong?'

But I didn't answer. I was not prepared to argue, not then, there was too much on my mind, nor did I want to stay with them. I put down my knife and fork and stood up.

'If you will excuse me, I am rather tired and I think I had better make sure arrangements have been made for our guests.'

'I have already done that,' said Fiona quickly.

'Thank you, but this does happen to be my house.'

'I am sorry if I have offended you.'

An angry retort sprang to my lips but I checked it. I was too much on edge. A stupid quarrel would lead nowhere.

Coll opened the door for me. 'What is it, Marietta?' he whispered. 'I know there is something.'

'I must talk to you, Coll.'

'Now? Shall I come up with you?'

And tempt me into forgetting it with his caresses. Never again.

'No, the morning will do.'

He would have kissed me but I moved quickly away from him. I closed the door behind me and went up to my room. I lit a candle and came down again and along the passage to the estate room. It was very quiet there, only the dogs sleeping by the hearth, no sound of the sea on the rocks below. The tide must be out. Wolf came lumbering across to me, thrusting his cold nose into my hand. I patted him abstractedly. There were papers on the desk, neatly stacked, but I was not concerned with those. I was looking for something else and after a second I found it lying beside the wafers, the sealing wax, the sandbox—my grandfather's big square ring. Who else would have worn it but Coll? Coll who had called up the devil to find out what the future held for him, Coll who saw himself as seventeenth Chieftain by right as much as by marriage with me, Coll who hated Richard and feared him as a rival and flogged him with his own hand, inflicting unspeakable humiliation on him. The cold feeling in the pit of my stomach made me feel physically sick.

Then there was a sound outside. Bran lifted his head

and growled. The door opened and Coll came in. I swung round guiltily.

He said, 'Whatever are you doing here, Marietta? I thought you had gone to bed.'

I held out my hand with the ring in it. 'Did you wear this on the night you tried to kill Richard Wynter?'

His eyes moved from the ring to my face. 'Did he tell you that?'

'He said the hand that held the whip wore the ring, the Gilmour ring. Who else uses it but you?'

He shrugged his shoulders. 'You forget, my dear. Neil is in and out of here every day.'

'Neil!' For an instant it took my breath away. 'Neil! That boy and Richard! I don't believe it. It doesn't make sense.'

'I told you, didn't I, that Neil is not the boy he seems. He is vicious. There are plenty of wild youngsters among the crofters and they were all of them drunk that night. Ready to get up to any kind of mischief.'

I stared at him remembering Neil's face when I met him outside the castle. It was plausible and yet I didn't believe it, not for one moment. Up there in the forest I had felt the evil like a palpable force. What had happened to Richard was no boyish prank.

I said, 'George Fergusson and Fiona, do they indulge in these wild games too?'

'What have they got to do with it? Really, Marietta, you are talking nonsense. You've never liked Fiona, have you? God knows why. But is that any reason to attack her because of her brother? You don't know what you are talking about.' He put a hand on my arm and would have pulled me to him but I jerked myself free.

'No, you can't get round me like that, not any more. You're evading the issue. You've not answered my question.'

'Don't bully me, Marietta. I don't like it.'

'And I don't like lying and cheating either. I learned something else this afternoon. You promised me that the people of this valley would be safe, that together we would work out how best we could help them and ourselves, and now I find you are planning to lease the land, my land, to a stranger who cares nothing for them, who will drive them out of their homes, burn the roofs over their heads, if they won't go . . .'

'Where did you hear all this?' his voice was dangerously quiet.

'It is true. Duncan Cameron had written to Richard. He is shocked at what is being done in my name, mine! How dare you act behind my back? My grandfather would never have sold his people for profit to himself and neither will I. I'd rather live in poverty all my days.'

'Damn him!' he said suddenly. 'God damn the Honourable Richard Wynter and his meddling ways! What a pity we didn't strike just a little harder!'

I backed away from him, horrified at the look on his face. In the flickering light of the candle, the blue eyes were cold as ice, the beautiful mouth twisted into a savage snarl.

'Yes,' he said, 'I held the whip. I flogged him and I enjoyed it, do you hear? He sneered at my challenge, too fine an English gentleman to fight with a Highlander, a bastard without a handle to his name! Do you think I was going to let that go by without punishment? After we had done, we stripped him, we rolled him in the mud and filth, there was not much left of his finicking airs and graces when we had finished with him!'

Now that I knew the truth, I could not endure it. I closed my eyes and he seized me by the shoulders, his face thrust close to mine.

'What else did he tell you? Did he let you read that letter? Did he?' I shook my head dumbly, too shocked to speak, and he went on. 'No, because he didn't dare. You admire him, don't you, so elegant, such fine manners, so much better than us poor devils. Has he ever starved? Has he been forced to humble himself, lick boots, crawl on his belly to an arrogant old man for the very bread he ate?' The bitter words poured out in a long stream. 'Oh no, he has lived on cream all his life and yet he didn't tell you that one of those bidding for your lands was himself. Oh no, he didn't tell you that, did he? It is only I who am the liar and the cheat!'

'It's not true. Richard would never do such a thing.'

'Wouldn't he? He's out for a good profit like all the other damned Englishmen who think Scotland is something they can plunder at their pleasure. And why shouldn't we enjoy some of the good things of life too? Why? Why?'

Then as suddenly as the rage had swept through him, it seemed to die. He released me and dropped into the chair by the table. 'Oh God, I am sorry. You made me so mad . . . I am sorry, Marietta, I didn't want you to know all these things.'

'I suppose you were waiting till we were married when I could do nothing.'

He reached out for me, groping for my hand. 'Marietta, try to understand, try to forgive. It was for both of us. Is it so wrong to want a little of what other people have always had? Think what it would mean to us.'

'I can only think of men, women and children, homeless, starving, with no one to care whether they live or die. I shall write at once to Mr Cameron.'

His expression hardened. He got up. 'Think it over. There's plenty of time. The mail boat does not call here for another week.'

'I shan't change my mind.'

'We'll see.' He took up the candle. 'Shall I light you to bed?'

'No, thank you.'

'Very well.' I took the candle from him and his hand closed over mine. 'Make no mistake, Marietta, I always get what I want in the end. I shall win, you know.'

'Not this time.'

He smiled. 'Goodnight, my love.' His lips brushed my cheek and I shuddered at his touch. Then he went out, leaving me shaken and sick and very much alone.

Chapter Fifteen

ichthyon

I did not realize at first that I was in a trap, that I was at the centre of a conspiracy that had begun from the very moment my letter had come to Glenlochy and been destroyed before it reached my grandfather. For so long I had lived with a dream that it was hard to awaken to the disillusioning reality. Truth stared me in the face and I still struggled against it.

Whether it was due to nervous reaction or whether I had caught a chill from my long walk in the rain, I don't know, but I woke from a disturbed night with aching limbs, a blinding headache and a nausea that would not leave me. Jeannie brought me food that I could not touch. Coll came knocking at my door and I would not answer. I lay in bed with the curtains drawn and fought sickness and an overwhelming sense of betrayal. Feverish and wretched I was haunted by Coll's face when he spoke of Richard. I had pledged myself to marry a man who did not exist. He had turned into a monster who had played a loving game and had deliberately deceived me, tricking me into something to which he knew I would never have willingly consented, and like a fool I had walked right into the net he spread for me.

I tossed on my pillow, fretful and tormented, because it seemed to me then that there was no faith or trust to be found anywhere. First there had been my mother, then Coll, even Richard. In his stern way he had seemed a rock of integrity. I knew now that almost unconsciously I had come to rely on him, to love him . . . I buried my head in my hands. I mustn't let myself think of that. And now if what Coll had said was true, he was just like the others. He had reproached me for betraying my trust

202

and at the same time he was planning to exploit the valley for his own profit.

For three days no one disturbed me and I fought a lonely battle. Then my natural resilience came to my rescue. To lie sick and moaning about the blow that fate had dealt me would help nobody. If I was going to put things right then I must pull myself together. I roused myself. I got up and dressed. I forced myself to drink the tea and eat the boiled egg that Jeannie had brought me.

'That's better,' she exclaimed in relief when she came to fetch my tray. 'That's more like yourself, Miss Marietta. You've been looking so peaky these three days I've not known what to do for the best and them downstairs not caring whether you lived or died, except Mr Coll of course.'

So I did matter to Coll, or was it just that I must not be allowed to die until we were married and Glenlochy and its lands safely his? And why had those others moved into the castle? I had an unpleasant feeling of being surrounded and watched.

I said, 'Is Miss Fiona still here?'

'Aye, she is that and ordering everyone about as if she owned the place. It's not right, Miss Marietta, and so I up and told her. She didn't like it.'

'Never mind, Jeannie, it will be different now when I'm about again, you'll see.'

I had made up my mind. I would go up the valley and talk to Kathryn. It would not be easy but I would swallow my pride. I would confess my folly and ask her advice.

There was no one about when I went downstairs and into the drawing-room. The portrait still hung there. Coll had not had it removed though I had spoken to him about it. I looked at the handsome ruthless face and wondered if that was how Coll saw himself, a man who rode roughshod over everyone who opposed him, who would permit neither humanity nor honour to stand in his way, who would not hesitate even to kill if it would get him what he wanted.

A mist hung over the valley that morning shredded by a light breeze from the sea and I was glad of the clean salt air after the stuffiness of my room. There was a curious stillness as I walked up the track. There were no friendly smiles, no cheerful greetings. The women turned away their faces and called their children to them. I had thought them my friends and now they shunned me. I was conscious of an intense loneliness that no reasoning was able to banish.

Some distance along the track I passed Hamish Kintyre's house. It was larger than the others, stone-built with a flower garden in front, unusual among the people of the glen. I would have walked on but just then he came round the corner of the outhouse carrying a basket of newly dug potatoes and I paused to speak with him.

'Good morning, Mr Kintyre. Is the crop good this year?'

He swung the basket to the ground without looking at me. 'It is well enough, Mistress Gilmour, for what good it will do us.'

I was determined to be cheerful. 'Where is everyone this morning? I have scarcely seen a soul. The beach and the fields are deserted.'

He looked at me with his deep-set eyes. 'And what use would it be to them to dig the fields with the printed notices distributed by Mr Fergusson himself lying on their tables this very morning?'

'Notices about what?'

'Do you need to ask that? Notices to say that since we cannot pay the rents that are asked, then the land is to be taken away from us. By September we must pack what little we have, take our children by the hand and leave the valley. The Chief but two months in his grave and his people scattered like leaves before the wind.'

Surely it was not possible for it all to happen so quickly. 'You must be mistaken. It is not so. The land belongs to me and I shall stop it being taken from you.'

He glanced at me pityingly. 'Ah, you talk bravely but what does a slip of a lass like yourself know of the ways of men? It is your husband who will be acting for you, him up there at the castle, speaking so fair and soft and waiting for the old eagle to die before he plunders his nest.'

'He is not my husband yet.'

'You are hand-fasted, pledged one to the other, isn't

that so? Now if it had been Mistress Kathryn . . . she had
the spirit of her father in her, brave as a lion . . . she'd not
have deserted us.'

'And neither will I. I am going to speak with her now.
You'll see. We will stop it.'

He shook his head. 'You're too late, Mistress. You'll
find no one at the croft nor at the Tige Dubh. She is
gone with the Englishman, she and the child.'

So Kathryn had gone with Richard and without a word,
believing with him that I had betrayed the trust my
grandfather had placed in me. I said helplessly, 'I didn't
know.'

He looked at me curiously, 'Mary carried messages to
the castle when she came to bid me goodbye. They told
her you were sick and could see no one so she left them
for you. Sorry she was to go, and Mistress Kathryn too.
Bitter they were at what is being done.'

Hamish had shouldered his basket and turned away.
Then he swung back, his eyes accusing me, his stilted
English stiff with reproach. 'On the day Mac'Ghille
Mhoire stood up there, bringing you to us from over the
sea, we rejoiced, we took you to our hearts, and so I give
you fair warning. There's some of us who will not go so
easily.'

'Is this a threat, Mr Kintyre?'

'You may take it as you wish, Mistress Gilmour, but we
are men, there is blood in our veins not water. Once we
were willing to shed it for our Chief, but now it will be
for what is ours. You'll not drive us from our fields
and hearth without a fight.'

I watched him go striding down the track but I did
not go back to the castle immediately. I wanted time
to think. Hamish Kintyre meant what he said. If there
was not to be bloodshed, I had to get a letter to Duncan
Cameron as soon as possible, but how? Neil or Murdo
had always taken the letters for collection by the mail
boat . . . supposing Coll made sure that nothing written
by me was included? Already he must have intercepted
the messages Mary had left for me. Had there been one
from Richard? The thought tormented me that he could
have waited for a reply that never came.

I had never felt so keenly how isolated we were at

Glenlochy. Anything could be done here and forgotten before ever it came to the ears of those in authority, and already George Fergusson had been at work, persuading the men and women of the valley to believe the harsh orders to leave came from me, relying on the fact that few of them could spreak more than two or three words of English.

I walked on trying to still my fear, trying to reason with myself. I was Mistress of Glenlochy, surely no one could take that away from me. I was so deep in thought that I had not noticed where I was going until I looked up and saw that I was on the verge of the forest. With sudden determination I plunged into it. I wanted to see the green dell once more in broad daylight. I wanted to rid myself of superstitious fear and see it for what it was, a place where vicious people had deliberately turned harmless age-old customs into something evil. It was there they had tried to kill Richard. Perhaps it was there they had murdered his brother too. I caught my breath, for the first time admitting to myself that Richard could be right.

I came quietly through the trees. The squat black stone was still there, sunlight slanting across it, and it was no longer frightening. It was just an ugly block of granite. I went closer, curious to see what lay in the shallow bowl at the top, and beyond it I saw the two who lay together on the smooth green turf under the shadow of the great oak. There was no mistaking the long black hair, no mistaking the passion that held them in each other's arms. For an instant my eyes blurred. I seemed to see my mother and the stranger in my father's bed, then once more it was Coll and Fiona. I wanted to cry out against them, but my throat choked. I turned and fled back up the path and along the track. How could I have been so blind? It was torture to know that I had never been loved, that it had all been a pretence, all those kisses, all those moments of tenderness were nothing but lies and deceit.

When I reached the castle I went straight to my room. I threw myself on the bed in an agony of tears. My world had crumbled around me. I couldn't face anyone yet. I needed time to pull myself together, to make up my mind what I was going to do.

When Jeannie came to tell me the midday meal was ready, I said, 'I don't want anything to eat.'

'But you must have something, Miss Marietta. You're not sick again, are you?'

'No. I'm just not hungry. Jeannie, please go down and tell Mr Coll that I want to speak to him as soon as the meal is over.'

She looked at me curiously. 'Why? What has happened?'

'Never mind that now. Just do as I ask.'

'Very well, Miss, if you're sure that's what you want.'

When she was gone, I dressed myself carefully, putting on a simple dark dress, brushing my hair until it shone red and glossy, as if somehow that would give me the dignity and strength I needed. Then I went down to the estate room. I seated myself behind the desk and waited. I could hear the roar of the sea under my feet. A long ray of sunlight pierced through the window across the silver ink-stand, the quill pens, the red sealing wax, the letter signed 'Mac'Ghille Mhoire' with a fine flourish. So Coll saw himself as Chieftain already. Well, he was not my husband yet.

He came in jauntily, looking so exactly as he had done when I came to the castle on that first day that for an instant my resolution wavered, then I saw that George Fergusson had followed him and purpose hardened.

I said, 'I would have preferred to speak with you alone.'

'Why? What crime am I supposed to have commited this time?'

The lightness of his tone, the faint smile on Fergusson's face, the vivid memory of those two in the glen that morning, brought my anger to boiling point.

I said, 'I'm not joking. If you want your friend to be here, I don't mind. You can fetch your mother if you wish, Fiona, the servants, the people of the valley, the whole world.'

'Marietta, my dear, what on earth is all this melodrama?' He pulled up a stool and sat facing me across the desk, smiling still though his eyes were wary. 'Go on, I am listening.'

'First of all,' I said, trying to keep my voice level, 'you

will tell your henchman, Mr Fergusson over there, to cancel that notice he has distributed without my knowledge or consent and inform the men and women of the valley that there will be no eviction and that the question of rents will be reconsidered by me before next quarter-day.'

'Anything else?' he said flippantly as if I were a child asking for the moon.

'Yes. You will write immediately to Mr Cameron admitting that you acted without my authority and that any arrangements entered into regarding lease or sale of land are to be cancelled.'

It was George Fergusson who answered. He came to stand behind Coll. 'I wonder if you realize, Miss Gilmour, that it can take three to four weeks for a letter to reach Edinburgh?'

'I am aware of that.'

'And by then a very great deal can have happened.'

'Such as?'

'Surely you have not forgotten. You will be married to Coll by then and after that it will not be you who makes the decisions.'

Now it was here, the moment I had dreaded but which had to be gone through and the veiled insolence in his manner helped me. I looked directly at Coll.

'I was coming to that. I have changed my mind.'

I don't think it had ever occurred to him that he had not complete power over me, that I was not a puppet only too willing to dance at his bidding. He got to his feet. He leaned across the desk.

'You don't mean that. You can't mean it. You must be jesting.'

'I've never been more serious in my life. I am not going to marry you, Coll.'

'Why? Why?' his fist came down heavily on the desk.

'Do you need to ask?'

His face darkened. 'It's because of Richard Wynter, isn't it? It is he who has put you up to this. All along I knew it. He has been working against me, feeding you with lies, making love to you!'

'After what you did to him, I wonder you dare to mention his name. Richard Wynter has nothing to do with it.

He has left the valley. You know that, don't you? It must
have been in the letters that never reached me.'

I saw the glance that passed between them and I knew
I was right. Fergusson took a step forward but Coll waved
him back.

'Leave it to me. I'll deal with this.'

'Then make sure that you do. I've waited long enough.'

'Waited for what, Mr Fergusson?'

He turned to look at me and the bland mask had vanished. It was as if I saw the real man for the first time.

'You will see, Mistress Gilmour. I advise you to listen
to Coll. It will be the worse for you if you don't.'

'Are you threatening me?'

He shrugged his shoulders. 'Please yourself.'

There was no mistaking the menace in his voice and a
tremor of fear ran through me. To hide my disquiet I got
up and moved to the window. The door closed and there
was a momentary silence before I sensed Coll come up
behind me.

I said quickly, 'Please don't touch me.'

'Very well, if that is what you wish. But you must listen
to me. I'm sorry all this has come between us. I tried to
tell you the other night. I wanted to come to you when
you were sick but you locked the door against me. It was
you I was thinking of all the time. Life has been so hard
here for so long. I wanted us to enjoy the good things together. I was jealous of Richard Wynter only because I love
you so much.'

I turned round to face him. 'Do you, Coll, do you? And
what about Fiona?'

'Fiona?'

'Oh don't deny it. I've been blind but now I know.' All
the pent-up feeling burst out in accusation. 'I saw you together this morning, you and she, in the glen . . .'

This time he was taken aback but he made a quick
recovery. 'That meant nothing, nothing at all. A moment
of folly . . . all men are capable of that . . . and Fiona is
free with her favours . . .'

'Don't put the blame on her,' I said contemptuously.
'What did you intend to do? Marry me and keep her as
your mistress?'

'No, no, I swear to you. It would have all been over and done with as soon as you were my wife.'

'I don't believe you. It has been Fiona all along, hasn't it? It was you I saw with her in Edinburgh before ever I came to Glenlochy.'

'In Edinburgh? No, you're wrong . . .'

But I swept on. 'Only you wouldn't marry her because she could bring you nothing whereas I . . . I could give you all you had ever wanted. Poor Fiona, no wonder she has hated me.'

'Don't pity her,' he said viciously. 'Fiona is a witch, a devil, I tell you. She gets her hooks into a man and won't let him go . . . Marietta please . . . please believe me.' He tried to catch hold of my hand but I moved away from him.

'It's no use, Coll. It's finished.'

'Not quite,' and for a moment there flashed across his face the ugly look I had seen once before. 'Not quite. I could make you listen to me.'

'You cannot make me do anything,' I said trying hard to keep myself resolute. 'I could order you to leave the castle now, this evening, you and your mother too, but I won't. I will give you time . . . and money . . .'

'To keep us from starving in the gutter, I suppose. How generous of you! And what am I expected to do? Go down on my knees and thank you? You are not your grandfather, my dear, I don't have to crawl to you as I did to him. I've not risked everything to lose it now. But for you all this would have been mine. I had persuaded the old man. He made his will in my favour after his daughter had made a fool of herself with the Englishman . . .'

'Is that why you killed him?' I said. 'Because he had found out that you and George Fergusson were selling the young men of the valley into slavery and you knew that once he had told my grandfather, he would have had you thrown out of the castle?'

It was a shot in the dark but it went home. 'I was not responsible for what happened to Graham Wynter,' he said sullenly.

'But George Fergusson was, is that it? You knew and you did nothing to prevent it and now he is demanding his price. What kind of bargain did you strike with him?'

'None, I swear it. It is you I want, Marietta, it has always been you,' there was desperation in his voice. 'You must listen to me . . .'

Before I could prevent him, he had seized me in his arms. He was crushing me against him, his mouth seeking mine. Now that I could see it all too clearly, I couldn't endure him even to touch me. I turned away my face and fought to free myself. He let me go but still gripped my wrists.

'Damn you, Marietta, you wanted me once, you know you did. You're mine, you've always been mine.'

'No,' I said, 'no, that's where you're wrong. I belong to no one.'

I jerked myself away and went out of the room, distressed and more than a little afraid but still determined to carry out my resolution. I did not yet realize that I was already as much a prisoner as if I had been chained to the wall in one of the dark cells under the castle.

Chapter Sixteen

❧❦❧

I sat up till dawn that night wrestling with a letter to Duncan Cameron. It sounded so incredibly foolish put into plain words. I wrote and tore it up and began again. How could I have let myself be so tricked? Coll and George Fergusson must have planned this for two years or more, simply waiting for my grandfather to die, knowing it could not be long delayed. My unexpected arrival must have come as an unpleasant shock until that first meeting when Coll knew he had an easy victim and played his part with consummate tact and skill. Over and over again while my pen scratched on, I fought back tears of bitter humiliation, but I must not weaken. If I did, I would be lost.

In the chilly light of the early morning, I folded the letter, sealed it and blew out the candle. Now it was done, I wondered whom I could trust. Once I had thought that Neil was my friend, but now I was not even sure of him. There was Murdo. But the old man had become very frail since my grandfather's death. Then I remembered Hamish Kintyre. There was something strong and unafraid about him. I had felt it from the time he had come to me at the funeral, an utter loyalty to his Chief and clan. But I dare not go to him myself. They would watch me now, I was certain of it. Jeannie must go. She could slip out of the castle unnoticed. I would write a covering note asking him to take the letter to Fort William. I knew there was a constant interchange between the garrison and Edinburgh. If it went in the official postbag, it would be sure of delivery.

Now I had taken the first step, relief flooded through me. I lay down on the bed and slept for a couple of hours so soundly that Jeannie had difficulty in waking me. I knew at once that she had sensed that something was wrong and was very curious.

'They're all talking downstairs, Miss Marietta. They're saying there's been a quarrel between you and Mr Coll.'

'Not a quarrel, Jeannie,' I paused. I didn't want to tell her too much, time enough later. I said carefully, 'I don't think I shall be marrying him after all.'

She sat down plump on the bed. 'I know I oughtn't to say it, but I'm glad. He's a handsome enough gentleman and soft-spoken with it, but I never liked him, not as I liked Mr Wynter, stern though he could be.'

I felt a sharp pang. Jeannie's shrewd eyes had been keener than mine. If only Richard had still been here. It would have been such a comfort to go up to the Tige Dubh. But by now he would be well on his way to Edinburgh and England. I knew now how much I regretted the last quarrel and the bitterness it had left behind it.

I explained to Jeannie what I wanted her to do and she listened eagerly.

'Don't you worry, Miss. I'll make sure no one sees me. I'll go round by way of the beach and I'll slip out now while they're still at breakfast.'

When she was gone, the precious letter hidden in her pocket, I went downstairs determined to go on as I had begun and not allow myself to be persuaded or frightened into submission by either Coll or George Fergusson. I had reckoned without Fiona. She and Ailsa Drummond were talking together in the drawing-room. They stopped immediately I came in. Then Mrs Drummond murmured something and slipped away.

Fiona said nothing. She had a way of remaining still and quiet and yet making you very aware of her presence. The two dogs had come rushing to greet me. It gave me an absurd pleasure that they had become as attached to me as they had been to my grandfather.

Fiona's silence drove me to speak first. I said, 'I am sorry if I seem inhospitable but I should be glad to have the house to myself.'

'Father is not well, I'm afraid,' she said calmly. 'He has been forced to keep to his bed again this morning. Besides Coll has asked us to stay until you are married.'

'In that case you are likely to be here for a very long

time,' I said dryly. 'There has been a change of plan. We are not to be married after all.'

'Oh that!' she snapped her fingers carelessly. 'A lovers' tiff. Coll will soon put a stop to that.'

Something about her cool amused tone enraged me. 'You're wrong,' I exclaimed. 'I have already told Coll. . have no intention of sharing my house with my husband's mistress.'

For an instant her eyes flashed, then she smiled and sauntered slowly towards me. 'So you know. I wondered how long it would be before you guessed. Did you really think that you could take him from me? Coll is like him up there, like Donald Ruadh. He's a man, my dear, he wants something more than your pretty baby ways. What do you know of such things?' She had come so close that her queer seductive perfume was all around me. 'You took from him what was his by right so you have to pay,' she whispered, 'but afterwards you can do what you please . . . run back to your mother in Paris or make eyes at your puppy of an Englishman . . . Coll will have no more use for you and neither will I.'

The insolent contempt on the beautiful face so close to mine stung me to fury. I struck out at it with all my strength. I don't think she expected it. Her hand went to her scarlet cheek, then she flew at me. We were tearing at one another like tiger cats.

'Fiona!' Coll's voice was like the crack of a whip. He came between us forcing us apart. 'Stop it, do you hear, stop it, both of you!'

He threw Fiona away from me so that she stumbled and almost fell. 'I did not start it,' she spat at him. 'It was your pretty little doll there with her fancy French ways. I was only telling her the truth.'

I was shaking now but I made an effort to pull myself together. I turned to Coll, my voice rising in spite of myself. 'I'll not endure this woman in my house a moment longer. She must go now today, I don't care how sick her father is. Get them out of here, get them both out now!'

'Marietta, please listen to me . . .'

'I won't have it, I tell you, I won't . . .'

Fiona watched us, her hands on her hips. 'What do

you expect Coll to do? Drag my father out of his bed in his nightshirt?'

The triumphant look on her face maddened me. I said wildly, 'I'll call Murdo, Tam, the stable boys . . .'

She laughed tauntingly. 'Try, Marietta, just try and see what happens. They'll not dare to lay a finger on me. Here we are and here we intend to stay.'

I swung round on Coll. 'I'm going to my room. I'll not come down again until she has gone, she and her father and George Fergusson. This is my house, mine, mine. Glenlochy will never be yours, never while there is breath left in my body . . .'

I was shouting into his face. I could feel my voice cracking and I could not control it. I ran out and up the stairs and into my bedroom, slamming the door behind me and leaning back against it, panting, my dress torn, my hair hanging around my face. I had never struck anyone in my life and I had been brawling with Fiona like some woman from the streets. I felt sick and degraded and very frightened.

I must get away, now and quickly, but how? On one side lay the sea and on the other the long journey to Fort William over an almost trackless waste of mountain, river and glen through which I could never find my way alone even if I could persuade Neil or Tam to saddle a pony for me. For an instant panic overwhelmed me. I wanted to run out of the castle and go on running. It was several minutes before I could force myself to be calm, to look reasonably at the situation, to persuade myself that Coll and Fiona, George Fergusson and Ailsa Drummond were not demons, but only four ruthless people who could still do nothing against me if I kept my courage high and my resolution strong. I only needed to hold on for a little. Once my letter reached Mr. Cameron, he would act and so long as I held the keys to Glenlochy Castle and its lands I was safe. Coll's one chance of winning them for himself was by marrying me and he would do nothing to endanger that.

Jeannie came back at midday running up the stairs, excited and breathless. 'I saw him and he asked a lot of questions, but he'll take it, Miss Marietta. He'll go off at dawn tomorrow. He says the distance is nothing to him. He has walked it often before and he can do it again.'

It was such a load off my mind that I felt almost light-hearted. Perhaps I was exaggerating. I was letting Fiona's jealous spite assume monstrous proportions. No one locked my door. I was not being held prisoner. I stayed in my room most of that day because I could not trust myself to face Coll or any of them at the dinner or supper table. But the next morning was bright and sunny so Jeannie and I spent a good deal of the day in the walled garden, weeding, hoeing, cutting off dead roses. I discovered a calm among the growing things and I liked the feel of the good dark earth in my hands, earth that was mine, that had been loved and fought for by so many past Gilmours.

It was late that afternoon when Mrs Drummond came into the garden. She said, 'Would you come in, Marietta? Coll has something to show you.'

'Can't he come out to me?'

She looked at me oddly. 'I think you had better do as he asks.'

I got up from my knees, determined not to betray anxiety or fear. I gave my basket to Jeannie and went in through the old tower and along to the estate room. They were all there, Coll, George Fergusson and Fiona. I went in boldly.

'What is it? I've already said I want nothing more to do with any of you.'

George Fergusson held out a letter between finger and thumb. 'Is this yours?'

I saw the name I had written so hopefully. I said in a stifled voice, 'Where did you get it?'

'Hamish Kintyre will not run any more of your errands.'

'He is not dead?'

'Now why should you think that? He met with an accident, that's all. It will keep him to his bed for some time.'

Anger and distress nearly choked me. I said, 'You devils! You have done this, all three of you. He is a good man.'

'Hamish Kintyre is a man with a grievance,' said Coll quietly. 'He has caused nothing but trouble. I told you that before. He needed to be taught a lesson.'

'Just as Graham Wynter needed a lesson, I suppose, so

you murdered him as you tried to murder Richard, and now Hamish . . .'

'Why will you go on fighting me?' he went on with a gentle exasperation as if I were a child battling against some imaginary threat. 'Why do you want to carry the burden of an estate tottering on its last legs? It's absurd. Let it go. You have only to marry me and it will be all over . . .'

'And you will shut me up, drive me out of my mind, throw me aside like so much rubbish while you flaunt abroad with your fancy woman.' The vulgar words poured out and did not seem to belong to me.

Then suddenly Coll leaned forward, pleading, the old Coll that once I had loved so dearly and now knew did not exist. 'Why won't you believe me, Marietta? Why do you listen to Fiona? It is you I love, you and only you . . .'

'Don't lie, it only makes it worse.' I turned away sickened because for an instant the old fascination stirred inside me.

George Fergusson brought his fist down on the desk with a force that startled me. 'Let us have an end to this nonsense,' he said harshly. 'We've let you have your way, Coll, and you've failed. Now it is our turn. Will you tell her or shall I?'

Coll sat back frowning. 'Do as you like,' he said sullenly and in that moment I knew that, strong as he was, he was not the prime mover behind their conspiracy. It was George Fergusson. I had been right all along. I had sensed evil in this man from the first moment and now it was here, the brutality behind the sly smile, the ruthlessness behind the ingratiating manner.

He looked at me for a moment, then he put his hand in his pocket and put something on the table. 'Have you ever seen this before?'

It was the blue phial of digitalis that Kathryn had given me and that I had not seen or even thought of since Coll carried it away in his pocket. Apprehension tightened inside me as Fergusson leaned forward.

'If you refuse to marry Coll, then we will bring an accusation against you of murdering your grandfather.'

'What!' It was so unexpected, it almost robbed me of my breath. I looked from one to the other as they sat there, unsmiling, implacable. 'But it is not true, you know it is not true. I did not even have the phial when he died. Coll took it from me, didn't you, Coll? You must remember the night I thought it was lost and we searched for it together.'

'Did I, Marietta? I remember how we hunted for it and how much you wanted me to leave it with you though I begged you to let me keep it because of the danger.'

'But that's not true,' I said frantically, turning to Fergusson. 'He's lying, you know he is. He put it in his pocket. He took it away with him.'

'It's your word against Coll's,' said Fergusson inexorably. 'On the eve of Sir Alasdair's death, it was you who insisted on giving him his broth.' He raised his hand and beckoned to Mrs Drummond who had been standing just inside the door. 'We have a witness. Ailsa Drummond will swear how you insisted on taking it from her against her will. Murdo too, he was there. He heard the quarrel between you.'

'But Murdo knew why. It was because grandfather didn't want her in his room . . . that was the only reason . . . and I did not wish him to be upset.'

'And who will believe that? No, my dear, you wanted him dead. You took the broth and made sure it was well dosed with the drug before you fed it to him because you knew that in his weak condition it would inevitably bring about his end before the morning.'

Suddenly it was all clear to me. I pointed a shaking finger at Ailsa Drummond. 'It was you, wasn't it? You put the digitalis in that soup because you hoped he would die before he changed his will, but he didn't, did he? He beat you all.' I swung around on them triumphantly. 'Why should I want him dead when it would only have meant that Glenlochy would have gone to Coll?'

Fiona's eyes were fixed on me with an intensity that sent a cold shiver down my spine. Coll was staring down at his hands. Fergusson leaned back smiling.

'Oh, you were very clever. Neil has told us what happened.'

'Neil!' I exclaimed.

'Yes, you didn't think of him, did you? It was Neil whom your grandfather sent for Duncan Cameron after you had worked on him, urging him, persuading him to change his will that night and when it was all over and done with, then you fed him the broth you had prepared and left him to die alone, an old man trusting to the granddaughter he loved.'

They were so calm, so deliberate, I felt like a fly struggling in the web of some monstrous spider. 'It doesn't matter what accusation you make, you can't prove any of it,' I said falteringly.

'We could have your grandfather's body exhumed, we could insist on a post-mortem—there is enough poison in his body to kill half a dozen men. Think how it will sound before the procurator-fiscal. A poor and friendless young woman who has quarrelled with her mother and her stepfather runs away from Paris and comes to Scotland. She finds herself an heiress if the inconvenient old man dies quickly, an heiress who can sell off the land left to her in trust and have all the riches she has wanted all her life, and the faithful servants, broken-hearted and deceived, come forward unwillingly to bear witness against her.'

It sounded horribly plausible, horribly real. I knew nothing of Scottish law, nothing of what it could do to me, but I could see myself standing in the dock, my grandfather's body torn from the grave, the shock and distress among the people of the valley who had accepted me and taken me to their hearts.

Coll said suddenly, 'None of this need happen, Marietta, if you are sensible. You have only to marry me and it will all be gone like a puff of smoke, and we will be happy, I swear we will.'

'Stop, stop! Don't go on!' I buried my face in my hands. 'Let me be. I must have time, time to think . . .'

'You've had time enough,' said George Fergusson grimly, but Coll had risen to his feet. He put a hand on the other man's shoulder.

'Let her be. You've said enough for one day. Tomorrow she will feel differently.'

'I won't be forced,' I looked wildly around at them. 'I'll not be threatened. If you do, I'll tell them what I know about Graham Wynter, about what you did to Richard . . . I am not friendless . . .'

'The case of Captain Wynter's suicide was closed long ago and the honourable Richard Wynter is on his way to England. It will be long before he cares to risk his precious neck in the valley again,' said Fergusson contemptuously.

'I will not listen any more. Do what you like to me. You'll never break me down!' Brave words! And about as much use as beating my fist against a stone wall! I turned away from them and they let me go, sure of themselves because they knew there was no way in which I could escape.

Up and down my room I paced while George Fergusson's threat hammered itself into my brain until my head throbbed and my courage slowly drained away. They had enmeshed me in a tissue of lies so that everything I did, every word I said only turned to my guilt. I could see the Scottish judge listening to the frantic young woman, the outsider, half French, shouting accusations at those who had served her grandfather loyally for more than twenty years. Why should he believe her rather than them? The inevitability of it sickened me. Only one thing puzzled me. Why had they not forced me into marriage before this? There was only one explanation. It had to be done legally and Mr McPhail was the only one who had the right to marry and register a marriage. Was he really sick or had he refused? I could not believe that the little gnome-like man with his transparent honesty could be a party to what was being planned.

I stopped still in my pacing. What if I went to him now, spoke to him, enlisted him on my side? It might be worth trying. I knew he slept on the other side of the castle. Buoyed up with hope I looked up and down the passage and then ran down it, across the top of the staircase and down the further corridor. At the door I stood with my hand poised. Should I knock or should I just go in? While I paused, uncertain, the door opened and Fiona was there, half smiling, saying nothing and I knew that to force my way past her would be useless. The old man lived in fear of her. He would do nothing with her in the room. I turned and walked away down the corridor hearing behind me the mock of her laughter until the door closed.

The hours crawled by and in the evening Kirsty came

knocking at my door. 'Would ye be wanting supper, Mistress Marietta?'

I had eaten nothing all day. It was no use starving. I said, 'Bring me something on a tray. Some milk and biscuits will do.' Then a frightening thought struck me. 'Where is Jeannie?'

The girl giggled. 'Locked safe upstairs. Jeannie has a way with the boys so Master Coll says, so she's been shut in to teach her decent manners in a decent household.'

How dare he say such a thing! Jeannie, that prim little body who had slapped the face of the gardener's boy for a saucy look, who would have died rather than 'make herself cheap' as she put it. My blood boiled with anger.

'She's not hurt, is she?'

'Nay, mistress, she is well enough but hammering on the door like a mad creature.' The girl giggled again. I had never liked Kirsty and her sluttish ways.

It was sometime during the short Highland night that I made up my mind to get out of the castle and make my way to Fort William. Better to die on the moor than be forced into marriage with a man I had grown to loathe and see everything that I loved destroyed before my eyes . . . even if they let me live to see it. For the first time I faced the thought of death. If they had not scrupled to murder Graham Wynter, they would not hesitate at doing the same to me when I had served their turn. The thought added wings to my feet.

I put on my riding dress, pulled on my thick boots, put together what money I had in my pocket and looked cautiously out of the door. Everything was very quiet. I crept along the passage and down the stairs to the door that led out into the courtyard and the walled garden. One of the dogs barked and whined. I had forgotten they slept in the downstairs room. I stood still but nothing stirred and all was quiet again.

In the grey chilly light of dawn I made my way to the stables. Some of the boys slept nearby and I dare not wake them. There was little light inside the stable and I fumbled over the saddle while the pony shifted snuffling against me. I had lifted the saddle on to his back when the door opened. I swung round and saw Neil standing there.

His face looked pale and his eyes were red and puffy as if he had been crying.

I said urgently, 'Neil, you must help me. You know what they are trying to do to me. Please, please, help me to saddle the pony and get away from them.'

'No, I can't, Marietta, I daren't.' He looked miserable but determined. 'It would be no use anyway. Fiona would know and have you brought back.'

'Fiona, Fiona!' I repeated in exasperation. 'Are you all in dread of her? Is she God that you have to run at her bidding?'

'Not God,' he muttered, 'not God but something worse. You don't understand, Marietta, she and George Fergusson between them, they would make us suffer for it, both of us. Why did you come here? Why didn't you stay away when I warned you?'

He was nearly weeping and it made me angry. 'Oh for heaven's sake, why speak of that now? Go back to the castle if you're so afraid and leave me to do what I must.'

I began to buckle the straps under the pony's girth and suddenly he was beside me, frantically trying to help.

'Quickly, quickly!' he urged. 'We must hurry.'

But with all our haste it was already too late. I don't know whether I'd been heard leaving the house or whether the dog had betrayed me, but the door creaked open and Coll strode in.

He said sharply, 'Neil!' The boy turned to him, white and shivering. 'What the devil do you think you're doing? Get back to the house and stay there.'

Neil looked piteously at me and scurried away. Coll leaned against the doorpost with a grim little smile. 'Why kick against it, Marietta? You will have to come to it in the end.'

I turned on him then. 'I'm a Gilmour and we don't give in easily. You ought to know that or did your mother cheat my grandfather about that too?'

I had touched him on a raw spot. 'You little bitch, why must you provoke me?' He seized me roughly by the shoulder pulling me out of the stable and marching me back to the castle and up the stairs. He thrust me inside my room.

'I never wanted this. You have brought it on yourself.

If you won't stay here of your own accord, then we shall have to make sure that you do.'

He went out and slammed the door. I heard the heavy key turn in the lock with a feeling of a despair. Now there was no escape.

Chapter Seventeen

The next few days had the eerie sensation of a nightmare from which there was no awakening. I was shut in my room and the only person I saw was Ailsa Drummond. She brought me food. She brought me water to wash with and took away the slops, but to all my questions as to what was to happen to me, she turned the same silent withdrawn look. At first I thought desperately of escape, but the windows on one side of the room opened out on to the inner courtyard and on the other there was only a narrow slit, no more than a foot wide, that looked straight down the castle wall into the sea. And even if I did get away, what was to prevent them bringing their lying accusation against me?

Confinement began to tell on me. My imagination invented strange fantasies. I started at every sound. Sometimes I heard footsteps outside and hammered on the door in a frenzy. Once I thought I heard Coll's voice followed by Fiona's rich sensual laugh and it turned me sick. I began to believe that the food they brought me had some kind of drug in it. Whether it was really so I don't know, but my head ached and my limbs felt so heavy that sometimes I could scarcely drag myself off the bed and I suffered from monstrous dreams . . . dreams of high walls from which I was falling . . . falling into darkness. I made up my mind to eat nothing but the oaten bread and a little cheese and I drank only water from my pitcher.

On the evening of the third day when Mrs Drummond came as usual to take my tray of untouched food, she said, 'What's the point of starving yourself? It will make no difference.' Then she looked directly at me. 'What's wrong with Coll? Isn't he good enough for you?'

'You know that is not the reason.'

I turned away from her and she came up behind me. 'You wanted him at first, didn't you? Do you think I don't know when a woman wants a man? It was in your face whenever he came near you. You're not so cool as you pretend with your "don't touch me" manner.'

I walked away from her humiliated because there was a truth in what she said that I did not want to remember. 'Please don't talk about it. My mind is made up.'

'Why are you so obstinate? Coll has it all, hasn't he? The good looks, the Gilmour charm, the Gilmour passion.' Her voice was low and excited as if she were pleading with me. 'I remember the first time I saw his father, tall and handsome he was, and a taking way with him that was hard to resist though I was a beauty then, I can tell you, and more than one man had wanted me, but none like him. In Edinburgh it was. I was in service at the White Hart and he came there one day, a Highland gentleman like no one I had ever seen before, his hair fiery red still though he was twice my age . . . the other girls laughed at me . . .'

Unwillingly I turned towards her. 'Twice your age? But I thought it was Andrew Gilmour . . .'

Her eyes came round to me, dark and smouldering. 'Andrew? Why should I look at a slip of a lad like that? It was Mac'Ghille Mhoire himself who was Coll's father . . .'

'My grandfather?' I stared at her, not wanting to believe and yet knowing it was true.

'Yes, your grandfather,' she said triumphantly, 'though he tried to deny it when I brought my boy to him. He had aged by then . . . his three sons dead as he believed, his estates half ruined by the English. "I've brought you an heir," I told him, but he'd not acknowledge him. He shouted abuse at me. He'd always been a proud man, too proud to acknowledge a bastard whose mother was only a maidservant though he was glad enough to take me to his bed.' An intense bitterness corroded her voice. 'He brought the boy up and he demanded his price but I wore him down. He gave in at last when he knew he'd not many years to live. He made his will . . . then you came and suddenly everything was for you, everything I had worked for and I was no more than the dirt under his

feet.' She was shaking me, her breath hot on my face.
'Don't you think you owe it to Coll? Isn't it his right?
You robbed him of what he'd earned by twenty years of
slavery to an old man's whims . . . But that meant nothing
to you, did it? Hot for him one minute and cold as ice the
next, driving him crazy with your cursed Englishman and
much good he has done you . . .'

'Stop it, stop it!' I shouted at her. 'It's not that at all.
You've got it all wrong.' I turned away sickened at what
she had just told me. 'Leave me alone, please leave me
alone.'

'Oh I'll leave you alone all right, but they'll not wait
much longer. Tomorrow you'll be married to him whether
you like it or not.' She drew herself up. 'It's we who have
the whip hand now and you'll dance to our tune.'
The door slammed and the heavy key turned.

That night and the next day were the worst that I ever
remember. I could not seem to think rationally. Pity for
Coll was mingled with loathing. I was appalled at what was
going to happen to me and very afraid. Mrs Drummond's
revelation was only an added horror. It was monstrous that
I should be forced into marriage with my father's half-
brother. Did Coll know who his real father was? He
must have done but he had not allowed it to stand in his
way.

The hours dragged by and it was about six o'clock on
the following evening when Mrs Drummond opened my
door.

'They are waiting for you,' she said.

'I'm not coming.'

'Do you want them to come and drag you down?'

It was with a feeling of utter hopelessness that I let her
grip my wrist and lead me down the stairs and into the
drawing-room. They were all there, all except Neil. God
knows where he had hidden himself. Mr McPhail stood beside Coll, looking old and sick and wretched. I broke
away from Mrs Drummond and threw myself at his feet.

'Don't let them do this to me, Mr McPhail, please don't.
You're a Minister of God, you cannot see me married
against my will. You must help me, you must!' I was clinging to his knees, pleading with him. I saw him look un-

easily at Fiona. She took a step nearer to him and he put his trembling hands on my shoulders trying to raise me.

'Don't distress yourself, my child. It will be better for you, really it will. You are distracted now, you don't know what you are saying, but Coll will take care of you and then you will recover.'

I knew then how they had persuaded him. They had told him that I was half out of my mind and to comfort himself, he had tried to believe it.

We went through the farce of a marriage service. 'Will you Marietta Jeanne, take Colin Alasdair . . .'

'No, no, no!' I repeated desperately but I might not have spoken for all the difference it made. It continued to the bitter end and Coll kissed my cheek and he slipped the ring on my finger. We might have been the happiest couple who were ever wed.

I wondered afterwards if it was Fiona or George Fergusson who added the last touch to that macabre ceremony. Food and wine had been laid out on the table. I was forced to sit with them while they ate and drank jesting with one another as if it were the merriest of marriage feasts. Only Mr McPhail sat silent and distressed.

Coll piled food on my plate. 'Eat up, my dear. Mother says you've scarcely touched anything for days. You must build up your strength.'

Sickened I thrust it away from me. George Fergusson poured the champagne and got to his feet.

'A toast,' he said with a twist of his thin lips. 'A toast to Coll and his lovely bride.'

They took their glasses and raised them. Coll pulled me up to stand beside him pushing the fine Venetian goblet into my hand. I looked around at my tormentors and then into the face of my husband. He stood there, flushed and handsome, happy now that he had got what he wanted, and all enchantment drained away. I saw only the ruthlessness that had murdered Graham Wynter, had tried to kill Richard and sought to turn a peaceful valley into a place of desolation and mourning. It was an obscene mockery of that moment barely three months before when I had stood shy and proud beside my grandfather.

'Is this what you call Highland honour?' I said bitterly. I hurled my glass into the hearth and fled out of the room.

· I threw myself on my bed too sick at heart even to weep. The fight was over. I had lost my battle and at that moment I only wanted to die. How long I lay there I don't know. I think that after a while out of sheer weariness I must have dozed a little. All I know is that I was suddenly sitting up and listening to footsteps coming along the passage. Panic sent me racing to the door before I remembered there was no key on my side. Then it opened and Coll was standing there, swaying a little, the light from the candlestick in his hand flickering over his flushed face, the hair tousled, the shirt open at the throat. I saw at once that he was very drunk. I backed away from him.

'Don't be afraid,' he mumbled thickly. He came in, kicking the door shut. I retreated as far as the window and he came after me putting the candlestick down on the table beside the bed. The draught from the open window blew out the flame and the room was plunged into darkness.

I tried to slip around him and reach the door but he caught me by the arm and swung me against him.

'Don't, Coll, don't please!'

'What's the matter? Is it Richard Wynter you want? Well, he's gone, my dear, I made sure of that and good riddance! It's I who am your husband.'

I fell back against the bed and he was on top of me, his arms around me, his mouth on mine. I fought him wildly but he was stronger than I. He lifted me on to the bed. He tore open the neck of my dress and kissed my throat.

'Darling, darling,' he was muttering. 'I've wanted you for so long and now you're mine, mine at last.'

It was horrible because in a way I believe he meant it. I think at that moment he did love me because I had given him what he wanted more than anything else in the world, but all I could think of was Fiona, of what he had done to Richard, of the lies he had told me. He was forcing himself on me, smothering me with kisses and I struggled desperately. I could smell the wine on his breath and my head swam. I flung out my arm to try and free myself and my hand touched the candlestick on the table. My fingers closed round the heavy brass base. Hardly realizing what I was doing, I hit him on the side of the head. His grip slackened. He slumped to one side. I dropped the candlestick and scrambled away from him intent only on escape.

I snatched up my father's plaid from the chest and flung it around my torn dress. Then I was running along the passage and down the stairs. I think I had a crazy notion that I might be able to get out through the walled garden.

The castle was pitch dark. I stumbled in my soft slippers and in my terror scarcely noticed where I was going. Instead of the garden entrance I realized I was in the corridor leading to the old tower. The door to the estate room was wide open. A candelabra burned on the table and silhouetted against it were George Fergusson and Fiona. I stood still, gripped by a memory of the old house in the Canongate and the two clasped in each other's arms. Even in my distraction a thread of pity flashed across my mind. They were tricking Coll just as they had tricked me.

Then George Fergusson looked up and saw me. 'By God, the little bride is running away from her husband already!' He began to laugh. 'What have you done with Coll?'

'I think . . . I think I might have killed him.'

'What!' Fiona spun round staring at me, her hair wild, her eyes gleaming. 'Is that true?'

'Would it matter to you if I had?'

Fergusson was still laughing. 'She's done nothing of the sort. Have you never seen a man drunk before, Mistress Marietta?'

There was something inexpressibly vulgar about him as if all restraint, all pretence of gentility had vanished. I turned to run but before I could take more than a step, he had caught me and flung me back into the room.

'Oh no, you're not running away, not just yet. We've not done with you yet, my lady. Besides Coll wouldn't like it, would he, Fiona?'

'I will tell him,' I said wildly. 'If you keep me here, I will tell him . . . he'll know everything about you both. If he finds out, you will get nothing from him, nothing at all, either of you.'

Fergusson snapped his fingers. 'Fiddlesticks! He wouldn't dare. You go back upstairs to him like a good little girl. Go back to your husband. He's yours now whether you like it or not, for better or for worse . . .'

They were mocking me deliberately, but Fergusson still held me firmly by the arm. I fought him fiercely with a strength I never knew I possessed. I dragged myself away but Fiona was at the door before me and threw me back. In the shadowy light of the candles we were playing a deadly game of blind man's bluff. I was being driven between them, thrown from one to the other and they laughed at me until I fell against the table. Quick as a flash I seized the heavy candelabra in both hands and raised it.

'Stop her!' shouted Fergusson. 'Put the damned thing down, you little fool!'

But I was beyond reason. In a frenzy I hurled it into the beautiful hateful face in front of me. Fiona dodged and it went spinning across the room. I thought I saw a lick of flame as I ran for the door. Then my feet seemed to give way under me. I was falling, falling into a darkness that never seemed to end.

I think that temporarily I must have lost consciousness because at first I couldn't imagine what had happened or where I was. Realization came slowly. I was shut into a blackness so thick that it could almost be felt. I stretched out a tentative hand and touched a wall of rock running with damp and icy cold. Pebbles crunched under my feet, water ankle-deep soaked through my thin shoes. There was a strong smell of the sea and rotting seaweed. I was in the pit where those early Gilmours, my own ancestors, had thrown their prisoners and presently the tide would come creeping up the shore and slowly, inexorably, fill it, rising higher and higher until I drowned. Sheer terror gripped me and I began to shiver. I lost all control. I screamed for help, hammering uselessly on the stone walls of my prison until I knew it was hopeless and sank down exhausted, my hands bruised and bleeding. I would never escape, never. I would stay there till death overcame me. I huddled myself into the wet plaid and gave myself up to despair.

I have no idea of how long I had been there, staring into darkness when I suddenly noticed something. Faintly at first, then more and more clearly, the walls took shape around me. I was in a rough hewn cave that narrowed at one end. Light was filtering through a long slit, gradually becoming brighter and brighter as I watched. Over the years the incessant pounding of the sea must have worn away the rock. Hope stirred inside me. If I could only squeeze myself through, then I might not drown after all, only I would have to be quick. I did not know whether the tide was on the turn or already racing up the beach. I was bruised and stiff with cold but fear lent me strength. The opening began about a foot from ground level and it was very narrow, but peering through it I saw that it led into a further cave and I remembered how weeks ago I had looked up from the shore and seen the dark hollow beneath the castle wall.

My foot slipped as I climbed and one of my shoes jerked off. I bent down to pick it up and saw something gleam among the sand and pebbles. It was a large silver badge in the shape of a brooch, a brooch that might have fastened a plaid. I stared at it in my hand and wondered if this was how Graham Wynter had died. Had he too been in this pit, stunned perhaps or believed dead? Had he gone this way before me and drowned as he tried to swim ashore? Was that going to happen to me? For an instant it seemed too great a risk to take, then I drew a deep breath, dropped the badge into the pocket of my skirt and squeezed myself through the rocky opening, feeling it tear at my thin dress and graze my skin before I fell to my knees on the sandy floor of the little cave. With a surge of hope I saw the blue-green of the sea and sky that I had thought never to see again.

I crawled to the edge and looked down. There was a sheer drop of at least twenty feet without a single foothold and my courage nearly failed me. The sea was already lapping at the base of the rocks and rising rapidly. It was a cool blustery morning and the waves hurled themselves below me in a flurry of creamy foam. There was a curious pink glow on the water but I thought nothing of it then. A seagull swooped past me into the cave and I shrank back terrified, but the moment had come. It was now or never. I pushed myself to the verge, held my breath and let myself fall. The water closed over my head. It was icy cold. Terror engulfed me, my ears thudded, I was suffocating . . . then I struggled to my feet. Pain immediately shot up my leg but I was lucky. I had fallen on sand and the water was no more than waist-deep. Coughing and choking I gritted my teeth against the agony of my leg and groped along the edge of the rock. The powerful drive of the water sucked at me and then threw me back against the wall. It was not really far but it seemed endless and again and again I longed to let go and allow the sea to take me where it willed. At last I rounded the corner and could see the long stretch of the shore. I staggered through the surf until I was free of the waves and then fell exhausted on the wet sand.

It was the noise that aroused me. A crackling roar louder than the beat of the sea at my back. I crawled further up the beach and rolled over. With a mounting horror I saw that one part of the castle was on fire. Flames shot up into the sky in a shower of sparks. Thick smoke curled and eddied in the strong wind. Dimly I remembered the fallen candelabra, the touch of fire. How long ago was it? Two hours, three . . . ? I struggled to my feet, tried to walk and collapsed again. I began to crawl painfully through the sandy shingle. Now I could see the causeway and hear the shouting. Everyone in the valley seemed to be crowded there, but I was still too far off to see what was happening.

With agonizing slowness I dragged myself across the beach. No one saw me. They were too occupied with the fire. I could see now that the whole central part of the castle was blazing but the stone tower had resisted the flames. The causeway was high here, more than seven feet. At its base were broken rocks, green and slippery. The pain of my ankle was so excruciating that it was torture to move. The rough stone tore at me and my hands slid on the slimy seaweed as I tried to pull myself along. I sank down on the beach weeping in helpless frustration. Then suddenly there was commotion. Someone had burst through the men standing near the edge of the path.

'Where is Marietta? For God's sake, where is Marietta?'

Unbelievably it was Richard. I thought I must be dreaming but it was he. I could not mistake that lean dark face. He was arguing fiercely with Hamish Kintyre. Then Coll was there, his shirt half torn off, his face streaked with the smoke of the fire. Richard seized hold of him.

'For Christ's sake, where is Marietta? What have you done with her, you damned murderer?'

Coll waved his arm to the castle and Richard thrust him aside. 'She must still be there. I'm going in.'

I cried out then, but only a croak came out of my throat. No one heard me against the roar of the fire and the pounding of the tide as it raced up the shore. It was like watching a scene in a nightmare when your limbs are paralysed and your cries go unheeded. Helplessly I watched the struggle between the two men. I heard Coll shout, 'She is my wife. Don't you understand? She's mine, mine!'

He flung Richard away from him so violently that he fell to his knees. Fiona had appeared, her dress in disorder, her hair hanging around her face. She was clinging to Coll's arm.

'It's too late. What does she matter? Let her go!'

'You bitch!' he snarled at her. 'You damned bitch!' He tore himself away from her and went running towards the tower.

I was screaming now, screaming to him to stop. I was clawing at the stone wall of the causeway, tears running down my face, my hands bleeding. Then with a sudden fierce roar a sheet of flame leaped up and engulfed the inner side of the tower.

I had loved and hated him and he had gone into an inferno to try and save me. A sick horror took me by the throat. I let myself fall on the rocks. The waves reached me and lapped all around me and I no longer cared.

A long time afterwards I thought I heard Richard's voice but I did not raise my head. Gentle hands were lifting me. I cried out once at the pain and then I let myself sink into merciful oblivion.

Chapter Eighteen

I don't really remember anything very clearly until I opened my eyes and found myself lying between crisp linen sheets in a small room with whitewashed walls and a high peaked ceiling. A face was bending over me, a familiar face with freckles and a snub nose.

'Jeannie!' I exclaimed. 'Oh Jeannie, I'm so glad to see you,' and stupidly I began to cry.

'There, there, Miss Marietta, don't take on. You're quite safe now, it's all over.'

'Where am I?'

'Mr Wynter had you brought back to the Tige Dubh and me too. He's been that worried about you. We couldn't think how you came to be on the beach and in such a state too, soaked through to the skin. What did they do to you, Miss Marietta?'

But I could not find the words to explain, not yet. Instead I said, 'Jeannie, what happened to . . .?'

'We all of us got out of the castle even the dogs, all except . . .'

All except Coll. I turned away my head and could not prevent the helpless tears running down my face.

'Don't you fret now, Miss, really you mustn't. I knew there was something wrong when that Kirsty locked me up, giggling like a mad thing she was . . .'

'Please, Jeannie, not now . . .'

'No, that's right. Perhaps it's for the best after all. Now don't you talk. You take a few mouthfuls of this nice broth and then when you're feeling better, Mr Wynter will come and tell you about everything.'

I ached with weariness. My hands were lacerated. I was covered with bruises and though my damaged ankle had been strapped up, there was a dull persistent throb of pain.

I wanted only to shut my eyes and put the last terrible week out of my mind, but try as I would, I could not forget the flames shooting up in the sky, the devouring roar of the fire and Coll running, running . . . Against all reason I was obsessed with guilt. It was I who had failed. It had all sprung from my own stupidity in allowing myself to be deceived. Even the fire had been my fault. I could not banish that last horrible scene in the estate room, the terror, the overturned candles, the licking flames. I slept at last but my dreams were disturbed and I awoke feverish and unrefreshed.

I did not see Richard until the following afternoon when Jeannie came running in, bustling agitatedly around the room. 'Mr Wynter says do you feel well enough to see him for a moment?'

'I suppose so.'

I had been lying in a half doze all the morning. Jeannie hastily shook up my pillows and smoothed the coverlet. She brought me a mirror while she brushed my hair. She had managed to salvage some of her own clothes from the fire. I was wearing one of her plain cambric nightgowns buttoned to the neck and my hair hung dank and lifeless. I stared dully at my pallid face with the dark stains under the eyes and did not care. I let her take the glass away from me and huddled into the shawl she put around my shoulders as Richard knocked and came in. He stood just inside the door and I thought his face had a grim unfriendly look.

'How do you feel?'

'Quite well, thank you.'

'And the ankle?'

'A little painful.' We were stiff and awkward with each other. 'I must thank you for bringing me here and Jeannie too. I thought you were going to England.'

'So I was. Janet and Kathryn are on their way to Laverstoke now. I decided to come back.'

'Why?'

He avoided the question. He came towards the bed and held out his hand. 'Jeannie found this in the pocket of your dress. May I ask where you found it?'

I stared down at the silver badge. It brought back vividly the nightmare hours that I was trying so hard to forget. I said slowly, 'It was in the dungeon under the castle. I saw it lying there when I fell into it.'

'Fell? Why should you fall?'

I buried my face in my hands. 'Please, please . . . I don't want to talk about it.'

'I'm sorry but I must know. If you like we'll leave it and I'll come back later when you are feeling stronger.'

'No, it's all right.' It had to be told so the sooner it was done the better.

He looked from the brooch to me. 'I know this well. It is Graham's regimental badge. Where is this dungeon?'

'It's under the tower where prisoners were kept in the old days,' I said reluctantly. 'When the tide comes in, the sea fills it but there is a gap in the rocks.'

'And that is where they threw Graham. Was he dead or alive?'

'I don't know,' I said unhappily, 'I don't know. I think he found out about the men being sold into slavery and threatened to tell my grandfather and so . . .'

'And so to silence him they thrust him into the pit and left him to drown. Who was it, Marietta, who?'

'George Fergusson and . . .'

'And Coll?'

'Yes.'

There was a pause before he said incredulously, 'You knew this and yet you still married him?'

I wanted to explain, to tell him what they had done to me, but the grim look on his face and my own pride kept me silent. He had warned me and I had flouted his warning. I turned away my head.

He straightened himself. 'Fergusson has taken good care to disappear and . . .'

'And Coll is dead.' I swallowed the involuntary sob in my throat.

'Yes.'

'What are you going to do?'

He was staring down at the brooch in his hand. 'What can I do? It was not the people of the valley who murdered him. Kathryn was right.' He looked up and met my eyes. 'I'm sorry if I have distressed you,' he went on more gently. 'Rest now and don't worry about anything. Plenty of time when you are feeling better. Tell Jeannie if there is anything you want and I'll try to get it for you.'

'Thank you.'

He touched my hand, nodded to Jeannie and went out of the room.

But rest was just what I could not do. He blames me, I thought, because I am a Gilmour he blames me in some way for his brother's death and I was angry at the injustice and at the same time wretchedly unhappy. There was so much to be done and yet I could not rouse myself. I lay there day after day taking refuge in sickness. Jeannie told me that one or other of the villagers came every day with little gifts; a few eggs, a handful of fresh baked oatcakes, a basket of raspberries, a fine salmon. I was touched by their loyalty and yet still could not face up to the responsibilities that had fallen on my shoulders. My dream had been brutally shattered and I was floundering in a deep sea of depression with nothing to hold on to, no anchor to which I could cling.

It was more than a week before I could put foot to the ground and even then my ankle was still painful. I had nothing to wear but a cotton gown belonging to Jeannie. She giggled as she hooked me into it.

'I'll have to take a tuck in it, you've grown so thin, Miss Marietta.'

It was a lavender print with a white muslin collar. I looked at myself in the mirror. Jeannie had washed and brushed my hair but my face was still pale and my eyes looked out of bruised hollows. It was not surprising that Richard had done no more than knock at my door each day and ask how I was.

It was a warm evening in late August when I ventured downstairs for the first time. It was after supper and I was feeling restless. I knew there were books in the sitting-room and thought I might fetch one, anything to distract my thoughts. I had seen Richard ride out earlier and the house was very still as I went slowly down the stairs.

I opened the door quietly. The room was half in shadow and it was a moment before I saw him. He was sprawled in one of the armchairs, a brandy glass in his hand, and in the glow of the fire his face had the haunted look I had seen long ago in Edinburgh. I would have gone out again but he must have heard the door. He stirred and sat up.

'Is that you, Jeannie.'

'No.' I hesitated. 'I came down to find a book to read.'

He got to his feet. 'Wait a moment. I'll strike a light.' He held a taper to the fire and put it to the candles on the mantelpiece. Then he turned to me: 'Come in. There is not much choice, I'm afraid, but there are a few books Janet left behind. I'm glad to see you out of bed at last. It's the only way, you know. Pull yourself together. Face up to things.'

I turned to the books, picking one at random, nettled by his tone. 'Do you think I have been shirking?'

'I wouldn't say that, but it is fatally easy. Believe me, I speak from experience. A couple of years ago I lay flat on my bed with only one thought in my head, to shoot myself and have done with it, but self pity doesn't help. Life has a way of going on in spite of shattered limbs, smashed careers and broken hearts.'

He thought I was grieving for Coll. Perhaps in a way I was but not for the reason he believed.

'You need not worry about me,' I said. 'I'll not be a burden to you much longer. I've been thinking while I've been lying in bed. I shall go back to France.'

'To your mother?' he sounded surprised. 'Do you intend to leave Glenlochy? What about the valley? What about the people here?'

'Mr Cameron will look after them for me. He will find a manager for the estate.'

'Another like George Fergusson?' he said dryly. 'So . . . at the first setback the queen abandons her kingdom and runs away to lick her wounds. Shame on you! I did not think you such a coward.'

'You don't understand.' I was stung to indignation by his criticism. 'How could you?'

'True. I'm only one of those damned English, not a Highland gentleman with charming manners and a delicate sense of honour!' The bitterness in his voice surprised me. He went on abruptly, 'I am going away for a few days. I'm riding north tomorrow and taking Neil with me.'

'Neil?' I stared at him. I knew that Mr McPhail and Fiona had returned to their house. That was one of the things that I dreaded having to deal with and I had assumed that Neil had gone with them.

'Yes, Neil. It was he who came here to fetch me on the night of the fire. He is wretchedly unhappy, poor boy, and he doesn't want to return home.'

'Why should you take an interest in Neil?'

He raised his eyebrows. 'Why not? Graham liked the boy. He has come every day to ask after you. He is afraid you are angry with him.'

'No, I'm not angry.'

'Good. I'll tell him. I'm leaving James behind. He will take care of you and Jeannie while I'm away. Then if you still wish to leave Glenlochy, I shall be happy to escort you to Edinburgh.'

'Thank you, but I wouldn't dream of troubling you.'

'No trouble,' he said coolly. 'I have to see Duncan Cameron myself. Won't you come and sit down by the fire? Make yourself comfortable.'

'No, thank you.' I turned towards the door.

'You're forgetting your book.' He came after me, holding it out.

I took it reluctantly. Our fingers met and he took my hand in his for a moment. 'Don't do anything foolish. Take care of yourself till I come back.'

'I will. Goodnight.'

I went back to my room and threw the book on the bed, furiously angry with him. How dare he attack me? What did he know of the agony I had gone through? I still could not forget Coll's brutal assault. I was still haunted by feelings of degradation and guilt. And yet, despite my anger, the astringency of his criticism did me good. It steadied me. Reluctantly I admitted to myself that he was right. I had been wallowing in self pity. It was time I lifted myself out of it.

A few days after he had ridden away I came down one morning and the two dogs came bounding in from the garden to greet me. They leaped up at me, barking joyously, licking my face, and I was extravagantly pleased to see them.

'Mr Kintyre brought them,' said Jeannie. 'He has been

caring for them since the fire. He is very anxious to speak with you.'

'Next time he comes, tell him I shall be glad to see him.'

'He told me something else,' she said hesitantly.

'What was that?'

'Miss Fiona has left the valley.'

So she had made her choice. She had gone to join George Fergusson. I should never have to see her again. It was like a huge weight being lifted off my shoulders. It seemed the sun shone brighter and the very air smelled cleaner and sweeter because of it.

As my ankle grew stronger, I took longer and longer walks and the dogs went with me. A touch of autumn had come to the valley already. I saw its beauty with renewed eyes, the fire of the rowan, the purple of the heather on the mountain, a gold leaf here and there among the trees, the clean peaty brown of the little river as it chattered over the stones.

It was just over a week later that I made up my mind to walk down the glen to the castle. I had no idea what I would see but I must know for myself. I must make decisions. Jeannie wanted to come with me but I shook my head.

'You have plenty to do in the house. I shall be quite safe.'

'I wish you'd wait until Mr Wynter comes back.'

'No,' I said firmly. 'This has nothing to do with him.'

'All right then, but you take care of that ankle of yours. Don't go climbing all over the place.'

'I won't, I promise.'

'And don't be too long or the dinner will spoil.'

I smiled and left her in the kitchen, baking bread. Jeannie vastly enjoyed being in charge and took pride in producing excellent meals out of whatever she had available.

When I followed the track along the stream, I thought how foolish I had been not to have done it before. The men and women of the valley came running out of their crofts, waving to me, calling shy greetings.

'Gu ma slàn a chì me thu!'

'May I see you well!'

'God go with you!'

George Fergusson's house was dark and neglected.

Someone had scrawled insulting words across the shutters. Let him go and Fiona with him. I wanted nothing more to do with either of them. I was sorry for old Mr McPhail. I must see that someone cared for him. I stopped still for a moment smiling at myself. So I was going to stay after all. My own decision took me by surprise.

The castle was a stark ruin but the bare stone skeleton still remained, walls that rose straight up to the sky, staircases that led to nowhere. I walked across the causeway and through the gaping door into the great hall. The roof had fallen in but someone had cleared it to make a pathway. It was foolish, I suppose, but I picked my way across it, went up blackened stone steps and saw the wreck of what had been the drawing-room. Here was where I had stood and seen my grandfather and Coll for the first time . . . For an instant tears sprang to my eyes and I shook them away impatiently. Richard had been right. The past was done and you cannot bring it back to life. I had tried to do that and it had led only to disaster. I was walking away when something caught my eye among the ashes and rubble and I bent to pick it up. The blood-red stone was cracked but when I wetted my finger and rubbed at it, the gleam of gold shone out unsullied. It was the Sithen Stone and it seemed almost incredible that it had survived the destruction. I put it in the pocket of Jeannie's cotton gown.

There was a gaping hole where the window had been. There the wind met me, the sharp smell of salt and the piercing cry of the gulls. In the distance women were gathering seaweed and the indestructibility of life struck me and made me feel very humble.

While I stood there, I thought I heard footsteps. I had the curious sensation that someone was watching me but when I turned, there was nothing, only the stirring of the wind along the dust of the floor. I shivered and suddenly wanted to get out of this dead place, out into the sunshine and the bustle of life.

I went down the stairs again and looked along the passage to the old tower. The ancient door that Coll had shown me on that first morning flapped backwards and forwards on broken hinges.

Something impelled me to go across to it. The wind

whirled around me as it had done then. The tide was up and the sea beat against the rock only a few feet below me. The dark pit must be awash with water by now. I thought how fortunate I was to be standing there and the future no longer seemed dark and without hope.

The next moment someone had seized me from behind. I was being thrust forward. My feet slipped on the slimy steps. I struggled violently, clinging to the swinging door. It gave way and swung outward.

I twisted round and saw Ailsa Drummond's face contorted with hate, the lips curled back in a savage snarl.

'You killed him,' she whispered, 'you murdered my Coll and now it's your turn.'

She was gradually forcing me through the doorway and I was fighting desperately to keep my balance. I got my foot in a crack of the rocky step. I pulled back with all my strength and tore myself free. She stumbled backwards and for one horrible moment I thought she would go over the edge and into the abyss. I saw the terror on her face and grasped her by the arms. For an instant we stood there, locked in an embrace, swaying to and fro above the surging sea, then the wind flung the door bruisingly against us. I staggered back, bringing her with me, and we fell to the floor.

Breathless and distressed, I knelt beside her but she thrust me away, weeping, screaming at me, horrible obscene things so that I got to my feet, running away from her, across the ruined hall and down the causeway until I reached the beach. I collapsed on the sand, huddled into myself, my ankle throbbing painfully, and it was there some time later that Richard found me.

'I saw the dogs,' he said dropping down beside me. 'Thank God I've found you. I've been looking everywhere. I returned at midday and Jeannie told me you had gone out and had not come back. She was very worried about you.'

I was still shivering with shock and he put a hand on my arm.

'Marietta, what is it? What has happened?'

'It was Ailsa Drummond . . . she tried to kill me . . . just now in the castle . . . because of Coll. Oh Richard, it was horrible. We were fighting with one another. I thought she was going to fall and then I would have had another death on my conscience . . .'

'You must not think of Coll like that. You were not to blame . . .'

'I was, I was . . . I can't bear to remember it . . .'

He put his arms around me and pulled me against him, holding me very close until I stopped trembling. Then he said quietly, 'Did you love him so much?'

'No, it's not that. It's not that at all.' I tried to pull myself together. I drew away from him. 'I'm sorry. I did not mean to be so foolish.'

'No, it's for me to say I'm sorry. I owe you an apology.'

'What for?'

'For what I said to you before I went away. Neil has told me something of what they did to you. I had not realized . . .'

'It doesn't matter. It's over now.'

'I was blaming you in my heart for Graham's death, blaming you because you loved Coll and defended him so passionately.'

'I did love him,' I said slowly, 'only the man I loved did not really exist and when I found out, I still tried not to believe it. And now . . .'

'Yes,' he said, 'and now . . .'

'Now I think I'm only sorry for him. You see I think he was two people and I don't know which was the real man. My grandfather has much to answer for.' I turned to look at him. 'You were right to reproach me. I don't know yet what I can do but I'm not going to run away.'

'That's my brave girl!' He reached out and took my hand. There was warmth and comfort in the pressure of his fingers. 'It's blowing cold. Do you feel strong enough to walk?'

I let him help me to my feet and we went on along the hard white sand of the beach, the dogs racing joyously in front of us.

After a little he said, 'Would you like to know where I have been?'

'If you want to tell me.'

'I've been looking at sheep.'

'Sheep?'

'Yes, sheep. Sounds ridiculous, doesn't it? But there's a man up in Ross who has tried sheep rearing on the West Coast and is finding it works well. It interested me. While my father lives, I'm not needed at Laverstoke and the army is over for me with this leg of mine.' He gave me a wry smile. 'I have decided to try my hand at farming in the Highlands.'

'Sheep?' I said and turned to look at him, all my doubts of him surging back. 'But you can't mean that, Richard, you can't. You know what they say. It means the land will have to be cleared, the people turned out of their homes ...'

'No, it doesn't, that's just the point. There are other ways of making the land pay for itself if you don't ask too much from it. I have been discussing it with Hamish Kintyre. He has ideas but neither your grandfather nor Coll would listen to him. The men here can be taught new skills. It is possible to sell wool and mutton. I believe that is what Graham intended to do.' His enthusiasm astonished me. It was the last thing I had expected. I was staring at him open-mouthed and he paused, smiling almost apologetically before he went on. 'It's a challenge, don't you see? It's what I've been searching for. When I came here in March, I thought life was over for me, now I know it is not. Can you understand that, Marietta, or do you think I am crazy?'

'No,' I said slowly, 'no, I think I understand. I felt like that this morning when I came down the valley. It's only that it seems so strange that you of all people ...'

'Because I am English, is that it?' He laughed a little. 'You forget ... I had a Highland grandmother. She used to frighten the life out of me but I still remember her saying that it was not Scotland's past that mattered but her future.' He was silent for a moment, then he said, 'There's a new breed of sheep being reared in the Lowlands among the Cheviots, a hardy breed that will survive a Highland winter. I'm going to look at them next week. Would you like to come with me?'

'I? But I know nothing about sheep.'

'You can learn. After all our lands run side by side. I thought we might make a successful partnership?'

'What kind of partnership?'

'Any kind you like.' He stopped to look down at me, the wind ruffling the dark hair, the grey eyes very serious though he smiled. 'Damn it, I've never courted a girl before by talking about sheep, but I suppose it is as good a way as any other. I would like it to be a life partnership but that will be for you to decide.'

I looked away from him. 'But I couldn't . . . you can't want it . . . not now.'

'I've thought of little else for quite a time now. After you ran out of the house that day, I knew what a fool I'd been to let you go. I wrote you a letter. It came back to me from the castle torn in half.'

'I never even saw it,' I said slowly.

'That's what Jan said, and that's what brought me back, hoping against hope that you might have changed your mind. I know you think of me as a brother, but you see, I already have a sister . . .'

'Oh Richard, what can I say?' I didn't know whether to laugh or cry. 'You must understand . . . Coll and I . . .' I could not speak of what he had done to me. 'I was married to him.'

'I know,' he said gently. 'I'm rushing my fences, aren't I? But I missed out once and I don't want it to happen again.'

I met his eyes. 'Are you sure?'

'Very sure, but there's no hurry. Think about it.'

He drew my arm through his. 'In the meantime we'll go and look at sheep.'

It is five years now and it has been an uphill struggle in many ways. Richard's father thinks he is quite mad but Kathryn has supported us steadily. There are sheep in the valley now, a great number of them, and our people are learning a new way of life. Bran and Wolf are still with us and there is a litter of puppies growing up in the stables. There is nothing they and the children like better than to race across the sands and fall in and out of the rock pools at the foot of the castle. Sometimes when I am walking there with them, I think of the great cairn of black stones under the shoulder of the mountain and the new one that

I have had placed there. He was a Gilmour after all. Then I hear the children shout with laughter. Richard is coming in from fishing and I remember to thank God for my happiness before I go to meet him.

About the Author

Constance Heaven was born in London in 1911, the daughter of a naturalized British citizen from Germany. An accomplished actress, Ms. Heaven turned to writing after the death of her husband in 1958, and is the author of historical novels, biographies, and romantic suspense fiction—for which she is most famous—published in the United States and in Great Britain. Currently a lecturer at the City Literary Institute in London, Constance Heaven now makes her home in Teddington, a riverside suburb of Middlesex.

Have You Read These Big Bestsellers from SIGNET?

- [ ] **THE KILLING GIFT** by Bari Wood.   (#J7350—$1.95)
- [ ] **WHITE FIRES BURNING** by Catherine Dillon.
                                             (#E7351—$1.75)
- [ ] **CONSTANTINE CAY** by Catherine Dillon.
                                             (#W6892—$1.50)
- [ ] **FOREVER AMBER** by Kathleen Winsor.   (#J7360—$1.95)
- [ ] **SMOULDERING FIRES** by Anya Seton.   (#J7276—$1.95)
- [ ] **HARVEST OF DESIRE** by Rochelle Larkin.
                                             (#J7277—$1.95)
- [ ] **SAVAGE EDEN** by Constance Gluyas. (#J7171—$1.95)
- [ ] **THE GREEK TREASURE** by Irving Stone.
                                             (#E7211—$2.25)
- [ ] **THE KITCHEN SINK PAPERS** by Mike McGrady.
                                             (#J7212—$1.95)
- [ ] **THE GATES OF HELL** by Harrison Salisbury.
                                             (#E7213—$2.25)
- [ ] **ROSE: MY LIFE IN SERVICE** by Rosina Harrison.
                                             (#J7174—$1.95)
- [ ] **THE FINAL FIRE** by Dennis Smith.   (#J7141—$1.95)
- [ ] **SOME KIND OF HERO** by James Kirkwood.
                                             (#J7142—$1.95)
- [ ] **A ROOM WITH DARK MIRRORS** by Velda Johnston.
                                             (#W7143—$1.50)
- [ ] **CBS: Reflections in a Bloodshot Eye** by Robert Metz.
                                             (#E7115—$2.25)

THE NEW AMERICAN LIBRARY, INC.,
P.O. Box 999, Bergenfield, New Jersey 07621

Please send me the SIGNET BOOKS I have checked above. I am
enclosing $_____(check or money order—no currency
or C.O.D.'s). Please include the list price plus 35¢ a copy to cover
handling and mailing costs. (Prices and numbers are subject to
change without notice.)

Name_____

Address_____

City_____State_____Zip Code_____
Allow at least 4 weeks for delivery